HOUSE OF BA
by C.J. Khe

BOWNE STREET PRESS

House of Badawi © 2022 by C.J. Khemi
First Edition published October 2022. All rights reserved.
No part of this publication may be reproduced, stored in a retrieval system, stored in a database and/or published in any form or by any means, electronic, mechanical, photocopying, recording or otherwise, without the prior written permission of the author, apart from brief quotations used in a book review.

For information about special discounts for bulk purchases, please contact Bowne Street Press at bownestreetpress@gmail.com
Bowne Street Press can bring authors to your virtual or live event.
Contact for more information or to book an event.

Library of Congress Cataloging-in-Publication Data
Names: Khemi, C.J., author
Title: House of Badawi / C.J. Khemi
Description: Bowne Street Press

Published by Bowne Street Press
www.bownestreetpress.com

Cover Design and Book Design by Franziska Stern
www.coverdungeon.com - Instagram: @coverdungeonrabbit

Map design © by C.J. Khemi
Author Photo © by Bianca Saikaley

Identifiers
ISBN: 979-8-9856977-0-4 (eBook)
ISBN: 979-8-9856977-1-1 (paperback)
www.cjkhemi.com

C.J. KHEMI

HOUSE OF BADAWI

Author's note

This is a work of fiction. While inspired by various cultures, including some geographical, historical, and culture aspects of the Caribbean at large (and my own Indo-Caribbean identity and experiences), the fictional lands in *House of Badawi* are not intended as a *truthful or whole* representation of one country or culture at any point in history.

Content warnings: branding scene, classism, explicit language, blood/gore/violence, sexual situations, misogyny, body policing and shaming. This novel is intended for New Adult/Adult audiences (18+).

On language

House of Badawi includes the usage of Caribbean colloquialisms that may be unfamiliar to some readers. I hope the following can help those who may be unsure of the following terms. Please keep in mind that the Caribbean is a hugely diverse place and that many areas have their own, sometimes slightly different spellings and interpretations.

Cobo – *also known as Corbeaux – a Trinidadian term used to refer to a bird of prey with a turkey-like bald or black head.*

Urni – *a kind of traditional scarf or shawl. While some may know this as a dupatta, the term 'urni,' is common among those in the Caribbean of South Asian descent.*

Dasheen leaves – *a kind of leafy green, similar to spinach. Dasheen leaves are commonly used in Callaloo, a popular dish often served with crab (at least, in the Trinidadian version).*

Pickney – *a West-Indian term most popular in country of Guyana.* It is most commonly used to mean 'child.'*

Obeah – *Alternative spellings: Obeya, – a West-Indian term of African origin. The term is used across various countries in the Caribbean including Jamaica, and Trinidad & Tobago, as well as the South American country of Guyana. It refers to a religious system of belief. However, the term obeah has also been used as a slang for voodoo or witchcraft.*

**While Guyana is geographically located in South America, it shares cultural aspects, peoples, and history with the Caribbean.*

CITY OF LAVENIA

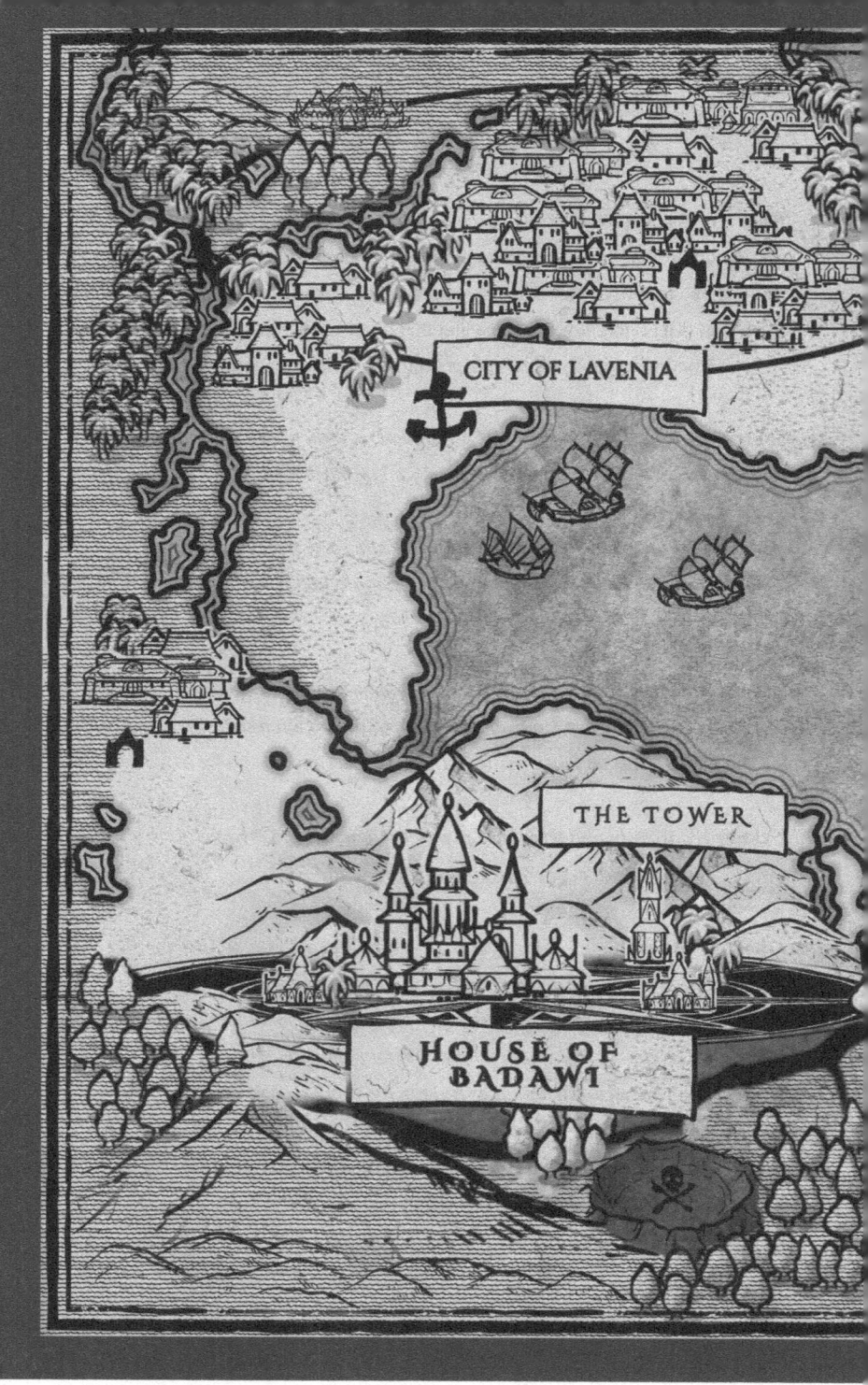

THE TOWER

HOUSE OF BADAWI

SAN'DIVOLAX

THE ISLAND OF QESHM

THE ISLAND OF QESHM, GIFTED TO THE BADAWI FAMILY BY THE LATE KING ELIJAH, SERVES AS THE HOME OF THE ETERNAL SPRING. IT'S COURT LIES AMONG THE MOUNTAINS, BUILT ABOVE THE GIFT FROM THE GODS THEMSELVES.

*To my own honey eyed human—
For you, I'd burn it down.*

Chapter 1

It was far too easy to attract the attention of the lord of the Badawi House.

The woman rose from the water like a nymph, her bare flesh dripping and her dark tresses slick. Her calculated gaze flickered to the man at the dais, at his crooked smile and nod of approval. She bowed her head slightly as the gong rang from behind. This scene had haunted her dreams for years. The water was so icy that she had to clench her teeth to keep them from chattering. But with the luxury that lay ahead, the cold did not matter. This was it, the moment she had been born for—the reason many of the women around her had been bred. But not her, she had *chosen* this. It was her ticket to a different life.

The woman lifted her legs from the ceremonial fountain with ease and measure, her reflection shimmering against the marble walls and candlelight. Every delicate tick of time seemed to stretch on the ivory clock ahead. She was not used to this, the attention. She had spent years hiding from the eyes of Court and sneaking away among the shadows. But Valxina did not permit signs of her discomfort to the surface—she locked it in, showcasing nothing but her fire within.

The scrolls of Roseau described the keeper's ceremony as one of the most primitive and principal protocols of the land. Whispers spread that women had drowned on the spot. The gods were fastidious when it came to the blessing of the keepers—they made their feelings clear, no matter how brutish the outcome.

Valxina had prepared for this night for years. She was convinced they would find her worthy—they had to. When the Court members shoved her head beneath the fountain waters, she did not struggle or spar with the burst of liquid. Like an old friend, she welcomed it. When she climbed to the top of the fountain ledge, her mouth lifted into a victorious and broad grin. Not only had she performed the task, not only had the gods deemed her worthy, but also had she been restrained longer than the others. It hadn't surprised her. The other daughters of the Court had pined over the position as long as she had. So, when they had the opportunity to possibly drown the woman they deemed unworthy in the ceremonial fountain, they had blood on their minds, or in this case, water.

Valxina lifted her chin and glanced around the room. Court members, the wealthy of the island, stood in their most formal attire, gowns, kurtas, and kaftans of threaded gold. They lifted their drinks into the air and shared delighted glances. Beads of sweat dripped down their temples, a consequence of the packed room and absence of windows. The onlookers laughed and smiled as they clapped. While other candidates spent years hunting for such applause, it unsettled Valxina. But the woman did not cower from the attention, no matter how much she wished to. They could not see her afraid. Instead, she lifted her chin higher. The attention, the applause, welcomed her in a soft embrace.

"Our new keeper, Valxina Kulrani—Protector of The Spring," the lord's adviser, Eno, announced. His voice, thick in his Qeshm accent, vibrated with such vigor the gods must have heard him. And if so, they now knew her name.

Valxina Kulrani—Protector of The Spring.

Valxina stood, bewildered. She had completed the oath and test; she would be a new keeper of The Spring... the very water that turned the king and her lord immortal. Pride seeped its way across her features. Her dark eyes widened, and her brows, thick and full, lifted with joy. Valxina now held one of the most respected positions in Court. She had been elevated for all of Qeshm to see. The waters blessed her with new status, and she now held a responsibility to the king himself. She was a protector—a defender of The Spring against enemy kingdoms and leaders, like Queen Chantara to the east.

Valxina felt exhilarated, until she remembered the brand came next. Valxina liked to believe she had a high tolerance for pain—especially after everything she had gone through to get here. The women of the Court had made sure she could bear pain—building up her tolerance in the name of the ritual. But she could not allow them to see her falter, no matter how much the hot steel approaching made her wince.

Valxina held her breath as the other women turned her body, moving her back to the crowd. The air kissed her exposed skin. The scent of burning incense and aromas of sandalwood wafted in the air. She tilted up her chin and thought of her future—of the privileges that would accompany her new life. She thought about the water, of the way it would feel against her skin. But no amount of daydreaming could save her from the burn—from the smell of her cooking flesh or the throbbing at her lower back.

Grimacing at the contact, she balled her hands into fists at her side in attempt to smother the scream that raced up her throat. She had never been more thankful for being drenched; onlookers would not be able to decipher her tears from the streams of water. She bit at the inner flesh of her cheek, allowing the bitter taste of blood to trickle down onto her tongue. The fire tore at her brown skin as the women pressed the metal against her harder. Fire to brand her to the water—an emblem of Lord Zessfar to identify her forever. Her heart banged against her chest in an attempt to break free. She did not dare protest the prolonged act, to tarnish her reputation before her responsibilities even began. She knew why they were doing this. A small part of her could not blame them. Valxina only turned her head to look at the lord. Her eyes did not plead, nor did they beg for an ending. Instead, she challenged him—she beseeched him for more. Spectators flashed their eyes about, hushed words traveling between them.

"What is she doing?" Valxina could make out the words of a man in the crowd.

"Is she allowed to *look* at my lord?" a woman questioned from the balcony.

Valxina lifted her chin at the chatter. She had never looked at the man—the immortal lord who ruled over their Court and island—not truly. Up until now, she had been forbidden to do so. Servants were not permitted to gaze upon the bonnie face of the sun-kissed man.

The look from the woman at the fountain either excited or chilled the man above. But Lord Zessfar only raised his hand in command. "Enough." His voice vibrated through the room with authority, sharp enough to cut through glass and steel.

The gentlest of the keeper candidates wrapped a delicate silk robe around Valxina. In the candlelight, she glimmered like a flowing stream herself. It was mere seconds before Valxina was ushered out of the chamber with the other triumphed keeper candidates. She tried to steady her breath as she walked down the hallway, into the catacombs of winding passages. But the skin on her back cried against the touch of her robe. The new keeper struggled to keep consciousness. Her bare feet left a wet trail behind her, from the darkness of her past to the light of her future.

Or so Valxina believed.

Chapter 2

Valxina's belongings had already been packed. Two boxes sat on her now-stripped bed in the room she had shared with the five other women. She was only a girl when she was brought to this room and introduced to them—all daughters of the Court from high-ranking families. Valxina had been brought to the former lord, Orin, at the age of six. But she hadn't entered *this* room until she was eighteen. She was four years into her twenties now. And in those years spent in this room, all she had collected were two boxes of belongings.

She grimaced at the sight of them and the women around her. Unlike the other women, she had not been selected from a family of wealth. Instead, her family had *won* a game of chance. The wording of the practice had always made Valxina scoff. On the island of Qeshm, each family was expected to enter their child into the lord's lotto. With the passing of each year, the House of Badawi blindly selected a new name from the lot, a new child to be brought to the Court and employed as a servant. If the child proved themselves worthy and passed a series of tests, they were considered for a variety of different appointments in the Court. Some strived to be a part of the Badawi House guards or an advisory role, while others hoped to catch the lord's eye for consideration as a lover. And while the former lord had many lovers they weren't what his son coveted most. It's the keepers, a select group of women who protected his most prized possession. A keeper from the child lottery had never emerged, not ever...not until today. And as Valxina reflected on the milestone, she toggled between disgust and gratitude. Where would she be now if she was never taken as a child? Would she be as safe as she was to be now?

Not all six women who entered had achieved protector of The Spring status. Valxina looked over at the three empty beds. The belongings of the failed candidates had not been packed neatly away. Her lips pressed together in a thin line as she studied the way their belongings had been tossed into the corner. Three women had drowned or forfeited during the ceremony. Drowned or forfeited—they were both the same, as those who forfeited were deemed a shame to the House of Badawi and the king himself and were drowned by the end of the night. The thought of dying in that bitter cold water caused Valxina to shudder. How many souls had been lost there? *Richelle, Shanice, and Kadejah.* Those were the names of the three who had not made it out of the chamber. All that would remain of them were their scattered belongings in the corner—an array of fine dresses, books, and some elaborately dressed dolls. The dolls always rang a cord with her. The wealthy women of the Court were allowed to hold on to childhood naivety. That innocence had been beaten out of Valxina years ago.

"Valxina?" A stern voice broke her daze.

A woman hovered in the doorway. She was dressed in a robe of the keeper's color, a mix of cerulean and the blue that glistened on a freshly torn berry. Images of waves in motion were sewn onto the woman's robe. While Valxina's robe seemed to be intended more for display, the woman's clenched cloth was made for utility. It was equipped with fasteners and buttons that would keep her secure even in combat. She wore her hair, black as night, in thick tight locs that twisted and collected together at the top of her head—her very own crown. She was santu—a keeper so holy she had been allowed past the crypt and to The Spring itself. A transparent veil in keeper blue draped across the lower half of her face and lay atop her dark brown skin and full lips. But the true evidence of the woman's santu status displayed in her eyes. Where the brown of her irises should have met white, they clashed against cerulean. The water from The Spring had been injected into her sclera. Valxina had never seen anyone like her before. But she had heard of her kind—the children of Qeshm were told stories of them, of their relentless dedication to protecting The Spring.

"Valxina?" the woman repeated.

"Yes? That's me." Valxina lowered her eyes to prevent herself from staring.

"Of course you are she." The woman laughed, her voice

rising and falling with the cadence of a true Qeshmian. It was always easy to identify the people of their island—they spoke as if in song. Beats and rhythm formed along with their words. "I heard about the dark-haired enchantress who drew blood with her eyes. Of course," she added as she looked around the room, "that would be you. Now bring your things and follow me."

Valxina lifted her boxes and followed. "You mean you were not in attendance?" she asked as the woman hurried her through the corridors.

The woman's features widened as if amused the words. "No. I have no interest in theater."

Theater. The word lingered between them like a held breath. Valxina made no effort to respond as she moved into the courtyard. Her wet hair danced against the wind under the shadows of the moon. Palm trees swayed in the light breeze, and the salt of the sea air whisked around her. Valxina noted the way others mumbled quiet remarks to one another, their eyes sharp as darts. *Gossips.* This Court was filled with them. She reminded herself of her new status. Life as a keeper would attract more attention than the life Valxina led as a fire-keep or kitchen servant. Now, everyone knew her name—no matter her birth. There would be no hiding in the shadows or cowering from crowds.

When they slowed at the tower, Valxina's feet scuffed. She had seen the tower before and had spent many hours studying the guards who protected the entry point. But Valxina had never come this close to entering through the doors. She had only watched from afar. Her breathing quickened, and her hands, still grasping the boxes, grew slick with sweat. The tower guards were a breed of their own, distinctive from the Badawi House guards. They were faster, deadlier—indestructible.

She watched as a man moved forward from the sea of tower guards behind him, his hand on his scabbard. Valxina stilled. She knew him as Ky—the man who trained with her in combat since she was eighteen. The moonlight glistened against his skin, dark and rich. He was wearing his uniform, an all-black kaftan threaded with Badawi blue, indicating his status as commander. *Commander.* As Ky approached, Valxina stiffened and wondered, *am I expected to address him as so?*

She knew this moment would come and yet she found herself ill-prepared. Nights had been spent devising the right plan, the precise words she would use when she saw him. She had planned to say hello—to reach out and let the memories of their past drift away. After all, her new status meant things could be different between them. But now, with the man towering over her, Valxina's mind wiped itself clear. Her thought-out sentences and witty greetings eluded her. She bit her lip as she looked up. The stars shimmered within his dark eyes.

"Sera," Ky said, making eye contact with the other woman. His voice was deep, his words clear. As he flickered his gaze to Valxina, she lifted her chin. "Who is this?" he asked.

Valxina's eyes widened. It took everything in Valxina to contain her bark. She gritted her teeth at the words. Ever since he achieved the status of commander, he seemed to forget them—Valxina stopped at the thought. No, ever since he achieved the status of commander, Ky seemed to forget *her*. But then again, she knew the reason behind his drift.

"This," Sera answered, "is Valxina Kulrani—Protector of The Spring."

The words sent lightning up Valxina's spine. She gritted her teeth in pain at the sensation of the fresh brand. She watched as the commander raised his brow. *Was he surprised?* Had he expected Valxina to fail in the tests that led up to the ceremony, or worse, did he expect the gods to deem her unworthy on this night?

With his free hand, Ky scratched at his beard. "She looks like a mouse," he said with a cocky laugh and the bow of his head.

A mouse. He used to call her that during their training with late Commander Hu. But besides the use of the familiar name, he did not show that he recognized her. "Keeper Mouse?" he said with a sly grin.

Beside Valxina, Sera sucked her teeth. "Absolutely not."

Ky laughed. "Keeper Val?"

Sera rolled her eyes before turning to Valxina. It seemed the woman had learned to illustrate a multitude of emotions with just her glare. "Commander Kyrad seems to have difficulty with our full names. Thank the gods we keep him around for his brute nature and not his brain."

Ky lifted a hand to his chest as if wounded by the woman's words. "Is that what you think of me?"

Sera rolled her eyes and continued, "He likes to call us as he wishes, but do not let his familiarity cloud your judgment. He and the rest of the tower guards are here for the same reason you and I are—to protect what calls this tower home."

Valxina nodded as they walked past Ky. Nothing could cloud her judgment here, not after she had spent years dreaming of this moment.

Each step the women took echoed in the stairwell. They seemed to climb to the heavens before they finally stopped at a wooden door marked with a "K1." Valxina glanced into the common room as the door opened. Books lined the walls, without a spare inch of blank space. They were holy volumes with legends as old as The Spring itself. Leather sofas were arranged in a circle around a stone fireplace in the center of the room.

Sera led her into the room before halting at a door with no markings. She turned its knob and pushed it wide, unveiling the small bedroom. Valxina had never had a room to herself—not even as a young child before coming to Court. She heard rumors that the keepers had the luxury of privacy, but she could not believe it—not even now as she looked it straight in the face. She took a silent step inside before turning to Sera in the doorway, her brow lifted.

"Yes, this one is yours," Sera answered. "Dry yourself and settle in. I will see you and the others in the common room in an hour." She placed an hourglass at a desk near the armoire. The woman's brown hands turned it, allowing the bits of sand to collide. They trickled toward the bottom of the glass like beads of sweat.

Sera reached for the door to close it. But her arm lingered, leaving it cracked for a moment. Valxina watched the way the light cast itself in from the common room. She could not see Sera's face, but she knew she was there. Valxina could sense her presence.

"Valxina," she said from behind the door, "I would leave the fire from the ceremony behind. This is no place for flames." And with those parting words, she shut the door.

Chapter 3

A room. Her own room.

Valxina slept in three rooms throughout her life: the chamber she shared as a pickney, a child with her mother and father; the room she shared with three other servants when she moved to the Badawi Palace; and the room she shared as a keeper candidate. Despite the lack of windows, no frills, and a damp odor, this room was all she had hoped for.

She placed her boxes on the bed. They fell softly. *Cotton.* Her new mattress had been stuffed with cotton, not the hay or straw her prior beds had been made from. Eager to test it, Valxina tossed herself beside her things, astonished at the lightness, at the softness. It rocked slightly, as the bed had been placed on rope—a common practice against bedbugs. But as she lay back, the hardness of the night weighed on her. Her back cried in pain, reminding her of the brand. In the moments outside with the fresh night breeze, she had tried to forget. As she peered across the familiar face of the commander, she had buried the pain. And at the sight of her living quarters, at the warmth of the common space and luxury of privacy, she had been distracted. She sprung up from the bed with a stifled yelp. *If this were no place for flames, why was her skin on fire?*

During her time as a kitchen servant, Valxina was in charge of the waste. She would pack the kitchen scraps into a basket and walk to the gardens. While the servants sometimes pecked over the half-eaten plates of curries and roti, not everything was as salvageable. The palace cook would toss bits of meat into a pot and stew what she could, but even then, produce went to waste. So, Valxina would be sent off to the outskirts of the palace walls and would not stop until she had passed the displays of roses and the lotus pond. There, away from the vegetables that grew on the premise, and the sweet hummingbirds in the gardens, was the pit. The pit was exactly as it sounded—a shallow but vastly wide hole in the ground that had been dug for kitchen waste. Valxina would dump the contents of the basket and sprint back to the palace. She would not wait for the creatures to appear—she did not wish to see the way they would slash, rip, and hack away at the trash. She had made the mistake of idling by the pit once. The sight of the wild animals emerging from the jungle left her shaking and running in fear. She wouldn't make that mistake again.

Tonight, by the way she tore at her robe to free her skin, Valxina resembled those very creatures. Her face as she did so resembled the wildest of vultures—feral and tormented. She dashed over to the small mirror in the room's corner and turned. The elongated mirror was mounted on a wood-paneled wall. Metal framed the edges, which were painted with delicate drawings of waves that appeared to be moving. Valxina held her breath. Although she recognized herself in the reflection, she shuddered at first glimpse. She looked... *different*. It was almost as if the night had painted a new face, a layer of grit and confidence she had never noticed in herself before.

Valxina hesitated as she turned to view her back. She had never seen the brand on anyone before. Going into the ceremony, she was unsure if it would happen. There were only rumors of the ritual that hushed their way through the Court halls. Attendees of the ceremony were always sworn to secrecy. *But why would the Badawi House trust the Court gossips with details of such an act?* Theater. Keeper Sera had referred to the ceremony as theater. *Had this harshness been done for the entertainment of others?* Valxina shook her head. *No. This was the mark of a keeper, a protector of The Spring. This was a mark of stature and honor, not an act of shock or entertainment for the noblemen and women of the Court.*

Facing her bed, Valxina shifted her head to the mirror. Like the stain of the darkest of gods, the mark watched her. It was blistered, a bloodied mark of barely recognizable waves. Three of them formed a deep triangle. Pieces of her brown skin had gone missing, bits near the edges screamed for relief. Valxina felt herself choking. Her heart quickened, and her body grew hot to the touch. She clenched her teeth and shut her eyes, but the mark could not be unseen. Valxina's flesh had been maimed. They had pressed into her harder, the iron hot with hostility and abhorrence. And the revulsion the others felt as they bore down on her would be present for the remainder of her life. While she was now their equal, she would never forget how far their prejudice took them. The entire Court had watched. The lord had watched. But she made sure he knew, by the intensity of her eyes, power was a thing not only for the rich.

Valxina squinted as she held her hand up before her. But her head had gone light, and her vision blurred. She braced herself against the wooden bedframe, bumping into it slightly as she moved toward her belongings. She shuffled through a box, tossing a card, an old dress, and a notebook of scribbles and nonsense to the side. She did not have much. The book held a list of rhymes and riddles, and the card gave her access, although limited, to a room of books held in the servants' quarters. A library for the people, by the people, an old friend had once proclaimed. And below it all was a wooden trinket box—a case that held a lock of coarse raven hair, not much different from her own, and a pair of pins. The pins were thin, the kind used to fasten blouses and drape urni scarves.

Valxina reached for a canteen at the bottom of the box. She rolled her eyes. This was madness. The rum was of low quality. Valxina had traded a week's worth of stolen apples from the kitchen for a tin of tobacco. Apples were not a fruit servants came by often; they were imported, as the island was too hot for such orchards. Apparently, the woman she had traded with had a child who worked the laundry room and had a taste for apples. She also had a husband with an addiction to the pipe and was eager to get rid of his tobacco stash. Valxina had then traded the tobacco with a fire-keep, a man who tended to the palaces' fires like she once did, who was rumored to make his own drink. He ran an entire operation that involved folks from all corners of the service. There was money when it came to the art and distribution of bush rum. But no number of berries could conceal its acidic taste.

Valxina unscrewed the lid. When she first traded for this, she had different plans for it. Two weeks ago, she decided she would celebrate once the ceremony was over. She imagined she would toast to her victory, to her success...to her new position in life. She hadn't expected to be surrounded by an ensemble of keepers or tower guards, although a small part of her wished she wouldn't be completely alone when she toasted to her newfound class and status. No, a small part of her imagined Ky beside her as she celebrated. But perhaps that friendship was long gone now. She found no one to blame but herself for that. Valxina scrunched her nose as she brought the canteen up. It smelled like rot and poison. Her eyes widened at the taste, and she fought back a cough. After the first gulp, she returned to the mirror, turning to locate the source of her pain—her mark. She drew a deep breath and held it.

"*Fuck!*" she all but screamed as the liquid contacted her flesh. Valxina's heart roared, hammering against her chest with barbarity. She felt her head lighten and fought against her eyes willing to turn themselves over. She reached to steady herself against her bedpost, but Valxina's fingers slipped. No words escaped her lips as her head hit the floor.

The new keeper, Val, as Commander Kyrad had called her, was late. Sera scanned the faces of their new recruits. Inara and Danae looked eager to please. They had entered the common room early. Inara's hair still sat in damp, tight ebony plaits across her shoulders. The collar and back of Inara's robe still appeared wet. It would take hours, perhaps even a full day, for her braids to fully dry. Beside her, Danae had dried her hair and wrapped it into a golden nest. It looked so tight Sera wondered how the woman could bear it.

"Just like her," Danae muttered as the last grain of sand hit the bottom of the hourglass before them. She leaned back, draping a relaxed hand over the arch of the sofa.

Inara lowered her eyes.

"Just like whom?" Sera asked. She waited for the woman's answer with bated breath.

Danae lifted her nose and answered, "Valxina—the servant girl. She'll make us wait like we haven't anything better to do."

Sera's eyes narrowed as she stood. The woman had no patience for petty rivalries. "This is no place for sharp tongues—especially towards one another." Sera watched the shared look between the two women. "There are no servants here. Only keepers—protectors of The Spring. There's enough of that out there, in the lives you have left. I will not allow keepers to speak of one another like that here. Get up!"

Like puppets on strings, the two women rose without protest. "We will check on her together," Sera added.

The doors of the tower did not lock. Especially not on this floor with the new recruits. Yes, they lived a life of privacy in contrast to the lives of those in the main Court, but there was a fine line between privacy and secrecy. And to Sera, a lock on the door represented the latter.

"Keeper Valxina!" she yelled as she knocked.

There was no answer from the other side of the door.

Sera peered over to the others before pushing the door open. Danae, the blonde one, kept her chin high and her face hard. But worry lingered under the eyes of the other—Inara. Sera pushed the door and stepped in.

Valxina was lying on the floor. *Had she fallen asleep? Had she lost track of the time?*

No.

Sera's brows furrowed as she hurried across the room. Blood pooled at the woman's head, a puddle so rich her reflection glimmered in it. She glanced across Valxina's bare back and turned to Inara. Sera trusted her more than the other. Maybe it was her own bias, as Inara seemed to resemble her, not only in features but also by the look in her eyes. Sera could hardly remember it, but she once looked like her—wide-eyed and devoted. Or perhaps the reason behind her choice was simpler—it was Danae who made her distaste for the fallen woman clear.

"Go to the door at the other end of the hall," Sera instructed. "Find the one marked with a P."

Inara disappeared.

When she looked down, Sera studied the mark that

scalded Valxina's dark skin. It was profound, a wound so distinguished it brought gooseflesh to her own. Her initial instinct was to look away—she was not in the business of peering at other keepers' marks. It was, in a way, a silent agreement among the keepers. They did not speak of the event that brought them such pain. But this one... this was a burn so disturbing that she could not look away. The brand inched itself into the woman's skin, reaching the tissue beneath it. It was bright red and swollen, and blisters bubbled up against its edges. Parts of it, the skin that had come in direct contact with the heated metal, appeared charred. Sera turned to Danae, her eyes ablaze.

"You and the others did this?" she questioned. Sera rose from her knees and grabbed the woman by her robe. It was a custom that Court members took turns branding the new keepers. But Sera had heard through the whispers of Court that this woman, Valxina, had been branded by her fellow candidates. She clenched her fingers at the thought. Was it because of Valxina's blood? Was it because she was not noble but a former servant to the palace? Keeper Danae was still wearing her ceremonial robe, thin and flimsy. "Let me see it!" Sera demanded. "Let me see yours. Were you branded as she was?"

The robe fell like a waterfall. The silk pooled at the woman's feet. She turned, her eyes panic-stricken and breathing erratically. Yes, she, too, bore the mark. But it was barely there. Bits of the iron hadn't come in contact with this woman. The brand was barely recognizable.

"Did it hurt?" asked Sera.

Danae gritted her teeth.

"I said, Did it hurt?"

"Yes, Keeper Sera. It did."

Sera dropped back to Valxina's side. Her eyes flashed between the boiled skin and the face above her.

"And yet, you and the others did *this* to her? Your pain wasn't enough. You made sure to inflict torment on to your fellow keeper?"

Sera shook her head. She had never seen a brand like this one, so wretched, so deliberate. The lord was cruel, and the Court members were monsters on their own. *But how could these women, vowed to protect The Eternal Spring, fail to protect their own?*

Inara reappeared with Keeper Pax not a moment too late. Any second later and Sera may have lost her temper altogether, or worse, cried in front of the new keeper. There would be no lessons tonight. Not formally. No, tonight their focus would be on the woman on the floor. They had a responsibility to her. She could not, she would not, die tonight.

Chapter 4

Sleep was no familiar friend of Valxina.
Her duties of fire-keep as a young child had her awake before the sun. Valxina would light the west wing fireplaces in time for breakfast. The inhabitants of the bedrooms would wake to heat, to comfort—a sharp contrast to Valxina's mornings in the chilly hills. Whether it was the morning breeze or the freezing water in preparation for the ceremony, the cold, numbing, unwelcoming bitterness was a feeling Valxina knew too well. Not many in Lavenia, her home, knew the cold—their city rested at the edge of Qeshm, an island rich with palm trees and heat. But even in paradise, even under the softness of the sun, one could find inhospitable chill. Valxina found it in the mornings, in the Badawi House atop the hills.

Valxina lifted her eyelids slowly. The room was unfamiliar and empty. She had been covered with a thin sheet and left to rest in bed. Shifting from her side, she grimaced as she propped her body up. Her head pounded in protest. She lifted a hand to her temple and traced the bandages that wrapped around her. Her eyes connected with the basin of blood-stained water at her side and at the faint stain in the center of the room. The stone spoke to her. It reminded her. She had collapsed. No amount of fighting had saved her from her own body, from its betrayal, as she slipped out of consciousness and collided with the floor. She looked over to the desk, to the boxes still left unpacked that occupied the small space. How long had she been asleep? How long had she been allowed to rest?

When she lifted her feet off the bed, she sighed at the throbbing. Valxina stalked over to the mirror. She let go of a contained breath as she turned. She was wearing a cotton nightgown. It was old, one that she had been gifted from an old friend, one who no longer walked the halls of Court. Fitted for her younger body, the material now clung to her curves, to her thick thighs and her waist. Someone must have fished it out of her belongings and placed it on her. Her dark tresses had been brushed, and her waves had been dried and pinned back.

Valxina tried to think of the last moment before she fell. She thought of the walk up the stairs, and the way her eyes widened at the sight of the room. She thought of the warning Keeper Sera gave as she left her to dress. Then, as if her senses wished to remind her, she sensed a faint whiff of bush rum in the air. Valxina shifted her weight. She could feel something against her skin. She lifted the nightgown to see if the brand was visible, but it was hidden. Over it, a bandage had been placed and tied.

The door opened without warning.

"Ah, awake at last." It was a woman she had not seen before. Her unnatural eyes radiated as Keeper Sera's did. She also was santu. The woman rested an elbow against the doorway and studied Valxina. She, like Sera, was only a few years older than Valxina. "I have been waiting for you."

The look Valxina gave her was that of a wounded bird.

"I'm Keeper Pax," said the woman. She, too, wore a thin veil across her face, but even so, Valxina could see that this keeper appeared delighted and happy, a stark difference from the woman who had walked her to her bedroom. "How are you feeling?"

It had been a long time since someone had asked Valxina how she felt.

"I'm well," Valxina lied.

"You're a terrible liar." Pax snickered. "You've been out for four days. Your... The mark became infected while you were asleep." Her playful smirk disappeared. "I have an earful for you. When you are fully recovered, I'd like to know what doltishness possessed you to wash a burn out with servant quality rum. It festered, and you wailed around that bed with a fever for days."

Four days. She had rested for four entire days.

"Thank you," Valxina said as she approached the woman. "I am sorry to have rested for so long."

Keeper Pax laughed. "Rest? You call a festering wound and fever fits rest?" She shook her head. "Are you well enough to dress?"

Valxina nodded.

"Good. Keeper Sera is on duty, so I'm here to tell you that Lord Zessfar would like to see you."

"My lord?" Valxina choked on the words. What would the lord want of her?

"Sera told him of your condition when he asked of you. I expect he would like to make sure you are well enough to continue—to enter into the crypt."

The Badawi lord. Valxina's eyes widened at the thought. *The crypt.* All that stood between her and the lord's most prized possession was this one meeting. But why would the lord care about her condition? Why would he ask for her? Valxina straightened her back as she grabbed for her dress, still boxed.

"No, that won't work," said Pax. "You're a keeper now. You should not be seen in anything but the keeper's sacred shade. It's a bit bloodied, but you should wear your ceremonial robe. We will get you sorted after you speak to Lord Zessfar. It's probably best to not keep him waiting."

Keeper Pax led Valxina down the stairway. She tried to avoid the gazes as they brushed past others dressed in robes and attire identical to Sera's and Pax's. She looked at Keeper Pax's outfit, which had a gleaming, almost snake-like sheen to it. Her skirt was high enough that any trace of her own mark was hidden behind its band. As they approached the bottom of the tower, Valxina simply nodded at the other keepers. With an extended hand, Pax indicated for her to step into the light—into the suffocating heat of the outside.

It was the middle of the day, though the interior of the tower had not indicated this. With no glimpse or glimmer of sunlight, the tight stairwells were lit by fire and flames. Valxina let out a suppressed breath as she stepped out of the doorway. She grinned as she allowed her eyelids to meet one another.

"Already craving the sun, Keeper Val?"

The voice startled her. It was Ky, standing in front of a formation of tower guards. He grinned and removed the stick of tobacco from between his lips when she didn't answer. Valxina watched as he tossed it to the ground and outed it with the heel of his boot. It was a bad habit, and she had hoped he'd outgrown it by now.

Ky followed Valxina's path of vision, and he tilted his chin slightly. "Rumors say you've picked it up too."

Valxina looked past him, past his dark coils of hair that curled right above his ears. So, the rumor mill had already begun about her. "I wouldn't be so quick to believe in the gossips of the Court," she said.

"I would not be so fast to *overlook* the rumors of these walls."

When Keeper Pax disappeared from the doorway, Valxina gazed back at her, confused. She turned to Ky with a raised brow.

"Every keeper has a designated tower guard," Ky explained. Valxina braced herself. "Inara's got Desil. Danae has been paired with Agnar. And you..."

"Surely the commander of the tower guards has better things to do..." Valxina countered.

"I've kept myself off the roster," Ky corrected.

A flood of embarrassment rose to Valxina's face. Her heart stopped.

"Mylo," Ky called out. She watched as a tower guard broke from the formation behind them. "Mylo, this is Keeper Valxina...Val. You are to escort her to the lord."

Valxina's heart sank. He had kept himself off the roster. And his tone, it did not match the kind and open man she once knew. Valxina glanced at the tower guard, Mylo. He appeared young. She studied his blue eyes. They were the same shade of the House colors. He looked eager and drenched in innocence. *How had he risen up the ranks of the tower guards?* Mylo nodded to his commander before turning to his newly appointed keeper.

"You have my sword, Keeper Valxina—Protector of The Spring," he said with the low bow of his head. "As long as I am alive, you shall be safe."

"Thank you, Mylo," she said as she moved toward him. When she reached him, Valxina lifted Mylo's chin with her fingers. She glared at the commander. "Thank you," she repeated to Mylo, "but bowing is not necessary. Not ever, not with me."

Life flickered beneath the gleam of Mylo's eyes.

Chapter 5

Valxina knew little about the young Lord Zessfar. He had only assumed his role two years ago, following the death of his father, the late Lord Orin. Lord Orin had been slaughtered during the attempted siege by Queen Chantara to the east. Since they had yet to take part in the ceremony, Valxina and the other keeper candidates had been forbidden from joining the efforts on that perilous night. House guards were placed at their doorway to prevent their exit. On the night Chantara's guards breached the palace walls, Valxina had waited in terror to hear of any news. The other women, especially Richelle, had an abundance of names to call Valxina and her eagerness for information. None were kind. But Valxina paid them no mind. She prayed for an opening, for a moment to slip out of the shadows and into the action. The moment never came. When a young fire-keep ran past their room, she screamed for his attention. His eyes radiated fear, pure panic, and horror.

He's dead. The child's words had rung through the chaos like a message from the gods. It cut through the noise, the cries, the screams, like the sword of Khal itself. He was a creature of the scriptures. Although the tower guards and keepers defeated Queen Chantara's people before they could set foot in the crypt, they had still done their damage. They had murdered Lord Orin, leaving his young son to take his rightful place in the House of Badawi. Rumors said the king slaughtered all the political prisoners from the East when he heard the news. Some say it was his decision to green-light the conversion of the Badawi heir, Zessfar. With the swords of Chantara's men sharpened, the leaders of the kingdom refused to leave the home of The Spring unprotected. For the king feared The Spring, in the wrong hands, could lead to an unstoppable army of immortals... an undertaking he, himself, had prohibited for his own lands. It was unnatural, the king believed, and an abuse of power to use the water for such a purpose. By their customs, Zessfar shouldn't have been blessed with the immortal waters so soon, but the king gave his orders, and Lord Zessfar followed. Zessfar drank from the waters just one week after his father's death.

Lord Zessfar was said to be maddened by his father's death, but Valxina could never make out the man in the brief glimpses she stole of him. He was always quiet, a stoic being who kept his face neutral and his lips sealed. At least, until he spoke the word at her ceremony nights ago. Enough, the man had commanded.

Some whispers even said Lord Zessfar possessed a jar of his father's heart and battled an obsession with the details of Orin's murder. But not all the gossip surrounding the young lord was so gruesome. Additional rumors said Zessfar was engaged to be married to the daughter of a wealthy Court member, although Valxina knew better than to believe in the whispers that spread behind the marble walls.

Valxina shook her head to clear her thoughts. The rumors were already calling her a dark-haired enchantress who smoked tobacco. She would not enter the lord's chambers with preconceived notions from Court whispers. She lifted her chin before turning to Mylo, who nodded slightly. Valxina's eyes narrowed at the scar that traveled across his neck. It choked him like a necklace, like hands hoping to block his breath.

Before she could say a word, the doors unlocked. Valxina swallowed her thought and stepped forward, her footing softening on the plush carpet. She kept her head down, studying the pattern of the floor, which was ornamented with images of soldiers engaged in combat. But as she moved forward, Valxina grew curious. She flexed her hands to rid their tension and lifted her gaze slightly. He appeared casual, hands clasped behind his back with a welcoming, warm smile on his face. She had never seen him smile. And when she accidentally locked with his gaze, she did not redirect her eyes. She feared doing so would display her as timid. *Had he remembered the daggers she had thrown at him during the ceremony? Had he recognized her eyes, her lesson on power?* When she saw his gaze shift to her head, to the bloodied cloth that still wrapped her, Valxina trembled. She looked like a battered mess.

I should have removed it before I came to see him, Valxina thought as her polite grin faded. Worry washed across her face as she lowered herself to bow to her lord. When Valxina's head kissed the carpet with a soft hiss of pain, she waited. Her body still ached from her fall and the brand that caused it.

"You may rise, new Keeper," Lord Zessfar finally said. He was dressed in a cream-colored tunic and slacks. The golden Badawi emblem adorned his chest, which was comparable to the mark Valxina now held. A necktie hung loosely over his neck, the only Badawi-colored item on him. As the lord stepped forward, Valxina remained silent.

"You look nervous," he said. The edge of his lips curled upward as he studied her.

Valxina lifted a curious gaze to him. He was taller than she had expected. And up close, in the light of the day, a glint of gold shimmered within his eyes. He appeared to be about her age—with a full beard cupping his face and features thinned out—no longer clinging to a roundness of a babe. His skin tone resembled her own, a sun-kissed brown, although not as rich as Ky's, Keeper Sera's, or Keeper Inara's. There was a tint of sand behind his complexion, and she wondered if he walked under the sun much—or did he avoid it? She had heard the wealthy of Court believed the wild notion that their paleness invoked auras of their status. Unlike the folks who worked the land, who farmed, who lived beyond their walls, they could avoid the rays of light. Zessfar's mother, who had passed soon after his birth, was even known to paste creams made by an alchemist—ones that claimed to lighten the complexion of her skin.

"You made quite the impression on me at the ceremony. Sera promised to bring you to me that night, but she said you were... unable?" His brown eyes pierced her, flecks of gold glinting in them.

"Yes, my lord. I came as soon as I was able."

Lord Zessfar stepped closer. He watched Mylo with a look of mild irritation. Expressionless, Mylo stood guard, feet behind his keeper.

"Your name?" Zessfar asked the tower guard.

"Mylo, my lord," he answered as he dropped to a knee.

Valxina shifted her gaze to her Tower Guard, noticing how the man's soft locks hid his face as he dropped his head. It displeased her to see another drop so, to watch anyone lessen themselves in the presence of others. Even as she had done it herself, she felt small and shamed. She wished that chapter of her life was behind her.

"And you, what happened here?" Lord Zessfar questioned. He lifted his finger to brush the bandage on Valxina's temple.

Heat radiated through her. "I..." Valxina paused. She took a step backward from the man, averting his touch.

"Go on?" he pressed.

"I am afraid I lost consciousness. I injured my head in a fall that made me... unavailable for several days."

She watched as the edges of Lord Zessfar's lips curved into a wicked smile. "A pity," he answered as he reached for her once more.

"My lord..." Valxina began, moving away.

But the man cut her words short, "You may call me Zessfar. You are a protector of The Spring now. You are a keeper, Valxina Kulrani." When he looked down at her confused expression, he continued, "What? Did you think I could forget the name of the keeper who dared to watch me during the ritual? I'd be careful if I were you, Kulrani."

Was that a warning, or was it a threat?

Lord Zessfar closed the distance between himself and Valxina. The new keeper shifted her feet against the carpet, but as she turned, her hands flailing to grasp at the nearby table, a stack of books tumbled between them.

"Shit," Valxina said, reaching for them. She braced herself for the man's reaction.

But a chuckle left his mouth. Zessfar brushed a hand through his hair, dark and curly, and kicked his head back.

"I'm sorry," the new keeper replied, kneeling to collect them.

Zessfar lowered himself. "It's not your fault. I've been meaning to have these reshelved. And I believe it was I who startled you into tossing books to the ground."

Valxina raised her eyes to him. With the exception of his golden armband and the crest on his chest, he looked nothing like she had imagined a lord to appear. She stopped to study the shelf of books that lined the man's walls. Zessfar followed her gaze.

"Do you enjoy reading?" he asked.

Valxina nodded. "I do."

"Let me guess..." the lord's voice trailed as they moved toward the shelves. "Other than the text of the scriptures, of course, you're a fan of epic adventures and, dare I say, *romance?*"

Valxina smiled. "In addition to the text of the scripture, of course," she repeated, "I'll read anything I can get my hands on."

"There's much time for reading as a keeper candidate?" the lord questioned.

Valxina bit at her lip. "Well, it depends." She paused. For the other women, the Badawi library was at their disposal. And while an impressive feat of its own for simply existing, the servants' library did not have the grandest of selections. It contained mostly books filled with recipes and old folktales scribbled down for the servants' pickney. "But no, not necessarily, at least... not for me."

"So what is your favorite?" Zessfar asked. "There has to be a genre you enjoy more than others."

Valxina thought back to her book of scribbles. She rose her brows as she answered, "I quite enjoy philosophy, my lord. Riddles and paradoxes have always been an interest of mine."

Lord Zessfar grinned. "Are keepers allowed to enjoy philosophy? Does it not clash with the teachings of the text?"

"Some may say that, sure. But perhaps there is more linkage between the two than we wish to believe."

Zessfar watched Valxina silently. He furrowed his brows at her words and lifted a finger to his chin.

"I have a riddle for you, Keeper Valxina," he said. "It's called the whisper."

Valxina nodded her head and gestured for the lord to continue.

"*Words leave my lips, but I never speak what consumes*

my mind. I hear chatter, but I do not listen to thoughts. When I rise, the world sees me. At night, when I slip into slumber, the world can hear me. Many, many heads are on my shoulders. I wear a multitude of masks. The strongest metals will not break my visage. But the quietest whisper can destroy me." Lord Zessfar paused. "Who am I?"

Valxina paused. She knew this one; she had heard it before and had even scribbled it in her book after hearing it once. She considered not confessing. *Would he be upset if she already knew the answer?* But Valxina shrugged and replied, "You are an actor." The edges of her lips lifted in a hesitant smile. "I am sorry, my lord, I should have told you. I have heard of this riddle before."

Zessfar shook his head. He smirked at her with delight. "They say the answer is a man in theater, yes. But I believe them wrong."

"You believe the philosophers wrong, my lord?" Valxina suggested. *There was that Badawi lord arrogance she had heard of.* "Then what do *you* think is the answer?" She paused. *"Who are you?"*

Zessfar answered, "I am a lord."

Valxina's face tightened, and her eyes lowered. *Words leave his lips, but he never speaks his mind. He hears chatter but does not listen to thoughts. When he rises, the world sees him. At night, as he slips into slumber, the world can hear him. Many, many heads are on his shoulders. He wears a multitude of masks. The strongest metal cannot break his visage... But the quietest whisper could destroy him...*

When she looked back at the man, Zessfar shrugged casually. "There are some parallels between being a lord and being an actor, do you not think so?"

Valxina shook her head. "I wouldn't know, my lord." It felt odd for him to ask her such a question.

"*Zessfar*," he corrected.

But Valxina could not bring herself to say the name—not so plainly. She had spent years learning the etiquette of the Court, of learning how to refer to the noblemen and women. It took her months to perfect the holiest bow, to learn the ways she could and could not refer to the Badawi family. His name... It was impossible for her to say it without recalling the agony of her teachings. Valxina grasped for her robe's sleeve, trying to hide the scars at her wrists.

When the lord removed a vial from his pocket, she asked "What is that?" She bit at the skin of her cheek and squared her shoulders with the words.

"It's my water, Keeper Valxina. It's the very thing you have vowed to protect." He lifted a brow. "You know, I do not do this lightly—I do not share my water so... openly. As you know, you are not allowed to drink the waters of The Spring. No one is permitted to do so without my permission. And even so, the circumstances must be dire. But I have spent quite some time asking about you, Kulrani. As you may remember, Commander Hu was slaughtered on the same night as my father, our late Lord Orin." Zessfar paused, lifting his gaze to the ceiling. "May they rest amongst the gods in peace." He took a step closer to her, the vial still in hand. "Commander Kyrad said he trained with you. He said Hu had high hopes for you, despite your..."

Valxina did not need him to continue. She knew what

his next words would be. *Despite her background.* Despite her class. Despite her poverty. Despite it all, Commander Hu had seen something in her.

The lord studied her shift and watched the way her hands clenched at her side.

"After what I witnessed that night at the fountain, and after Kyrad's praises, I think this is more for me than for you," Lord Zessfar continued. He lifted the glass. "While you may not drink the waters of The Spring, I will allow you to be washed with it. You are allowed to be healed by it." He reached for the bandages that wrapped around her head. The contact was unexpected. She shuddered at the touch.

"And the king?" asked Valxina, taking a step back. "How would he feel about this?"

The lord chuckled. "Do not worry about the dealings between myself and His Highness. This Spring is under my protection. These waters have been in my family for generations. This is my decision to make. Now, tilt your head back."

Valxina held her breath. Why would the lord of the Badawi House wish to heal her? She analyzed him with curiosity but bit down at her nerves. How could she tell him no?

"You want to heal... me?"

Lord Zessfar lifted a brow and inclined his head at her. "Yes, if you will allow me to." His eyes softened with the words.

Valxina held her breath as she nodded. She shut her eyes and allowed the lord to touch her—to remove the bandages that wrapped around her head.

Three drops. Three drops were all it took against the crest of her hairline. The throbbing discomfort from her fall vanished within seconds. Valxina's eyes darted around the room in astonishment. The pain beneath her skull existed no more. Her eyes widened at the revelation. It was magic, the kind of alchemy she knew existed but had never experienced herself.

"There," the lord said with a victorious smile. "Mylo, get her back to the tower."

If Mylo felt as she had, he did not show it. He stood, still feet away from the doorway, his hands still on his scabbard. His eyes focused ahead as if in waiting. *But what for?*

"My lord," Valxina said as she turned for the door.

"Come on," Zessfar replied, edging her on to call him by his name, not the title.

He was not driven with madness... not anything like the whispers and rumors claimed. She focused on his eyes. They were soft yet impenetrable. Valxina's glance shifted to the shoulders that held the lord's head up high. He had asked about her. The lord of the Badawi House had asked about Valxina Kulrani. And it wouldn't be the end of his inquiries, not by a long shot.

"Thank you," said Valxina.

"Hold your thanks, Keeper. Now, go protect my Spring," his voice rang through the room with authority.

She nodded as she headed out the door. Relief bubbled from within her.

Chapter 6

Valxina entered the changing chamber for the first time, still covered in bloodstains. But it wasn't the blood that caught the attention of those she walked by; it was her smile. Mylo had walked her straight to the tower. He did not say a word about the happenings with the lord—with Zessfar. He kept his hand on his scabbard and his eyes ahead. Every so often Valxina would catch the way he looked around, the way he scoped out Court members as they walked past them. *But what danger would truly lie inside the palace walls? Was there really a need for such vigilance?* That was the thing with young guards; they were always so eager, so possessed with their desire to impress their commanders that they lost grip of reality, of true danger. Mylo had walked her down the winding stairs, but his feet froze at the last stairwell. He could not go farther. As the keepers swore an oath to The Spring, the tower guards swore theirs to the structure and the women inside. They were not permitted past the last set of stairs, past the chambers to the crypt. And they certainly were not sanctioned to enter the water.

Valxina pushed past the door and into the changing chamber. A bustle of women buzzed around the room. Most moved rapidly, tossing garments off and on. Bare bodies moved openly in the space, free from prying eyes and sinister gazes. The walls were lined with compartments, open shelves with hooks all adorned with clothing in the keeper's shade of blue that glimmered in the light. Valxina glanced around the room; she sought the woman who had brought her to the tower that very first night. But when she noticed the bare backs of keepers shifting through the room, she tensed. Valxina lifted her gaze and released a deep breath. She felt it rude to lay eyes on their brands. And if she could avoid it, Valxina did not want to see another mark for the remainder of her life.

"Keeper Valxina," Keeper Sera's voice called to her from an empty compartment. Beside her, Keepers Danae and Inara dressed.

As a way of greeting, Valxina dipped her head slightly. She lifted her hands to her chest in attempt to make herself smaller as she maneuvered through the sea of women. Keeper Sera's brows scrunched at the sight of Valxina and sighed, her eyes connecting with a faint scar that had been left on the new recruit's temple. It was barely noticeable, as most of it lay covered by Valxina's dark hair. But the bit that traveled out of her hairline would not do.

"It looks good," Keeper Sera said.

Valxina smiled. "Lord Zessfar helped heal—"

But Keeper Sera's scoff cut her words short. "Zessfar

healed this for you?" She shook her head. "You did not drink the water? Tell me you did not drink the water?"

Valxina shook her head. "No, he only washed my wound."

Keeper Sera released a deep breath. She rubbed a hand against her chest and whispered, "Thank the gods."

Valxina studied the woman. She held her breath before she asked, "Keeper Sera? What would have happened if I drank it?"

Keeper Sera gazed ahead. "The Spring has the magic to heal, to preserve, to grant a life of eternity—but there is a dark side to it as well. It can even kill. It can take life away from those it believes unworthy."

Valxina tilted her head. "The Spring water... It can *kill?*"

Keeper Sera nodded. "Everything in moderation, you know. And your brand? Did he touch you there?"

Valxina froze. "No."

Keepers Danae and Inara shared a silent glance.

"As I thought," said Keeper Sera. She sighed a breath of disappointment but said no more on the matter.

In her hand was a pile of garments. Sera lifted the first one, a skirt of iridescent fabric and a matching choli. The attire would leave her midriff exposed. It was a replica of the clothing Keeper Pax had worn when Valxina woke from her rest, or fever-induced fits as Pax had called it. The next item was a collection of fabric. There was no shape or cut to it. Valxina let her fingers glide along the silk. It felt like butter, much softer than the other. Golden embroidery danced through it, images of florals and scaleless, slender water snakes intertwined.

"You'll learn how to drape it," Keeper Sera told her. "It's about six feet in length. You would be surprised by how many ways the women have learned to fashion it."

The last garment was a new robe, not one like she had worn at the ceremony but one that resembled Sera's. It had buttons and fastens, but the most unusual aspect of the garment was its pockets. The item had been made not for show but for practicality.

"You have the choice of these three for daily wear. You'll see every keeper has their preference. It is up to you to decide."

Valxina had never owned such fine things. The thought of these choices sparked a flame within her.

"And in the crypt?" Valxina asked. *What was she expected to wear once she entered the caverns?*

"Some of us go bare; other keepers go with skirt and choli. I enjoy my robe. The other is in no way conducive to swimming or fighting, so I'd advise you against that choice." Keeper Sera paused, her mind elsewhere. "I'll have to acquire something for your head."

"My head?"

"Court members won't like to see you walking around with that..." Sera's fingers brushed against the scar at Valxina's temple. "When in public, outside of the tower, you will have to cover it with a wrap."

"Will I be the only keeper with a bandeau?"

She nodded. "I'm afraid so. But it's nothing to cry about—I'll see that there's one laid out for you by the end of the day." Sera's bright eyes flickered. "Oh, and here you are." She handed Valxina a thin veil. When Valxina brushed her thumb against it, she added, "You can pin it above your ears like the rest of us."

Valxina glanced over at the other women, the ones who had pressed the hot steel against her skin. When Inara's dark eyes met her own, the woman lifted her lips in a wry smile.

"How are you?" Valxina asked, polite but hesitant.

While Danae kept her eyes forward, Inara moved to face Valxina. She always seemed the kinder one of the pair.

"Fine."

Keeper Sera had stepped away from the group, leaving Valxina to change.

"Fine? We weren't allowed into the crypts until you recovered. We've been waiting four days," she said.

It didn't make sense. New keepers were expected to enter the crypts the moment the sun rose following their ceremony.

"What...What do you mean, you weren't allowed to enter?"

Neither woman answered.

"What did you do for four entire days?" She had never heard of keepers waiting days before their entrance. The women must have maddened at the order—she sure would have grown upset. After all those years, all that work... to be forbidden to enter?

"We made sure you didn't choke on your own bile." Danae sounded exasperated—like she had spent the last nights with little sleep.

"You looked after me?" Valxina asked.

"Keeper Sera made it clear I didn't have a choice."

But there was something about Danae's words that stuck with Valxina. *"I didn't have a choice."* She didn't seem to be the kind of person to do anything she hadn't wished to do.

Chapter 7

Valxina's stomach plummeted as the women entered the artillery chamber.

It was yet another moment she had awaited, a moment she had fantasized about. This was the point at which she could choose her own weapon. While the other keeper candidates had the funds to book private sparring lessons, Valxina did not have that luxury. That was the basis of her joining Commander Hu's training of the guards. Hu trained them all, the Badawi men and the men destined for the tower. It was said that Commander Hu sculpted boys into artillery—weapons more powerful than any sword, crossbow, or cannon. With Valxina, he held none of his tests back. Once, when he was making his rounds, his usual notes of who he deemed becoming of the tower guards, he stopped at her. *Bewitching* was the word he used to describe the way Valxina prowled around in combat. She was slick with a sword in hand—a stealthy fox that could creep up in silence and swipe with the brute of the mightiest of warriors. Ky had laughed at the description. He seemed to think Valxina looked more like a rabid armed mouse. He'd even call her so on occasion. It was Commander Hu's idea to separate her, to give her semi-private lessons once he saw her potential. The lessons were always free. And when Hu asked Valxina to pick a mate, an opponent to train with her under the night sky in lieu of a sit-down dinner, she selected Ky.

All keepers had been trained with artillery. Some favored the crossbow, while others selected the dagger or sword as their weapon. Valxina had never seen any of the other women in combat. Their private lessons had made sure to keep their skills secret. But she had heard rumors, particularly of Danae.

Valxina scoured the shelves with a certain item in mind. She headed for a collection of javelins in the center when Valxina spotted them. Valxina allowed her eyes to roam the room, to watch as the others perused the walls of arms. Inara's fingers grazed the golden handle of a sword. Valxina watched as she lifted it, testing its weight in her hands. Her muscles seemed to bellow under the weight of it. Too heavy. It was apparent in the way Inara's muscles tightened under her skin. Her shoulders tensed as she flicked the weapon from one palm to another. But alas, she placed the weapon down. Inara lifted another, this one with ease and grace, and made swift, circular movements with the broad saber as if the air laid laden with invisible enemies.

Valxina gazed at the javelins. She had trained with all the weapons under Commander Hu's watchful eye, but there was nothing more familiar than the feeling of a javelin in her palm. She studied their difference in sizes; some were thinner, and others bore only one sharp edge. And then she saw it. Valxina stopped when her gaze landed on a particular javelin. There were no singular arrow edges on either side. Instead, the weapon had been made as a sole sharp blade. Both edges bore the end of a sword, leather wrapping its center.

Valxina reached for it. The material was just thick enough for her hand to wrap over it. She lifted it in test. The weight did not make her muscles roar. Valxina swayed the item, testing its agility. It moved with her, like an extension of her arm, a part of her body she could control and manipulate with ease. She grinned. When she first began training, Hu had recommended it to her. He believed Valxina needed a weapon as swift as she was. She was short in stature, so a weapon with the advantage of reach was necessary. She would be able to stab a person feet away before they ever had the opportunity to swipe at her. It would do perfectly.

She reached for a strap, searching for one in her size. Behind, Inara fastened a scabbard around her. Valxina buckled the javelin across her back, the double blades tucked behind her. When she looked up, she caught sight of Danae with a surujin. With the weighted chain in her hands, the woman turned. She seemed untroubled as she reached for a belt and fastened the chains around it.

"What is it?" Danae said. Her eyes burned holes into Valxina.

"A surujin?" Valxina asked.

Danae rolled her eyes. "What did you think? I am here too, aren't I? Did you think I would faint at the sight of the artillery room? Did you think you were the only one deserving of the keeper title?"

When Valxina turned to Inara, she shrugged. "A javelin?" Inara asked, pointing to the weapon strapped across her back.

Valxina smiled. "A cutlass?"

She nodded. "My father was a tower guard. He trained with all the weapons, as they all do. But I always liked his cutlass—the way it curves slightly like a crooked smile."

Valxina bared her teeth at the words. *Had Inara just compared a weapon to a smile? And had she just shared a bit of her life?* In all the years they had spent in the same room, under the same regimens, none of the candidates had ever shared a glimpse of their life with her. Of course, she would overhear their conversations in the dead of night. But they had never shared information willingly with her. Not even Inara had done so... until now.

As they left the room, Valxina desired more.

"How are your tower guards?" she asked, hesitant. She tried to recall the names from her conversation with Ky in the courtyard. "Desil and Agnar?"

Danae scoffed. "Why? Isn't the boy enough?"

Mylo. She was referring to Mylo.

"The boy?" Valxina echoed.

"Do not tell me you don't know?" Danae lifted a brow. When Valxina stayed silent, she let out a breath laced with irritation. "You know, for someone so agitated during Chantara's attempted siege, you truly do not know much."

Danae had remembered Valxina's behavior on the night of the attack.

"Mylo is..." Inara paused, her eyes flickering with thought. "He is known for his actions during the night of the late lord's death. He cut down more of Chantara's men than many of the men combined. The only reason he obtained that scar in the first place was in an act to protect the commander. Everyone was sure he would die. And yet... he didn't."

"And who did that fucking commander deem important enough for Mylo to protect? Who did he assign the most notorious tower guard to? *You.*" Danae spat the words out.

Perhaps Ky did remember her. While he had kept himself off the roster, he had assigned someone just as notable, someone just as vigorous.

"Danae is just jealous," said Inara. The words invoked a sharp gasp.

"Jealous?" Danae said.

"You only wish the commander put as much thought into your tower guard," Inara replied.

"All the tower guards have been trained the same," Valxina said. "I know Commander Hu made it a point that no man would set foot out of the training circle until they were ready. I'm sure Ky does the same."

Danae's eyes lifted with intrigue. *Ky.* Valxina had said the name with such informality. She raised a brow at the sound of it.

Chapter 8

Prior to the ceremony, Lady Masha was the woman in charge of preparing the candidates for their lives as keepers. She was not a keeper herself, just a wealthy cousin of the lord who had acquired the position from birth. Lady Masha's lessons were to be focused on the scripture, on the history of The Spring, and the legacy of the Badawi House. But Lady Masha was not a woman without her bias. She had her own ideas on what constituted at lessons. She had her own thoughts on whom she served and what she believed were effective teaching methods.

Valxina allowed her eyes to adjust to the stifling darkness. Years ago, this would have made her shutter. It would have made her tremble with panic and distress. She allowed her feet to take pilot. She followed without thought, heading toward the sound of Keeper Sera's voice ahead. They had entered the crypt, which lay at the very bottom of the tower. The gods themselves had dug the tunnels beyond the surface, according to legends. But even Valxina knew that part of the story was untrue.

Years ago, the members of the Badawi family were known not as lords and ladies but as expeditionists. They would search ancient ruins and hunt for remnants left from the gods' time on land. Even the grand temple of Lavenia had been discovered by the family. They discovered the sword of Khal, the gem of Vashti, and other items of magical properties. Each grand House now protected one of those items. But it took generations for the Badawi family to discover their last bit of history. And when they came across The Spring, it was enough to leave the world of travel behind. Instead, they were welcomed into Court life. Their pockets were lined with gold from the late King Elijah, the man known for his obsession and hunt for immortality. And while many believed it was the gods who carved out the tunnels, Valxina and her family knew the truth: It was not.

The rocks had been carved by the hands of the people, by the very folks of Lavenia, by the first who lived under Badawi rule. For Valxina, the history had been passed on through generations. Her ancestors had been brought to the island of Qeshm from the continent to labor and work the tunnels. They had migrated on contracts, with empty promises of a better life post-servitude. The Badawi promise of gold, of plots of garden lands, and of class—it was never fulfilled. But even them, even her ancestors were lucky, as they were left to live. Not all the folks brought to Qeshm to work the tunnels had the same ending. Not all had come on promises or signed contracts. But one thing was true: It was the people, all of them, who built the tunnels, not the gods.

Valxina narrowed her eyes in the dark. A keeper could fulfill three different posts. They comprised of crypt duty, lake duty, and Spring duty. Keepers were expected to remain on crypt duty until deemed worthy of the lake. Then only the best of the keepers, the most trusted by the lord and king, would move forward to The Spring. They would be considered the holiest of them all, and they would be named *santu*. Valxina thought back to Keepers Sera and Pax's eyes. They held the position of Spring duty.

As the women fumbled their way into the darkness, they knew there was no light for them. Darkness would be their only friend today. Shadows would be their companion until they were deemed worthy.

"Here," Keeper Sera's voice echoed. Valxina's bare feet froze. "About thirty keepers are spread from the entrance to the lake. That now includes you three."

Torches were not allowed in the crypt; they were all told so during their lessons. For Valxina, the lesson was learned through a sequence of events involving closets and luggage chests. When she was eighteen, Lady Masha started locking Valxina into palace closets to acclimate her to the conditions of the crypt. Masha said it would bring Valxina closer to the gods. The first few times, Valxina had screamed, trembled, and cried herself to unconsciousness. The tight space, in addition to the suffocating blackness, terrified her beyond anything in her life. And when she finally found a way to calm herself, to control her breathing, and gather her thoughts, Lady Masha only tested her more. That's when she began instructing her into luggage chests. Valxina had protested at the start, but Masha knew how to coerce Valxina. *"You won't last,"* she would tell the young candidate. *"The gods won't find you worthy. No keeper can be afraid of the dark."* And so, time and time again, Valxina would climb in.

"Five hours," Sera said. "Five hours today. You'll hear the sound when you can leave your post. But until then, you are here. You are not to step away from this very spot, understood?"

"Yes." The words of the three women echoed.

When the sound of Keeper Sera's footsteps drifted off into the distance, Valxina shuddered. She could do it. She had once gone forty-eight hours in the darkness of a closet. She had once gone six hours crammed into a chest. *Five hours... five hours would be nothing.*

There was no sound but the dripping of water, no sight but the darkness. Valxina's eyes had adjusted enough to see slight shadows but nothing past an arm's length. Commander Hu had his own lessons in preparation for the crypt. She recalled the blindfold her partner, Ky, would tie across her face. She had once thought it silly. But here, staring into nothingness, Valxina felt differently. She felt grateful.

"How did you two train for the darkness?" Inara's voice broke the silence. "Commander Hu would blindfold me."

Valxina stilled at the question. "Me too," she answered. "He would have me blindfolded and stick Ky on me."

Danae sneered, "I knew you were too poor to afford lessons of your own, but sparing with Commander Kyrad? Are you saying you have known him since training?"

"I..." Valxina hesitated. Had she known Ky? Their last interactions had made her question her memories. He hadn't addressed her as she expected. He hadn't acknowledged their friendship. Had her memories betrayed her? He did not seem to know her in the way she felt she had known him.

"Valxina?" said Inara.

"Yes—yes, sorry," Valxina answered. "We sparred. I would not say sparring is knowing someone." She could hear someone murmur in response. Valxina shifted on her feet. Desperate to redirect the conversation, she continued, "Lady Masha prepared me for the darkness." The words, fresh off her lips, filled her with instant regret. *Too personal. Too dark.*

"Don't remind me of that insufferable bitch." Danae's voice rang clear. Valxina's brows rose, and her eyes widened.

"I..." Inara started. But the woman could not continue her sentence.

"I thought you might have liked her," said Valxina.

Danae replied, "And why is that?"

"Because she was like you... like all of you," Valxina said.

"Of course," Danae replied. "We're all the same, aren't we? I'm just as depraved and malevolent as the rest of them."

"I..." Valxina began.

"You what?" Danae replied before adding, "You are probably happy to hear of the news of Fazia."

Valxina lifted her chin at the name. "Who?"

✦ 69 ✦

"Have you been too preoccupied to hear about the girl who went missing from Court?"

Preoccupied. The word lingered between them. Valxina had been knocked out because of what the others, what Danae, had done to her. And the woman described her illness as a mere preoccupation?

Valxina blinked slowly. She bit at her lip and released a fiery breath. "A girl has gone missing?"

"You have heard about them, haven't you?" Inara cut in. "She hasn't been the first."

But Valxina knew all too well that disappearance was no stranger to the palace. "I hadn't heard—"

"Fazia is the daughter of a noble family. She was a family friend of ours. She wants to become a keeper herself, that is, when she becomes of age," said Inara.

"And how old is she?" Valxina asked.

"Fifteen," said Danae. "But we are all the same, Valxina, aren't we? What does it matter if a noble girl goes missing? What does that mean to you?"

"Danae," said Inara, "that's enough. Valxina did not mean to assume we are all—"

"That's just it," Danae replied. "Regardless of if she does so by choice or not, she makes assumptions about us."

"And you do not make assumptions about me?" Valxina scoffed. She winced at the words. She did not want to hear Danae's answer because she already knew the truth.

"I know everything I need to know about you," Danae replied. "I don't need to make assumptions. Why have you even bothered to drum up conversation with us? Since when do *you* care to speak with me—or even Inara?"

Valxina paused. "What is that supposed to mean?"

"I think I made myself very clear—you have never bothered to speak to us before. You always stay to yourself, creeping around in the shadows like a palace rat."

Valxina balled her hands into fists. "If you say I never spoke to you, it is because of *this* right here. I don't make assumptions about noblewomen, but I know *you*. Your memory of me doesn't seem to match mine."

Danae's laugh echoed. "Fine. Play the victim here. But if you ask me—"

"Enough," Inara whispered.

Danae huffed. "What, you don't think she owes me an apology?"

"An apology?" Valxina spat. Did the woman forget what she had done to her? Did she forget how she pressed the metal to her skin only days ago?

"Enough!" Inara repeated. Her voice crackled as if holding back a sob.

Silence fell between them once more. It was charged, explosive silence. A fallen palm leaf would have boomed in comparison to the noise between them.

✦

Hours went by without another word. But Valxina knew how to pass time. First, she counted sheep—only it made her feel as she was willing herself to sleep. She barely reached fifty before she changed the imagery of sheep to visions of jumping steeds. She gave up at two-hundred and forty-three. After the steeds, Valxina spent some time on exercise. She didn't wish for the others to hear her, to recognize her sounds of exhaustion. So, after a few minutes of squatting, lunging in the dark, and lifting herself off the stone ground, she called it quits. Somewhere ahead in the dark, she could hear Inara sharpening the edge of her cutlass against stone. Valxina reached her fingers for her weapon strapped across her back. She traced the leather across her chest and reached behind. She practiced removing her javelin from its holder in the dark. And when it was free, she slid her fingers across its flat edge and spun it like a baton.

Surprisingly, it was Danae's voice that broke the silence between them.

"Fuck," she said, "after all that training, all that reading..."

"What?" Inara asked.

Danae cursed under her breath. "All that time spent on scripture, and no one told us what to do when we have to fucking piss?"

A broad grin spread across Valxina's face.

"Stop it," Danae said.

"Stop what?" Valxina answered.

"You would enjoy this, wouldn't you? I bet you're grinning to your fucking self like the little freak you are."

She was.

"I may be a freak," Valxina said, "but I'm not the one about to piss myself."

"I'm serious!" Danae snapped. "What am I to do?"

Valxina held out her hands and swished them around

in the air. She did not come in contact with anything or anyone.

"It doesn't feel like you are that close to me. Hold your arm out. Are you doing it?"

"Yes, I'm doing it."

"You too, Inara," Valxina continued, dropping her title. She knew Inara had done so when she felt the wind of motion to her right. "Ok, everyone, take two steps back."

"This doesn't help my situation."

But the women all moved. They could hear each of their steps in the dark.

"Well?" Valxina said.

"Well, what?" Danae replied, her voice clearly farther.

"Well, we can't see you. You're far enough that we can't touch, and close enough that we won't lose an arm for abandoning post. Go ahead, take your piss, Danae."

"I can't piss on the ground!" she protested. "Y-You may be accustomed to such behavior, but I cannot. Behind a tree, fine. In a stream, ok. But out in the open? Not with you just standing there."

"Fine," Valxina muttered. "If you are so much better than me, piss yourself."

Inara said, "I'll tell you what; I've got to go too. If we both go, we won't be able to tell who's who. We won't be able to decipher where the noise is coming from. It'll be less... pressure."

Danae huffed. "Tell anyone outside of the crypt about this, and I'll fucking kill you."

With Inara's eager countdown, Danae relieved herself. Inara held her word—she, too, went. But even in that moment,

Valxina could not shake off the words the woman had spoken earlier. *You always stay to yourself, creeping around in the shadows like a palace rat.*

Chapter 9

Mylo was already waiting in the stairwell when Valxina stepped out of the changing chambers. She watched the way he propped himself against the wall, his hair now tucked away and tied behind him.

"He knows he doesn't have to follow you around in the tower, right?" said Danae. "He looks like a sad little puppy awaiting its owner."

Valxina watched her. Danae's golden tresses and blue eyes resembled Mylo's features. The two could have been siblings. But by the way Danae spoke of him earlier, it was clear the resemblance was just that, nothing more.

The remaining hours had gone by quietly. There was no more talk of the Court girl who had gone missing. And nothing as exciting as Danae's piss had occurred. When the gong sounded, announcing the end of their shift, Valxina had shuddered. She hadn't heard a gong since the night of the ceremony.

As if the moments of conversation had not taken

place, the women changed out of their clothing quietly. While Danae and Inara opted for a full bath in the shared pool, Valxina washed with a rag in her compartment. She didn't wish for anyone to lay eyes on her mark. She wasn't even sure if it was ready to be unwrapped or washed, so she left it just so. When she was done, she reached for the skirt and choli.

Fresh from the crypt, Valxina said hello with a soft nod. "Mylo."

"Keeper Valxina," he replied with a lifted chin. She much preferred that to his kneeling and bowing. "Dinner has been set out in the courtyard tonight."

Valxina's eyes narrowed. "I'm sorry?"

"Commander Kyrad likes the keepers and tower guards to dine together. He says it promotes a sense of community—that it breaks the barriers between us."

Valxina grinned. Not everything about her old friend had changed—it seemed he still carried around his idealistic notions and dreams. "And what do you think about that?"

Mylo's eyes scanned hers. "I believe the commander has his heart in the right place. Class is a thing that can divide and split even the strongest of armies. There is no place for separation in a unit."

"And we are a unit?" Valxina asked.

"You and I are a unit, Keeper Valxina. The keepers and the tower guards are a unit. Or at least, that's how it should be."

Valxina looked at the man before her. He did not appear so young anymore, not with the information she had learned about him. And with the words that left his lips—those were certainly not the beliefs of a young boy.

"How old are you, Mylo?" she finally asked. Patience was never one of Valxina's strong suits.

Mylo chuckled. "You know, just because I haven't been blessed with a beard like the commander or the wrinkles of the others does not mean I am a babe." He shook his head. "I know what the gossips say about me. I know they call me a child—*a boy.*"

Valxina smiled. "And are you?"

Mylo brushed his hand against the back of his neck. "No, Keeper Valxina, I am no boy. What if I asked of your age?" He laughed.

"Four and twenty," Valxina said.

Mylo raised his eyebrows. "One and twenty."

So, he wasn't a child.

"But that would make you..." Valxina's brows furrowed. The two continued up the steps. That would have made him nineteen during Chantara's attack.

"Youngest member of the tower guards, Keeper Valxina. That is right. I was a child of the lottery, just as I've heard you were. But I wasn't taken to the servant's quarters. I never once served as you did. Hu took me in when I arrived and taught me all he knew. I ate and slept with the guards. I was destined for this even if everyone around me and I stood blind to it."

Valxina nodded. "It's Valxina. You can drop the 'keeper,' please. If we are to be a unit, then perhaps you can let go of the formality."

Mylo nodded. "Commander calls you Val."

Valxina laughed.

"You can call me Val if you wish, Mylo. The commander does not own the name."

When they reached the doorway, her feet stopped. Mylo studied the way Valxina's fingers reached for her head. She muttered a soft curse beneath her breath.

"Keeper Sera told me to give this to you," he said, extending a hand. A bandeau in glistening cerulean laid in his palm.

"A life saver," Valxina whispered as she took the item from him. She shaped the material into a triangle and wrapped it around her head. Although never made of such rich material, Valxina had worn her hair like this quite regularly as a fire-keep and kitchen servant.

"How's it look?" she asked, hesitant.

Mylo looked down at her with a subtle nod. "It looks great, Val."

The name sounded so familiar on his tongue. It was the sound of one friend to another. It was something she had not experienced, had not heard, in a very long time.

When the two stepped out of the doorway, the moon had already risen. Valxina's stomach growled, twisting beneath the surface of her skin. Under her veil, her mouth watered at the aromas of dinner. In all the days occurrences, she hadn't eaten a crumb. Her stomach had growled in the dark of the crypts, but there was nothing she could do but count her steeds.

"Mylo," Ky called out to them. He stood from a table, one positioned at the center of the space, and motioned to the empty chair at his side.

The courtyard had been set up with long wooden tables. It was a sea of keepers and tower guards, all of which sat side by side. Torches burned bright around them, sprouting out of the ground like blades of grass. It was beautiful—a sight she had never seen before, a meal arranged as if to be shared by a family. The smell of spices lingered in the air. Valxina bit at her lips at the stacks of roti, and at the spread of curries and stews. When her stomach growled once more, Mylo looked down at her.

"Hungry?" he asked with a raised brow.

"Starving. I can't remember the last time I ate."

"They tried while you were sick. Sera and Kyrad had callaloo sent up to you. In fact, Kyrad insisted and fetched the crabs fresh from the shore himself. But you only vomited it out."

Valxina's eyes darted between him and the others. Sera sat at the other end of the table, situated at the head. The woman looked cross. Valxina could see the rise and fall of her chest. Across from her sat Ky. When they reached his end, Mylo pulled a chair out for Valxina. She took the seat between Mylo and the commander.

They had tried to feed her while she was resting. The thought made her head spin. Sera seemed like a fair person, but kind? She had not thought her so nurturing. And now, looking at the way she seemed to glare into the sky—like the moon itself had vexed her—it was hard to imagine. And the commander... *Had he remembered her love for the dish?* She had mentioned it to him in the past, how fresh crab in callaloo reminded her of childhood dinners with her parents. Her father caught the best crabs on their street, and her mother always knew where to find the healthiest dasheen leaves to cook with. Her brows pinched together at the thought. Had Ky truly remembered?

"It was Inara and Danae who fed you," said Mylo. As if the last bit of information was not confusing enough. "Actually, Danae wouldn't leave your side."

"Why?" she replied.

The two women took their seats farther down the table. Valxina eyed them. She could not recall a moment from her rest—no matter how much she wished to.

Mylo didn't reply; he only shrugged as he reached for the roti and passed the basket to her side. Valxina ripped a piece in her hands. They were soft and still warm to the touch. The scent of roasted garlic danced into the air.

"How was your day, Mylo?" Ky asked, his voice low.

"Good, Commander, and yours?"

"Better than yours, I expect. Did she give you any trouble?"

Valxina cleared her throat. She swiped a bit of roti across the plate, drenching it in curried peas and aloo. "I hope you aren't speaking of me, Commander." When she looked up at him, his dark eyes flickered.

Valxina watched as Ky passed the tower guard a tankard of rum. Mylo shook his head and waved it away. "Still working, Commander," he said, his mouth full of geera pork. He nodded toward his keeper.

"And you?" Ky asked Valxina.

She huffed. "She... You... I have a name, you know, or have you forgotten it?" Heat rose within her.

The commander grinned. "Would you like some, *Val?*"

When she nodded, he placed the rum at her side. She reached for it, but the smell took her back. The last time she had a drink was in her bedroom, and she had only taken a sip as a prelude to wash out her mark. The memory clouded her thoughts. The smell, like rot and acid, rose to her nostrils. Valxina clenched her teeth. She could feel the turns within her stomach. The bitter taste pushed its way up.

Valxina pushed the drink aside and brought the back of her hand to her mouth. For a moment, she was there again. Her back tingled in recollection. It was dark. Her hair was still wet, drenched from the ceremony. Her heart banged against her chest, demanding to be free. Valxina forced the memory out. *Not here, not now,* she told herself. She squeezed her eyes shut and cursed beneath her breath.

Mylo noticed her behavior first. "Is something wrong with the food? Something is wrong with the food..." he repeated louder.

"No," Valxina replied. She forced a crooked smile to raise to her eyes and reached for the pitcher of water. She counted in her head. *One steed. Two steeds. Three steeds.* "It's not the food. It's me... I'm afraid the rum's stronger than I expected."

The tower guards around the table chuckled and glanced at each other with mocking grins. Valxina did not need to look across the table to know Sera's eyes rolled. Beside her, Mylo nodded, shifting back into his seat. But Ky's eyes remained on Valxina. She glanced over at him, noting the way his features hardened slightly. Did he not believe her? Did he see through her lie? When Valxina lifted her vision, she stilled.

Another watched her, their eyes intent and their chin raised. *Danae.*

Chapter 10

An hour had gone until the table was cleared. Valxina had drunk four glasses of water, freshly removed from a coconut, and eaten her weight in the perfectly rolled roti. She watched and listened silently as Ky forced conversation around the table. He asked his tower guards of their days and the keepers of their lives. She noted the way their faces gleamed at the questions. And while even Inara seemed taken with him, Danae stayed true to her form. The woman only answered his questions with a curt yes or no, even to inquiries that required more.

Valxina scraped the jelly from the inside of her coconut. It was a habit she had acquired through the years. Even now, she couldn't let the sweet treat go to waste. She surveyed the way the others nodded and smiled. It was as if they were waiting for his attention, wishing for someone to ask about their life prior to their ceremony. But Ky had always been that way—he always sought to make people feel comfortable. Creating friendships and comrades out of the most unlikely of souls was a gift the gods had bestowed on the commander.

Valxina recalled the first time she had met him. Ky was only a new recruit, a trainee from the womb of a noblewoman. She had been so worried about joining the men in the ring. Valxina recalled the way she kept her head down and her arms behind her back. She was just a girl then—a quiet girl with no friends and one wish. When he sauntered up to her and asked her name, she had turned red.

"Sera!" Keeper Pax's voice echoed, shattering Valxina's memory. Every head turned to face the woman standing at the edge of the table. Conversation halted as a wave of silence washed across the space.

"What happened?" another voice questioned.

Sera reached for the edge of her robe and tightened it. Her eyes darted around the table.

"What is it?" Inara's voice mumbled to Danae beside her.

Mylo turned silently to Valxina and the commander.

"Nothing is the matter," Sera replied, her voice booming down the table. And as if willing the table to return to normalcy, she sat back down. No one dared to ask further questions when she shot a glare across the space. The blues of her eyes silenced them. All except for the commander.

"Sera?" His voice was low.

"Not the time," Sera replied with a hiss.

Heads turned again, this time toward a figure. A man was entering the courtyard. Valxina's hair rose from the back of her neck.

"Mylo?" she said as the tower guard moved to stand.

"Stand down, Mylo," Ky muttered to Valxina's right. "It's—"

"It's only me," the voice replied.

Valxina recognized the voice. She knew that calculated, horrid cadency too well. But she hadn't heard it since the ceremony—since he had announced her name.

"Adviser Eno," Ky said as he stood. Valxina watched the remaining tower guards rise from their seats. They all greeted him with a nod.

Eno was the greatest gossip of them all. Some members of the Court had even gifted him the adoring nickname of "Serpent's Tongue." Valxina turned in her seat.

"Keeper Sera," Eno said as she stood, "please, no need to stand." He motioned for all to return to their seats. They did not.

"I didn't know we were to expect your company tonight," said Ky. "If I had known, we would have pushed our meal back."

Eno shook his head. He rubbed his rough hands together with eager eyes. "No, no—that is not necessary, Commander Kyrad."

"I hope all is well with the lord?" Ky said.

Sera's face tightened at the mention. She lifted her chin higher. It was a move Valxina knew too well.

"Lord Zessfar is very well, Commander. In fact, it was he who sent me here."

Ky tilted his head. "Oh?"

"It seems he had some visitors to his chambers today," the adviser continued, his voice strange.

Mylo's head snapped to Valxina, and her eyes widened. She watched as Mylo reached for his scabbard. *But surely... surely, this was not about her? And if it were, why would Valxina be in harm's way?*

Silence prowled across the table. The keepers studied Eno. They noted each movement he made, each breath he took. The air grew thick. The question vibrated through them. None needed to say it; none needed to put voice to words. Valxina straightened her back as Eno moved forward. He flashed a wink at Mylo.

"Who?" Ky finally asked. His voice was harsh, demanding even. He knew Eno was not here for dinner. He had been sent for *someone*.

Eno lifted a hand into the air. It was a slow movement, like the decaying of the pit. He said no words as the Badawi House guards moved out of the shadows behind him.

"Adviser Eno?" said Ky. "Surely, if we have a problem, there is no reason, no need, for collision? House guards surrounding tower guards..." Ky shook his head. "I do not think the lord—"

"Do you question his authority? Are you doubting my lord's judgment?"

Valxina's heart quickened. She stood, ready for her name on his vile lips. Mylo stepped in front of her, his free arm extending to push her back.

Ky moved forward. "Who?"

Eno grinned. "Keeper Seraphine."

Valxina's heart dropped to her stomach, and she released a deep breath. But when the name echoed within her head once more, she lifted a brow. *Keeper Seraphine?*

"Sera?" Pax questioned. "At the lord's chambers?" There was more to her words, like the very event could not happen. Whispers broke out between the women.

Ky's face hardened. "Sera?"

Keeper Sera moved forward silently. She kept her head held high. The moon seemed to illuminate her pathway. No tower guards moved to protect her—to stop the Badawi Guard members from grabbing her.

When Valxina turned to Ky, he seemed to understand her eyes—to read the question that raced across her mind.

"Seraphine has denied herself a guard. She asked that she be removed from the roster... Ever since hers fell in Chantara's attempted siege," said Ky.

"And you allowed that?" Valxina snapped.

She watched as Ky lowered his face to match hers. His hand wrapped around her wrist swiftly. She had never seen his face like this. It was a reckoning. Valxina tried to break free of his grasp as he tugged at her. She dug her heels into the ground as he whispered, "For fuck's sake, little mouse, keep your damn mouth shut."

"Commander?" Mylo whispered. His eyes widened at the sight.

Ky shook his head. Under the night sky, with his fingers wrapped around her, and his eyes demanding, the commander looked unrecognizable. He almost looked wicked. "Stay out of it, Brother."

Before his exit, Eno gave one last glance towards the others. He let his eyes linger on Valxina for a moment too long. He looked her up and down with a smile. "Remind your keepers to be careful," he said in parting.

The commander didn't lift a finger as the House guards removed Keeper Sera. He didn't say a word as they rushed her to the palace. And through it all, Ky kept his grip firm. Valxina held her breath as they took Sera away under the watch of the stars. *What could Keeper Sera do to invoke such aggression? Did Zessfar have a reason to act with such vigor?*

"Inside," Ky commanded. Valxina fought the instinct to tremble at the sound. His voice echoed through the courtyard. "Now."

CHAPTER 11

When the commander yelled "inside," Valxina expected to be sent to her room. By the way Mylo's eyes bore into her, she half-expected the tower guard to escort her straight there himself. But when Ky's fingers wrapped around her arm, his fingers tense and his skin pulsing, she imagined he could fling her up the tower with the slightest of maneuvers.

What she did not expect was to be taken to Ky's quarters. When Danae and Inara raised their brows and questioned why Valxina was needed, Ky directed Desil and Agnar to bring their keepers into his quarters as well. Danae swiped away at Agnar's hand and rolled her eyes at the order. Pax was the only keeper who had entered Ky's quarters without being commanded to do so. She stormed straight through the doorway. It seemed the woman had also forgone a guard of her own. No one told her to enter; she did so herself.

"I'm going to be sick," Pax said as she slumped into the

armchair in the corner. When she snapped the veil off her face, Valxina stiffened at the sight. They were out of public eyes, but Ky's quarters were outside of the tower. She did not expect the woman to remove her covering so casually.

"Why the fuck are we here?" Danae shouted. She shrugged as Agnar tried to take grip of her.

Inara hadn't fought Desil off the way Danae had. When Desil motioned for her to move toward the commander's quarters near the east side of the courtyard, Inara had abided. She steadied herself against the wall and watched the others. Confusion plastered across her face.

"What did you see?" Ky asked. "Pax, when you called out at the table, before Eno emerged like a rat in a sewer... What did Sera mean, *not the time?*"

Pax buried her face in her hands. She rocked herself, letting out a muffled cry. "I... I don't know."

Valxina walked over to her. "Did you see something?" she asked. "Was there something wrong? Something that you saw?"

"She pulled at her robe, Pax," Inara interrupted. "Was she hiding something? Did—"

"She was bleeding," said Pax. "She wouldn't tell me what left her dripping with blood..."

"Who knows why they took her. There's probably some good reason behind it all," said Danae. When they all turned to her, eyes wide, she shrugged. "I don't see why we are getting all worked up about this. Just count our blessings we weren't the ones that got pulled out of here."

Inara opened her mouth, but it was Valxina who interrupted this time. "Count our blessings?"

"A keeper was removed from the tower by force," said Ky. "House guards were brought against us. Like we don't serve the same lord and king..."

"So this has never been seen before?" Mylo questioned.

Desil and Agnar were at least ten years his senior. They both turned to one another and shook their heads. When they glanced at Ky, he mimicked them. "No, I don't believe this has ever happened before."

"So why now?" asked Keeper Pax. "Why Seraphine?"

Danae rolled her eyes. "Clearly, she went to go see the lord today. Lovers' quarrel, perhaps?"

Inara gasped. Valxina's jaw dropped. The room filled with tension.

Keepers were not meant to be touched by any man or woman. The ceremony was supposed to represent that shift to holiness.

Pax jumped to her feet. "Listen here, if you don't keep that mouth of yours shu—"

"You know the implications of such an accusation," warned Ky.

Agnar stepped between Danae and Pax. Danae's eyes widened, and she grinned at Pax's response. "A-Are you two..."

Pax rolled her eyes and covered her face in her hands.

"Eno kept looking at you," Inara said to Valxina. She said the words softly, as if unsure whether they should leave her lips. "I thought he was going to call out your name."

When Ky looked at Valxina, his eyes willed an answer.

"Val... Mylo... Is there something you should tell us about the day?"

Mylo's eyes narrowed. "You told me to escort her to the lord."

"And where did you find him?" Ky responded.

"In his quarters."

The commander hissed. "You brought her to his bedroom?"

Valxina moved between them. She positioned herself in front of her guard. "Nothing happened."

"Nothing needs to happen," Ky replied.

"What do you mean?"

Danae shook her head as she moved forward. "Because the rumor mill has already started. Are you truly doltish enough to enter the lord's rooms alone?"

"She wasn't alone," said Mylo.

"It doesn't matter," Danae said, with no compassion behind her eyes. "You cannot just walk into a man's bedroom and not expect whispers to spread."

But he wasn't a man—he was the lord. And when the lord of the Badawi House calls you to his chambers, how could you explain the impropriety of it all?

"I did not realize I had a choice in the matter. I did not think I could refuse to see him. You all sent me there," Valxina said, her eyes fixating on Keeper Pax.

Pax pressed her lips together. She sighed and shook her head. But the movement made her uneasy again.

"And Keeper Sera? Had she truly entered the lord's quarters? Or is she the victim of the Court's gossip?" questioned Pax.

"Pax, please. You know Keeper Sera better than the rest of us. Was there something, anything, strange about her today?" Ky moved towards the woman in the corner. His words were soft and his movement slow.

"She was upset," Pax replied. "After she left the crypt."

Ky rubbed at his temples. "What was she upset about?"

"I don't know. All she said was, 'He healed her, but not where it mattered.'"

Valxina's blood ran cold. Her eyes widened, and her breathing quickened. In her hands, she gathered bits of fabric from her skirt and squeezed at it, her hands growing slick with sweat.

"Does anyone have any idea what that could mean?" Danae replied, her arms crossed in annoyance.

Mylo turned to Valxina. When she looked up at him, her breath caught. She walked over to the commander's desk and gripped its edges. Her fingers pinched at her nose, still concealed under her veil. "It was about me," she said through gritted teeth. "It's about what Zessfar did to me."

"Zessfar?" Danae repeated, her brows raised at his name.

Ky grasped the edge of his desk. His nostrils flared as he gritted his teeth and directed his gaze at Valxina. His glare traveled, settling on her tower guard. "Mylo," Ky growled.

Mylo moved forward. He rolled his eyes at Ky's actions. "It wasn't like that. You can calm down."

"Calm down?"

"Can someone tell me what is going on here?" Danae's

voice called out. A storm brewed beneath the surface of her eyes. She turned to Valxina. "You." Danae sucked her teeth. "You are the reason for everything, aren't you? And why? Has Keeper Sera been put in the dungeon because of your poor peasant cunt?"

A slap passed across Danae's face. Danae's mouth dropped. She reached for the burning red spot. And then she looked at the woman who had laid her hand across her flesh. It was Keeper Inara.

"You, of all people, know better than to say such a thing to another woman," Inara said.

Danae stared at her silently.

Agnar's eyes widened, and he stumbled back. Desil, as if concerned for his keeper, moved Inara behind him. And while Valxina expected Danae to reach for Inara's face, she did not. Danae lifted a shaking hand to her cheek, and her eyes softened. If Valxina did not know better, she would have believed shame, maybe even embarrassment, flooded over the woman's features.

"Enough," said Pax. "Tell us what happened with the lord, Keeper Val."

Valxina kept her head hung at the commander's desk. "H-He told me that I impressed him at the ceremony," Valxina started. The words felt foolish. "He pulled a vial out of his pocket and said it was water from The Spring. He washed the wound on my head with it. He healed it. That is it, that is... that is all at happened."

"He used Spring water on you?" Ky asked. "And what did Sera mean, when she said he healed you—but not where it mattered?"

Silence dissipated through the room. Valxina knew what Sera meant by the words. Danae and Inara knew what the keeper had referred to. And with the new information, Pax shook her head. She, too, knew what Sera meant. The men in the room had no idea—they had no knowledge of the mark that had turned Valxina sick. They had no awareness of the severity, of the mangled skin, or of the putrid smell of the burnt flesh. Valxina shot her glance towards Danae and Inara. Inara lowered her head, but the other held her glance. Valxina balled her hands into fists at her side.

"What did she mean?" Ky repeated.

But Valxina stayed silent. She shook her head, waiting to see if either of the new keepers had it in them to share. But they didn't. Danae and Inara stayed quiet. Even now, the secret ritual of the keepers would remain unknown.

"It doesn't matter," Keeper Pax said. "What matters is what we do now. How do we know Sera is ok?"

"I can make an inquiry," Ky said.

"And what if the House guards turn on you for asking such questions?" Mylo asked. "I do not think it wise."

"I'll do it," Valxina replied.

Ky rolled his eyes. "And what do you have in mind?"

"I'll speak to Zessfar."

Zessfar. The name rolled off her tongue like she knew him.

"You'll do no such thing," Mylo said from Valxina's side.

"I'm going," she replied, head held high. She turned to face the commander. Ky ran his fingers through his dark hair and took a deep breath as he fumbled in his pocket for a roll of tobacco.

"But we need to speak first."

"I knew this was coming," he said. "Everyone out. Except Val."

Chapter 12

Kyrad Varma became commander of the tower guards two years ago. The last time Valxina had seen him was the night of his appointment. She wasn't allowed into the room—the space was reserved for noblemen and women. But Valxina had snuck into the balcony and watched from above. He deserved it. With all his talk of unity and his beliefs in equality, no one was better equipped to command the tower guards. The late Commander Hu would have been proud to see him, to know Ky was his successor.

"I'm going to Zessfar tonight, regardless of what you think, regardless of what Mylo wants."

The commander shook his head. "Zessfar," he repeated. "You say his name so casually."

Valxina forced a smile. "He asked me to." She watched the way his brows raised. "I know it sounds ridiculous. Trust me, I could barely do it when he asked me to. It's like after all these years of wishing and wanting... of working so damn hard and keeping my mouth shut. It was strange to be spoken to the way he did." When Ky dropped his head. Valxina added, "Don't do that."

"What?"

"You aren't allowed to be jealous, *Commander* Kyrad."

"I'm not jealous."

"I believe I know you better than that." Valxina lifted a brow. At least, she thought she knew him. "What's wrong?"

"I'm not jealous. I have no right to be jealous. I know that. Am I not allowed to care for the well-being of an old friend?"

Valxina huffed. "I certainly do not need you to protect me. I thought I made that clear on the night of your ceremony."

"The last time you saw me, you said you never wanted to lay eyes on me again." Smoke circled around the commander as he drew from the tobacco. In the darkness, he looked different—like tension had built within his muscles and beneath his dark eyes. Gone was the look of childlike mischief, replaced with the weight of responsibility and duty. Valxina thought back to the night their friendship had shifted.

Following Ky's appointment, Valxina had followed him into the courtyard. There was a spot near the gardens, far enough from the palace but not close enough to the pit to despair. The two would occasionally go there following their sparing practice. Something about that night told them to go there. And when Valxina saw him up close, when she saw how he stood in his new uniform, with the bead of gold, an emblem of his status, weaved into his hair, she froze. She knew heartbreak lingered around the corner. She knew how their friendship would end. And while she was the one who spoke the words, she did not expect him to abide, not truly. Even now, as she looked at him and the way he watched her, longing ripe at his lips, she wished he had not listened.

"The last time you saw me, I was stupid," said Valxina. She reached for the roll of tobacco. Ky watched silently as her fingers grasped it from his. She stood only inches away. When she leaned over the table and outed the roll on a plate, he did not object. He only sighed. He didn't need her to protect him either. But she always did even when he willed her not to, even when it was at her own expense.

"I'm going to see Zessfar."

Ky shook his head. *"Zessfar."* He crossed his arms across his chest and leaned against the paneled wood wall. "What exactly do you plan to say to the Badawi lord?"

"The truth. That Sera was taken by Badawi House guards."

"You do not think he already knows this?"

"Do you? Would you be serving our lord if you thought he was capable of arresting keepers without stated reason?"

Ky lowered his face. He lifted a hand to his chin and rubbed his fingers over his beard.

"I serve The Spring and you keepers—I'm not a House guard."

Valxina released a deep breath. "Even so, I know you would not be here if you truly believed Zessfar was some sort of malicious ruler."

Ky nodded. "Val, I get your point. So you do remember me."

Valxina grinned. "Me? It was you who has been acting as if you have no knowledge or recollection of me. So you will not try to stop me?"

"I know there's no stopping you, no matter how much I may disagree with you. No matter how hard I wish or pray." It was clear in his tone that the man wasn't speaking of Valxina's wish to visit their lord. He said the words with another encounter in mind.

Valxina smiled. "You were never a praying man, Ky. I've never seen you set foot in the palace temple or the ones out in town. I've never even watched you light a diya lamp on our holiest of days or respond to the daily prayer calls of those who worship the other."

"Well, a man can change, can't he?"

Valxina nodded. He certainly had changed.

"What's your plan, anyway?"

Valxina released a deep breath before answering, "He likes me. I know it probably sounds wrong, but perhaps he'll open up. Perhaps he'll help... if he thinks... you know..." She scrunched her face, preparing for Ky to interrupt her. "It doesn't hurt to ask."

Ky lifted a brow. "Val, are you saying you plan to seduce the lord of the Badawi House?"

Valxina smiled. "I guess I am."

"And you think it'll work?"

"You don't?"

"You know, I am familiar with the force you can

emit—I know it all too well. Zessfar had his serpents asking for you. A Badawi guard came to my door after your ceremony asking of your history—of whether I thought you were someone worth attention."

Valxina narrowed her eyes. "He mentioned your praises. I did not realize you thought so highly of me."

Ky laughed. "You didn't? I think you know exactly how I feel about you." When Valxina looked away, he continued, "I do not doubt Zessfar would say anything just to get closer to you, but how could you be sure that it just isn't *anything*? How are you sure he will tell the truth?"

Valxina shook her head. "I don't know." She released a deep sigh. She knew how foolish the words sounded, but she needed him to see her as more than the girl he once knew. "Just let me get close to him. Besides, what do you have against the lord to believe him a liar?"

Ky walked over to her and rested a hand on her shoulder, trying to ignore the way she shifted under his touch. Her words bellowed between them. *Let me get close to him.* Valxina hesitated for a moment but stilled. It was only Ky. She had trained with him. She had no reason to shy away from his contact. In fact, she longed for the familiar grasp of his hand. But she would never admit so, not out loud. Not to him.

"Nothing," he said. "Only that he is a man... and I know men."

Valxina rolled her eyes. "I think he already has a soft side for me. You can ask Mylo; he was tender in his chambers today. He was filled with Badawi arrogance and the confidence that only comes with wealth."

The commander lifted a brow. "You speak as you hate them so."

"Hate who?"

"The wealthy of the Court. The noblemen and women... the lord himself."

Valxina looked into the commander's eyes. A knot traveled up her throat. He looked like he wanted to say more. Ky watched her with a heavy face. She knew his question had nothing to do with the lord.

"That night," Valxina began, "the last time we saw each other... You don't know this, but I snuck into your ceremony. I watched them pin that crest to your chest." She lifted a finger and outlined the item on Ky's uniform. "When you stood from your kneel, it was like something I had never seen before. It looked like rebirth. The colors suited you so well. The adornments looked like they were forged for you and only you. When you turned to the crowd. I saw you smile. It was a grin I had only seen when you were with me. That's how I knew you were right where you ought to be. I swore, the way the candlelight flickered across you, and by the roar of the crowd, I was sure I was watching a man blessed by the gods."

She let out a stifled breath before continuing, "I know I told you about *her*." Valxina could not say her name out loud. "The person I loved before... someone who was kind and bright, and when I looked at her, I swore I was in the presence of an angel. But life was cruel to me—it always has been. We were both poor. We were both untouchable. But I was a servant below even the lowest of ranks. I was a lotto child." She watched as Ky withdrew with the words...

lotto child. "I lost her because of our ranks and the whispers that dragged us down. When I saw you in that uniform, when I saw the way you reached for me in the gardens that night..." Valxina lifted her chin. "I knew if you were to achieve all you wanted in your life, all the wonderful, selfless things you longed for, you would not be able to do so with me. I knew rumors and gossips would destroy you if you were caught with a friend... a partner... *a lover*... of my class."

She paused, savoring the truth and gut-wrenching stain of the word on her mouth, lover. "So, when you reached for me in the gardens, I told you to forget about me. I told you to move on. When you say I speak as if I hate the wealthy of the Court, the noblemen and women... Maybe I do. I know you are bred from them, Ky. But I have never considered you so. Because where there is ice and vile evilness in them, there is warmth and righteousness in your veins. I knew it then, and I see it now. Ky—I have to do this. I must find out why someone would send guards to detain a woman blessed by the gods, a woman who has vowed to protect The Spring." Valxina shrugged her shoulders and stood up tall.

"Why?"

"Because I was not safe," Valxina said. "I was not safe as a child nor as a servant. I thought I'd be safe as a keeper. But after the ceremony, after Keeper Sera... I'm not so sure that is true anymore. I am a woman surrounded by powerful men. And no change in rank or title could ever protect me, truly protect me, from them."

"I can protect you," Ky muttered.

But Valxina released a stifled laugh. "And when you are not around? Am I to rely on the muscles and hot heads of men until I am dead? No." She bit at the edge of her lip. "I need to do this on my own."

"And I'm supposed to watch you flirt around the lord?"

Valxina smirked. "Yes."

Ky leaned closer to her. "I have missed you, mouse."

Valxina grinned at the familiar name. "You still think me a mouse?" she asked with a raised brow.

Ky shook his head. "No. Maybe Commander Hu was right all along. Maybe you really are a stealthy fox... a woman brave enough to go to the Badawi lord and ask for answers."

✦

The palace was built for gossip. It was made for secret rendezvous and whispers in the dark. Archways and hollow halls echoed, carrying rumors on the backs of dust. At night, the House of Badawi was notorious for its debauchery. Any sliver of darkness could conceal those who took advantage of the cover of shadows. Court members treated the night like a blanket, a shield from the clarity of day that resulted in such gossip. But Valxina knew true gossip did not come with the sun. It was the night—the cast of the moon that brought the juiciest of rumors. The wildest of tales were born under the stars. The cruelest of stories came out of the dark. In a Court deprived of privacy, the night was a slice of freedom its people could not turn down.

She, too, had taken advantage of it on occasion. When she was sixteen, she would sneak off to meet a fellow fire-keep Eleni under the stars. Eleni was the first person Valxina felt seen by, cared by, loved by. Fire-keeps were not allowed a life outside of their duties; none of the servants were. But under the protection of the stars, the two would sneak out into the archways. They'd dare to hold one another. Valxina thought of her often. The west side archways brought the brightest of grins to her face. She could still see them, see their bodies pressed against one another. All the fires they'd light by day lit no match to the heat between them. It was young and tender love. They had even exchanged lockets of their own hair. The heartbreak was devastating. It's what propelled Valxina to the path of a keeper—it's what made her wish to never experience love again.

Valxina hurried under the archways. Eleni's voice, calm and sweet, seemed to encourage her further. She swore she could feel her fingers caress her cheek. She swore she could hear the woman scold them on the night they were caught. The rumors had reached the entire Court by the next morning. Two fire-keeps had dared to love, to find a scrap of privacy and compassion for one another. How dare they? They didn't deserve such a luxury—not according to the others. Especially when the noblemen and women themselves hunted for that feeling, hungry for what they had.

So, when Valxina decided she needed to speak to Lord

Zessfar, she knew her only chance was to do so at night. Perhaps the shadows of the eve would bring her that same protection that it once did with her, with Eleni. When she reached the doors of his rooms, her feet scuffed against the carpet. The guards looked down at her, brows raised. They glimpsed behind her at the glint of her javelin.

"Please tell the lord I am here," Valxina said with her softest of voices. "He'll want to see me."

Mylo lingered in the shadows. She had instructed him to stay there—to not enter the room with her. He had protested at first, stating that a keeper should not be in the presence of a man without her guard. But alas, when the order came from Ky's lips, Valxina's tower guard abided through gritted teeth.

Valxina watched as one guard whispered to the other. "I was here just earlier," she added.

The guard who bore the tattooed house crest on his arm disappeared behind the door. The crest, like the one Valxina now bore, included images of waves in motion. At the center lay the delicate "B" adorned with creeping water snakes. It was an ode to the Badawi family history. It was the same crest Lord Zessfar wore.

The other guard lifted his chin. His dark eyes scanned her.

"The lord isn't expecting any maidens tonight."

Valxina concealed her irritation. He was testing her and her temper.

"As I am sure you know by my dress and veil, sir, I am no maiden. Keeper Valxina Kulrani is my name."

The second guard returned. He turned to his partner

and shook his head. "Your weapon stays here," he said as the other moved aside.

Valxina felt her heart quicken. "I am a keeper. I am required to hold my weapon on me at all times. It is at the request of my lord and king that—"

"Let her in, boys." Zessfar's voice spilled through the doorway like honey. "Are you truly afraid of a woman armed?" He chuckled.

The guards moved aside. Valxina lifted her head as she moved forward. *The doorway. She had made it to the doorway. It was farther than the others had anticipated.*

Chapter 13

The lord's chambers transformed at night. Slivers of moonlight illuminated the walls of portraits in a way that made them almost appear alive. Valxina allowed her eyes to roam the room once more. She had been so fixated on him, on Zessfar, when she came through the doors, she hadn't noticed the largest portrait, the image of him that hung in the entryway. It was distorted, a painting of him where half appeared true to life, a man of flesh and blood, and the other appeared of him in death. The portrait seemed like a reminder of mortality. *But what was life and death to an immortal lord? Why would any of it matter?* She turned her head between the portrait and Lord Zessfar before her.

Valxina lowered herself to the ground. She moved to outstretch her hands before her and bow, but Zessfar shook his head and spoke, "No need, Valxina. You may stand."

Valxina's muscles tensed. She watched him curiously

as she rose to her feet. It was not common for lords to wave off greetings of power.

But Zessfar only grinned at her. "A javelin?" His brows raised. "Impressive." Zessfar stalked over to her. Just as he had been earlier, he appeared familiar. He wore a white sleep shirt and plain pants. The first three buttons of his shirt lay undone against his chest. Just days ago, before her ceremony, if Valxina had seen her lord like this, it would have been considered abhorrently inappropriate. Even now, as a keeper, she found it wrong to see him like this under the guise of the night. But perhaps the false sense of safety, the feeling of freedom that accompanied the darkness, perhaps that pertained to Lord Zessfar as well.

Zessfar's eyes glimmered under the candlelight as he studied the keeper in his room. He raked over her as if to memorize her. "What are you doing here?"

Valxina swallowed the knot in her throat and looked up at him. "Keeper Sera." She analyzed the man's reaction to Sera's name, but if Zessfar knew anything of Sera's arrest, he did not show it. His face was still, and his hands remained relaxed at his sides.

"Seraphine?" He said her name like a song, like a gospel from the scriptures. "I hope all is well between the two of you."

Valxina stilled. "Adviser Eno has taken her."

"Eno?" Zessfar said, his brows pinching at the words. "What do you mean, he has taken her?"

Valxina titled her chin towards him. "Adviser Eno brought the House guards and took her away tonight, my lord. He had her removed from the courtyard without a spoken reason."

She watched as he blinked slowly. Zessfar shook his head and moved toward her. Valxina studied the way Zessfar rubbed at his face, at the scruff of his beard.

"I'm sorry, Kulrani. I was not aware of this. I—I'll get to the bottom of this."

"You did not give the command?"

"I certainly did not." His chest rose and fell deeply. This was not a man of madness. This was not a man of cruelty. This was a young lord unaware of his adviser's actions. But even so, Valxina was not entirely convinced.

"I am sorry, That must have been a terror," he whispered, flexing his hands. She did the same thing when anxious or overwhelmed. "You say the House guards took her?"

Valxina nodded. "That is correct. Commander Kyrad felt it was—"

"Commander Kyrad must be enraged," said Zessfar. "Rightfully, I am. Badawi House guards surrounding tower guards? It's unheard of. It's—"

"It's wrong, Zessfar." She said his name again, hoping the familiarity would be enough to have him overlook her critique.

Zessfar's eyes lowered. "Are you close with Keeper Sera?"

Valxina bit her lip. She diverted her response. "Are you? They are saying she entered your chamber today? That this might have to do with something between you and me?"

"*You and me?*" Zessfar said softly. It almost embarrassed her. Was the thought such a joke to the man? He brushed a hand through his dark curls. "I don't know what to tell you, Kulrani."

Valxina looked through the window and examined the way the moon shone through the crevices of stone. She hoped the night would protect her and propriety would be shaped and bent because of the shadows. She prayed her next words would be safe.

"Why did you heal my wound this afternoon, my lord?"

Zessfar released a deep breath. "I favor a good underdog story, Kulrani. I know what it is like to be underestimated and I... well, I do not know what it is about you, but I have a feeling you may also understand what that feeling is like."

Valxina nodded. She had. Every moment that led her to the keepers was filled with doubt, both from others and herself. But how could a lord feel underestimated?

Zessfar turned and walked over to the cart in the center of the room. She watched as he filled a glass of wine. When he faced her, brows raised, she could hear his question; he did not need to speak the words. Valxina nodded. As the lord stalked over to her, glass in hand, she steadied herself, studying the eels etched into the glasses. She pressed the edge of the glass against her lips. The wine tasted of peaches, like a faint island breeze, and like rays of sunlight. She pressed her lips together, savoring the moment.

"Better than the servants' rum, isn't it?" Zessfar laughed.

But how would he know? Valxina's eyes widened. "What's that?"

"Oh, don't be coy with me, Kulrani."

Valxina sighed. "Don't tell me that rumor has reached the ears of my lord."

Zessfar shook his head. "I don't suppose it would have... if I hadn't gone around asking about you."

Their eyes locked. "And what else have you found out about me?" She hoped he could not sense the fear behind her words. Who knew what other rumors lay dormant on the lips of those who wished to see her fail?

"Lotto child, fire-keep, kitchen servant turned enchantress." Valxina rolled her eyes.

"I don't understand that last one."

"No?" Zessfar asked. "I do."

"You think me a witch?"

He shook his head. "I do not believe I know, truly, what you are, Keeper Valxina. But I saw you that night at the ceremony. I felt the way you looked up at me. It was bewitching. I am not surprised at the gossip that has stemmed from it. I don't suppose you are surprised by it, truly, yourself?"

Bewitching. Even if this was a part of her plan, hearing that word leave the lord's lips quickened Valxina's pulse.

Valxina released a sharp breath. "Zessfar," she said, the name all too familiar on her tongue.

He smiled at the sound and lifted a finger to the corner of his mouth. He wiped at the wine that sat at the edge of his full lips. And when he lifted his chin toward the empty chaise, she moved toward it. Her body sank into it, falling deeper than she expected.

"I have a riddle for you," she said. "I know it is a strange moment to bring it up, but would you indulge me?"

Zessfar nodded.

"In a far-away kingdom of only liars and truth-tellers, you meet the two most beautiful women to ever live. Azami, a woman with dark coils of hair and skin as smooth as silk, comes up to you first. Behind her, the other woman, Gisele, watches, studying you with eyes so rich and deep you risk falling into them if you aren't careful. Azami says, 'We are both liars.' What is the truth?"

Zessfar raised a brow. "Are you calling me a liar?" While the question was a blow to her chest, his tone was light as if half-laughing. Zessfar did not see her as a threat.

Valxina held her breath. She shook her head as she replied, "No. Not at all. But who in the riddle is a liar? Is it Azami, or is it Gisele? Are both of them liars, or is it neither?"

Zessfar studied Valxina's eyes. He inched closer as he thought, pressing a finger against his lip. "They cannot both be liars. It wouldn't be possible. It would mean a liar would have to tell the truth. If Azami is the liar, that would mean her statement is still a lie. Gisele is the truth-teller, and Azami is a liar." He leaned back, pride plastered across his grin.

Valxina smiled as she nodded. "It took me ages to figure that one out," she lied, surprised by the lord's intellect. "And then there's you, solving it on the spot." Zessfar's smile widened at her words. They might not have been in a far-away kingdom, but here, Valxina knew the room had at least one liar—herself. She wondered if Zessfar could tell the truth. She wondered if he could see through her.

"Your riddle is unbelievable, anyway."

"And why is that?"

"Because, if you don't mind me saying, the most beautiful woman to ever live stands before me in the House of Badawi."

Liar. Cunning, flirtatious, silver-tongued liar. Valxina winced at the far-fetched comment. But while the compliment was far too much for her to ever believe or fall for, a small part of her warmed at it. No matter how she felt, no matter her true motive, hearing such words from the lips of a lord took her aback. She narrowed her eyes at the compliment, unsure of how to respond. He was bold.

"Ok, maybe that came off a bit too..." Zessfar started.

But Valxina hushed him and smiled. "No, that was sweet. But Seraphine... Tell me the truth, Zessfar. Please. Tell me the truth." The words danced out of her and lingered in the air.

Lord Zessfar rose from his seat. Valxina knew one scream would summon Mylo here. But she prayed it would not amount to that. No, perhaps the lord was misunderstood. Yes, he definitely had the faults of every man of wealth, but was there a possibility the rumors were wrong? Valxina straightened her back at the thought. She wouldn't be fooled, no, not by him. But if what he said was true, the lord did not know of Eno's actions. Valxina bit at the edge of her lip; she had to get to the bottom of this. *Why had Keeper Sera been taken?* And what did this have to do with her?

Her name sounded so familiar on his tongue. "Seraphine..."

Chapter 14

Valxina was used to hearing about the most personal aspects of people's lives. It came with the territory of being a lotto child, a servant, a person who, to some, was not even a person. As if they were alone, most people spoke to one another frankly in her presence. Even information that one may deem private was ok to be said in the presence of Valxina—for she was a servant. Who could she share the news with? She was no one. Only a few people in her life shared information about their lives with Valxina purposely. Ky was one of those people. She remembered the way he would gush about his mother to her. A noblewoman with the heart of gold. Who knew they existed? He would even share the darker of memories, the motivations of his that weren't as pretty. Much of those stories involved tales of his father and of the death of his younger brother.

Eleni often told Valxina about her siblings—of her brother and sister who lived on the farm. Eleni would paint vivid illustrations of her life before guards took her. She wasn't a child of the lottery, not like Valxina. Instead, the late lord had taken her at the age of eight. She was collateral for late rent payments and farm fees. When Eleni's parents failed to pay the guards, they were instructed to take a child to work the debt off. Eleni hid her baby sister in the barn, leaving her behind a pile of hay. Her older brother couldn't go, Eleni had said. She thought it better for him to stay on the land and work it. If he continued to help, they stood a stance to make the money up. So, when it was time, Eleni ran right up to the guards and sacrificed herself. Valxina knew people from all walks of life had issues—problems with families, with friends, with work, and with lovers. She heard the problems of many. But as she sat across from Lord Zessfar, she froze. She never expected to hear the problems of a lord.

"Seraphine. She did visit me today." The lord lifted his palm to his face and wiped a bead of sweat away from his brow. "I know you probably see her as rigid. I know other fresh keepers perceive her as harsh or unapproachable." He sighed. "But she wasn't always that way."

Valxina tilted her head towards him. "Zessfar?" she said, pushing him to continue on.

"Seraphine came to my chambers today. She... It is hard when two people have history. Years can pass by, people can grow old, responsibilities can weigh on your shoulders... yet sometimes, you'll see them as they were. But it's an illusion. It's a coping mechanism we create for our own happiness. It's a way to convince ourselves that even the things that can't work will work, that maybe there's a chance."

"So you and Keeper Sera?" Maybe Danae was right after all.

"We were young. She was a daughter of a wealthy nobleman, and I was the heir to the Badawi House. She hadn't even thought about becoming a keeper, and I surely had no idea the position would pass to me so soon. Hell, I thought the responsibilities would never pass to me. My father was immortal; he had drunk from The Spring. How was I supposed to know someone would get close enough to cut his head clean off? Even an immortal man cannot live without his head." His face twisted in pain. "She was smart—probably the brightest woman I have ever met. We'd sneak off the palace grounds and into the town taverns." Zessfar smirked. "I'd steal money, Badawi funds, and gamble them away with her."

It was hard to picture Sera running around with Zessfar, gambling in a tavern of all places. "What happened? What changed?"

Zessfar lowered his head. She watched as he stared into his wine. "Her parents found me unworthy... They, too, did not believe I would ever ascend to the throne. They knew I gambled away funds, that I was a far cry away from my father. You see, my father was smart, he was tough, and he was... fit for the position. Everyone believed I was not."

Even the lord before her knew the feeling of being underestimated. Valxina lowered her gaze. "Years ago, I had heard rumors you were to be wed to the daughter of a nobleman?"

"Yeah, I got so desperate I got on my knee for her, for

Sera. I proposed. And she said no."

Valxina bit the inside of her cheek. He was being so... candid. She hadn't expected it.

"She did not want me when my future was uncertain. She let the words of her parents and gossips of the Court sway her decision." The lord met Valxina's eyes. "I loved her—but she chose another path."

Seraphine had chosen the path of a keeper, the life of a holy woman.

"And today, why did she visit your chambers?"

"Seraphine visits every so often. She visits to remind me I am not my father. She visits to remind me why she did not say yes. I do not know why she continues to do so, why she feels it necessary to scold me like a child. Perhaps she was jealous when she saw I had healed the wound on your head. I've never used the waters for her. She came here in a blaze about it all."

Valxina moved to sit next to him. She reached a hand out and touched his. She could see Seraphine was taut, but this... she had never expected this kind of heartlessness from the woman. And she knew all too well what it felt like to be pushed into the shadows.

"I have no idea why Eno has done this. Please trust me, Kulrani." Lord Zessfar's eyes grew glossy.

Trust him. Confusion whirled through her head.

Why would the lord lock Seraphine up when he had once loved her? He did not break his gaze with her and wrapped his fingers around Valxina's. Though hesitant at the touch, Valxina leaned closer.

Keepers were not to be touched by others. Wedding

bells and the cries of babes were not in the cards for them. But this was not marriage. It wasn't even real.

"I told you to be careful, Kulrani. I told you so just today."

"And what do I have to be careful of?"

When he closed the distance between them, she did not falter. Zessfar cradled her face in the palm of his cold hand. While accepting this act went against the rules of a keeper, this was the Badawi lord. They were his rules.

Valxina drew closer to him, feeling his breath. *It is all part of the plan.* His eyes traced her features under the veil—her lips, her chin, her nose, her thick brows. He stopped at her brown eyes—they were as dark as his. *It is all part of the plan.*

"I am a disappointment to many," he whispered, "and a target of so many rumors." He stopped to motion to her veil. "May I?"

Valxina's brows furrowed, but she nodded. "I am not afraid of rumors," she lied as he unclipped the veil from behind her ears.

"I'll speak to Eno in the morning," Zessfar said. Valxina held her breath as the tip of his thumb outlined her jaw. She lowered her gaze and moved to look away, but he only tightened his grip and willed her to stay put. When her lips parted slightly, Zessfar grinned. A lonely finger glided to her ear and wrapped around her head. "What is this for?"

Valxina exhaled and lifted a finger to where the scar lay hidden. "You healed me, but the scar..."

Lord Zessfar gathered the material in his hands. She

closed her eyes as he reached behind, undoing the knot near her neck. When he removed it, she broke eye contact. She chewed her lip and looked down at her lap. While this act was all a part of her plan, she wondered, *Is this fair? After all his honesty? And why did this touch, a feeling that should have her bolting for the door, feel so familiar and right?*

"Are you upset with me?" he asked.

"What reason would I have to be upset with you, Lord Zessfar?"

Zessfar lifted a brow. "For not healing it properly—for leaving a scar."

Valxina shook her head. "That would be a very foolish reason to be vexed."

His eyes searched for answers in hers.

"So what do you say, Keeper Valxina Kulrani? I knew from the moment I saw you, from the second your eyes connected with mine, that I would not sleep until I knew you. You are the kindness I have sought. You are the fire I have longed for."

"This is no place for flames," Valxina muttered, thinking back to the words of Keeper Sera on the night of the ceremony.

Lord Zessfar narrowed his eyes. "Who would tell you such a foolish thing? Flames need no invitation; they do not need open doors. They may enter as they wish; they may destroy whomever they please." His lips hovered above hers. "And you, Kulrani, you are welcome to destroy me."

Lord Zessfar smirked as Valxina reached out. Her

fingers traced his chin, running over the sprouted hair of his beard. Valxina's heart pounded against her flesh. Filled with nerves, she flexed her fingers.

"I would not destroy you," she answered. "I am not the destroyer of lords or grand Houses." The words, so soft and true, fluttered off her lips. Those words were not a part of her plan.

Valxina allowed Zessfar a moment to admire her once more. It was a hollow second under the spotlight of the moon. When his lips reached hers, she steadied herself. She wrapped her hand around his head and savored the taste of the wine. Perhaps the lord was just as the others; perhaps he, too, yearned for stolen moments in the darkness. When his hands reached behind her to undo her javelin strap, Valxina did not protest. She lifted her hands and allowed his fingers to graze her. He was so gentle it hurt. Valxina searched him for more. His eyes glistened, and kindness radiated from him. This was not the man from the gossip. When she lifted herself closer to him, he stilled.

"I think that is enough, Kulrani." He panted the words into her lips. When her eyes scanned his features, his fingers, once tight around her, let loose. "I'll speak to Eno in the morning. And I hope to see you tomorrow too?"

Valxina closed her eyes as he pressed his lips against her head—against the scar that marked her temple. When she moved to stand, she struggled to catch her breath. She nodded and reached for her javelin, collecting the harness from the ground in one quick stride. Zessfar reached for her and held her hand as they walked across the room. It was soft but cold. And when she lifted her fingers to push the door, he pressed himself against her. Valxina held her breath as he reached for the brass doorknob. Zessfar leaned in closer, placing his lips against her cheek.

"Promise me I'll see you tomorrow?"

Valxina nodded. "I'll see you tomorrow, Zessfar. I promise," she said with the widest of grins. But confusion swirled beneath her plastered smile.

Chapter 15

Adviser Eno's head was found on a spike outside of the tower.

Last night, Valxina had waved Ky and the others off. She swore to them that Sera would be released the next day. *Zessfar will look into it in the morning,* she told them. By the time the rays of sunlight dissipated the shadows of the night, the lord's adviser was already dead. He had been displayed so early that a layer of dew collected over his face. His eyes remained wide open, pools of terror that had watched its murderer without a blink. Adviser Eno's blood leaked down the spike, creating a small pool in the grass beneath. His mouth was open, and his skin color had faded.

Mylo had rushed up the tower stairs, right up to Valxina's bedroom door, and knocked wildly. He's dead, the tower guard said to his keeper. Visions of Chantara's attack flashed before Valxina. The image of the young boy, the fire-keep, who had informed her of the late lord's passing overwhelmed her vision.

After she shrugged her robe on, she descended the winding stairwell, which seemed never-ending. The keepers feet scurried beneath her, her heart a drum within her. *He's dead.* The words echoed once more. She wrapped her head as she took a step out. And then she saw him—a fraction of him. Eno's head seemed to cry, to scream. *What had he said, and what had he tried to say in his last moments of life?* Had he wasted his breath? When Valxina looked up, the crowd had already gathered. Inara and Desil, Danae and Agnar... keepers' feet were glued to the ground, to the stone around the tower's base. Valxina turned to look at Mylo. His eyes seemed heavy. Had she done this? Had the lord done this? No, it couldn't be. And Sera...Where was she? When Valxina's eyes met the commander, she shuddered.

"Keeper Sera?" she asked as she marched over to Ky, Mylo trailing behind her.

Ky shook his head. "No sign." Whispers broke out among the crowd. His eyes narrowed. "You swear you were not seen last night?"

Valxina huffed. "I don't think so. But what does it matter? What would it matter?" Mylo and the commander exchanged a glance. "They'll speak no matter what is done."

Ky moved towards her. "What are you saying? Is there something for the Court to talk about?" He shook his head. "Val?" he whispered.

When he looked over at her tower guard, Mylo only lowered his head. He seemed to study his feet. "After everything with Eleni, to hear you speak as if rumors could not touch you." Ky's voice was soft. "You hover over a dangerous path, little mouse."

Valxina bit the inside of her cheek. She released a breath, irritated at him for tossing Eleni's name over to her so easily. "It's not what you think."

Footsteps came from behind. Valxina turned to see Inara. Danae followed, but she hovered a few feet away.

"Keeper Sera?" the young keeper muttered. She looked as if she had not slept, like she had been dragged from her room and down the tower steps. She still wore her night dress under her robe and the head wrap she slept with at night.

"Zessfar said he would speak to Eno this morning," said Valxina.

"Do all your conversations end with the disappearance or death of a Court member?" Danae interrupted. Her words cut through the air like blades.

Perhaps there was reason for her check, but Valxina could not let it end there. Maybe the lord had done this, and perhaps Keeper Sera was recovering in the palace near the heat of a fire and with the luxuries of medicine, tea, company, even. *Was it feasible that Zessfar had spoken to him and that this was a justified punishment?*

Keeper Pax's eyes glued to the pike in the grass. The morning breeze lifted her skin like gooseflesh. "You must go again," she said. When her bright eyes lifted, she flattened her lips under her veil and crossed her arms. "He spoke to you?"

Valxina nodded as the woman squeezed her eyes closed. She looked up at the sky. The clouds had parted, and three large vultures circled above.

"They'll come for his head," Danae said, eyes scanning the bird. The group watched as the woman waltzed over to Eno's remains. Her eyes remained indifferent. Her golden hair lay too perfectly across her shoulders, she must not have had time to pin it up. As she walked, the morning breeze scattered strands across her face. Danae approached it with ease, like she had seen the severed heads of many men before him. And when she reached for the face, she did not shudder. She noted his missing part—a serpent without a tongue. Whispers heightened.

"He was a shit of a man," Danae said to the others. "Do not interpret this as anything else." Her fingers clenched at the bloodied head. "I'll dump it in the pit for the creatures. I do not wish to battle crows and cobos each time I step foot into the courtyard." And like a goddess of death herself, Danae strolled away with the head of the lord's late adviser.

✦

Breakfast was a glum affair. Valxina sat in the common room of her chambers with an apple and a muddled look. She could not get his face out of her head. She kept seeing Adviser Eno and his greyed expression. She kept wondering, questioning, where his body lay. The act reminded her so much of the night Queen Chantara attacked. It reminded her too much of the little boy who ran through the corridors. He was young, a lotto child himself, and she recalled the soot of his face and the burns on his hands. Valxina took a bite of the apple. It reminded her of blood. So much blood had shed that night, the night she was instructed to stay put in her chambers with the other candidates. Guilt crept into her in the most unlikely of moments. She was not responsible for the death of Adviser Eno; the man was known for his malicious behavior. While Valxina did not believe the whispers of the Court with haste, she believed every word about the lord's late adviser. He was cruel and notorious. He would often invite himself into the servants' quarters and make wild demands.

Mylo hovered in the corner.

"Are you not hungry, Mylo?"

The tower guard shook his head.

"I'm not so sure myself how I have an appetite after... after what we've seen out there in the courtyard."

"It's not that, Val." When she looked up at him, he continued, "I've seen far worse, you know?"

"What could be worse than a man's decapitated head?" she muttered. She didn't expect him to hear her.

"Fifty decapitated heads," Mylo answered. "Feeling the blade of another slice across your own skin."

Valxina blinked, and her breath quickened. Heat rose to her cheeks. Foolish—of course there was worse.

"I-I am sorry, Mylo. I cannot imagine what that must have been like."

The tower guard blinked. "I hope you never have to, Val."

Valxina watched the way he propped himself on a stool, the darkness of the tower stone cast over him. She fidgeted. "They say you saved Commander Kyrad's life?"

Mylo's grin held no vexation. He looked up at her with a shrug. "That may be the wildest of rumors about me."

"So it isn't true?"

Mylo shook his head. "If I saved Kyrad's life, it was only a mistake... a mistake that I am truly glad to have made... but it was not planned. It was not calculated."

Valxina raised a brow. "So it was a move of passion?"

She watched as Mylo released a deep breath. "I saw the man, the blade that was fated for the commander, and knew he was blind to it. I can't say I remember what was running through my head. Perhaps nothing truly was. I remember knocking down the man in front of me. I didn't wait to confirm his death. I did not plunge my sword to make sure of it. I was rushed. I did not stop until I felt the warmth of blood on my face and Chantara's man was cut down. But the one I had left, the one I did not finish and left lying in the mud, he caught me by surprise. But are there truly any surprises in battle? Maybe I was not completely bewildered when my head was yanked back. I don't suppose I was actually taken aback by the cold glint of the steel on my skin." Mylo shifted his glance and dropped his head. "I thought I was dead. I swore I saw death. But she was a goddess I was not ready to see. I woke up in Kyrad's quarters days later, with forty-eight stitches..."

"Is that why the commander calls you brother? Does it have to do with your saving of him?" When Mylo flashed a tired grin, she stuttered, "I-I heard him at dinner. Sorry, you don't have to answer my questions if they—"

"No, no. I suppose you already know of Ahmed?" said Mylo.

Ahmed. Of course Valxina knew the name. Ky had told her all about his young brother.

"Commander says I remind him of his brother, in spirit. He says if Ahmed had grown old enough to join the guards, he wishes he would have turned into someone like me. He probably would have too. From Kyrad's stories, it sounds like Ahmed would have pummeled me to the ground without so much as breaking a sweat."

Valxina smiled. "That is quite a compliment. I know Ky was devastated when he learned of Ahmed's passing." She paused, remembering the turmoil and grief that had plagued her friend when his brother passed away from sickness. "But it is lovely to hear how he feels about you."

Mylo nodded. "You know him well, don't you?"

The edge of Valxina's lip lifted. "I cannot imagine I know him any better than you."

"As well as he knows me, Kyrad does not look at me the way he looks at you." Mylo laughed. "And I sure as hell don't wish him too."

"Ky doesn't look at me in any particular way." She rolled her eyes. "There is nothing between us, you know? We're just good friends, like he is with you."

"Well, if that is true, I am sure he wishes for it to be different. He's told me—"

Valxina's cheeks were growing hot. "Please, Mylo. I know you mean well, but perhaps it best for us to leave what little past Ky and I had behind us?"

Mylo lowered his gaze. "It's not my place, anyway."

An awkward pause of silence pulsed through the room.

Valxina proposed, "So if it isn't the head in the courtyard, what has you so... You look lost away."

Mylo lifted a brow. "I... It's..."

A figure swaying in the corner caught their eyes. Mylo stood as Valxina turned to face it.

"It's for you," Keeper Pax said. She held a piece of parchment in her hand.

Valxina's brows furrowed. A letter? She had not received a written note in years. "For me?" Her heart lifted.

Pax moved toward her. Her face looked grave, scared even. She placed the note in Valxina's palm, the keeper traced her name along the surface, dancing across the exterior like a tango—its letters soft, winding, suggestive. She did not know her name held the ability to appear so beautiful. It did not bear her first given name but the name of her family, Kulrani. Valxina held her breath as she turned it over. The Badawi House crest sealed it. When she looked up, Keeper Pax took a seat across from her. And while Valxina knew it was not real, that it could not be real, that it was all a part of her plan, the paper illuminated her heart. Valxina broke the seal and opened it.

Chapter 16

I could not sleep. I thought only of you, your eyes, and your fire. Please forgive me. I could not wait for the sun, for each second of inaction dragged on like an eternity. After your departure, I was guided to the ceremonial fountain where I prayed. I feel inclined to tell you that I do not know what came over me, but that would be a lie. You are too bright to fall for deception. I found Eno in the dead of the night. You were right. The whispers of the palace tell me you once were acquainted with the pit. Meet me there, and I'll explain.

Valxina folded the parchment. No one had ever written a note to her like this. The room spun before her. It was a note from Zessfar. She reached for her javelin and strapped it against her back with a grunt. The mark under her skin no longer cried, but a whimper still echoed. The reminder seemed to weaken with each passing moment.

"Val?" Mylo whispered.

She did not answer, for he wouldn't believe her nor

understand. And the last thing she wanted was to be talked out of it. Valxina walked over to the door. When she looked back, her tower guard was already moving.

"For fuck's sake, Val," Mylo called out, "stay in the fucking tower!" He tossed his chair out from under him as he stood. His face darkened as he moved toward her. But when Mylo saw the look in his keeper's face, he stilled. "I-I'm sorry. I-I have these moments where darkness creeps into me. I shouldn't have taken that tone. I shouldn't have... I'm just concerned about you, Valxina. Where are you going?"

Valxina studied the man in front of her. There was nothing he could say to stop her, no amount of chair tossing or wide-eyed claims of concern would keep her in place.

She would have to lose him.

✦

Below the palace halls, under the throne room and the rooms of Court members, lay a bustling maze of the workers. Servants lived a cramped life. The kitchens and rooms where servants polished silver and washed laundry were not planned to be as open and lavish as the palace above. There were other ways to the pit, of course, but Valxina knew if she stood a chance of losing her tower guard, she had to do it through the servants' mazes.

When he called out and asked where she was going,

Valxina did not answer. When he reached for the letter in her pocket, she swayed away. When he demanded to know who had written it, she rolled her eyes and continued on. "I'll get the commander," he even warned. *As if she were afraid of him.* Valxina dared Mylo to do so. It would give her moments alone, more minutes to spend getting lost underground. Plus, Ky had agreed to help her. He would know this was all a part of her plan even if she herself knew it wasn't.

"Valxina!" Mylo yelled, his voice irritated. He followed her, his hand tight against the hilt of his sword. When she descended the stairs, she heard him mumble a curse under his breath. He might have been a child of the lottery as she had, but Mylo had never spent time in service. He had never worked under the palace nor lived with the others. This was hers, the home she had grown to know like the back of her hand.

Valxina lived in the mazes under the palace until she passed her exam, the first trial to becoming a keeper—an oral exam encompassing the history of The Spring. While no one ever spoke of it, the test held another purpose. It was a test of pressure, of stress, and of obedience. The Court members involved were cruel. But in the end, Valxina emerged victorious. She had obeyed their demands and stayed the quiet, compliant servant girl they expected her to be. The thought made the new keeper scoff. She could not believe she had allowed them to treat her the way they did. She could not believe all she had endured to end up here—on her way to meet Lord Zessfar, his letter and the Badawi seal in hand.

Valxina knew it was strange. She was no fool. And she did not pretend to believe this was something like she had shared with Eleni or even her friendship with Ky. Those were deep and uncomplicated as they could be. Those relationships were innocent. But they were with someone she no longer resembled. When she emerged out of that water, when she felt the heat of the metal press against her skin, when she shot that glare at the man at the dais, she was reborn. A keeper now, she was the kind of woman she never thought she could be. Once afraid of the rumors, of the whispers in the shadows, of bringing those around her down, she could feel those fears dissipate, at least when she was with him. Valxina had spent years hiding herself. She had hidden in the shadows and kept her head down. She allowed the people of the Court to treat her like a child, like she was less than human, like a child of the lotto and nothing more.

Valxina ducked into a room. It was dark and filled with laundry—white linens and towels embroidered with Badawi blue. She knew the mazes better than Mylo ever could. She snuck behind a line of cloth, reaching for the end of the room. As Valxina ducked behind a hanging sheet and ran for the exit across, she could hear Mylo struggling behind. Valxina held her breath as she pressed her body against a crate of produce. It was a box of corn from the providence of San Divolax, the sister island to Qeshm that consisted of a small strip of farms and gardens. She hid between it and the wall. When Mylo's footsteps softened, when she was sure he had moved forward, she turned back.

She snuck through a servants' dining area and into the oven room. When a kitchen maid caught sight of her, Valxina smiled. The young girl gasped at Valxina, and her eyes roamed her robe in keeper blue and the veil that hung across her face. Valxina lifted a finger to her lips and whispered a soft *shhh* before moving toward the back door and running into the open air. It felt like an entrance into a different life. Valxina did not look back. She only prayed she had lost him.

When Valxina saw the stables ahead, she sprinted toward them. She concealed herself behind a stack of hay until the man who occupied the stables turned. She walked through the space and hurried out the other end. Dust collected at her sandaled feet. They rose from the ground filled with optimism and hope. Valxina held her breath at the sight of the gardens, and she moved past it. She ran beyond the pond as memories of the last time she had stood here flooded through her. She thought about the last person she had stood here *with*. And when she reached the vegetable garden, Valxina's hands shook. She wiped the sweat on her palms against her robe. Upon reaching the hill, the crest at the outskirt of the pit, she paused.

Lord Zessfar stood tall and dark against the light of day. She watched the way he fidgeted with his hands. She smiled at the thought that he, too, battled with nerves. When he turned, Valxina watched the way his eyes widened. Under her veil, she allowed a smile to spread across her face and moved toward him.

But the smell of the decaying pit, sour and diseased, halted her.

Chapter 17

The pit smelled worse than she had ever remembered. Its scent of death and decomposition lingered in the air. Trails of the smell whisked around Valxina. She swatted away at the air as the hot breeze moved her hair. She lifted a hand to her nose to ward off the grimness. Her brows furrowed as she moved to step closer. When the lord extended an arm to bring her in, she accepted feverishly. He smelled of lavender and honey.

"I know," he said. His eyes were miles away. "It's horrific."

Valxina looked up at him with a dazed look. "Why are we here? What happened here?"

Lord Zessfar raised his arms into the air. When Valxina looked down, she saw it. Them. *Bones. Bodies.* Tangled and mangled bits of human flesh and trash soggy with blood scattered across the pit.

"You were right in your inquiries of me. I was tasked with the pit dumps when I worked in the kitchens. But it never looked like this..." Valxina's eyes widened. "What happened here?" she asked again. The pit had frightened her as a kitchen servant, but it never appeared like this. This... this was unholy. Her face whipped around to face Zessfar.

Zessfar took a step back from the crest of the pit. With heavy hands and lids, he held her shoulders. Valxina shuddered slightly at the touch. He noted it; it was obvious in the way his face dropped.

She watched as Zessfar surveyed the area and said, "There were too many bodies for individual pyres following Chantara's attack. There wasn't enough time or space..."

But it had been two years since the attack, and some of the bodies looked too fresh to have been dumped two years ago. Valxina shifted on her feet.

"I know it's dreadful. We've been burning in batches but have not gotten to all the bodies. They lay here until the next group pyre. I- I won't bother you with the political details behind it all."

When he turned away, Valxina followed. She detested his insistence to keep the details to himself. "I-I don't understand," said Valxina. "Something like this... this stench should hover over the entire Court, the entire island. How has it been contained?"

"I may have commissioned the work of the king's obeah women."

Valxina's brows pinched together. The king was rumored to have a group of women at his disposal with combined powers and magical knowledge that had been passed on through generations.

"His obeah women masked the scent for you?" she asked.

Zessfar nodded. "They created an invisible barrier—a force to contain the smell, the sounds past the barrier—a containment of it all, really. It was a coronation gift to go with my immortality. So the world wouldn't know of my... my failures."

Valxina took another step away from the death.

"But I did not bring you here to chat about the king or my issues with the pit," Zessfar continued. "I brought you here to tell you that I spoke to Eno. He had heard rumors about Seraphine. He said she was spreading gossip through the halls, speaking of me with ill intentions." The words stirred intrigue within Valxina. "He..." Zessfar shuffled another step away from the death. "I am afraid I do not know how to say this, so I will do so frankly. Keeper Seraphine is missing. Eno would not tell me what was done with her. I had my guards search the pit to make sure... to make sure she was not here."

"She can't be dead, my lord."

Zessfar shuddered. Was it the use of his title that unsteadied him? "I've opened an investigation into it. But in the meantime, I am afraid I cannot report any good news to you. That is... other than the absence of her body in the pit."

Valxina looked up to him. "And Eno?" The words brought visions of the man's head, his eyes wide and his mouth agape. Valxina inched away from Zessfar.

Zessfar sighed. "I know peace cannot be found until

Seraphine is safe and sound. But I cannot allow members of Court to take matters into their own hands—not even advisers." Zessfar reached a hand out and rested it softly on Valxina's shoulder. "I sent his head as a gift to the keepers—to let them know that they are safe. Anyone who dares to hurt them will be punished. I'll make sure of it."

Valxina shook her head. "You've shaken most of us. It did not make us feel safe."

Lord Zessfar ran a hand through his hair. He mumbled a curse under his breath. "Shit. I've fucked this up, haven't I?"

Valxina watched the guilt flow through him. She observed the way he squeezed his eyes shut in disappointment. It was vulnerability—open vulnerability for her eyes to see.

She knew it wasn't ok, not exactly. The man delivered a severed head in hopes to lay worries to rest. *Who would do such a thing?* But then she remembered he was different. He was not just a man but a ruler. Valxina studied the pit before her, the way the mangled bones and bodies seemed to form valleys of death.

"It's ok," Valxina said. She watched as his head lifted. Lord Zessfar pounded a clenched fist against his forehead. "Your heart was in the right place." Once he stopped, she faced the pit once more.

"I have the guards searching for Seraphine. But I've also had an idea of going into the town. Maybe if the people knew she was missing too, maybe if they knew she meant something to me, there would be a reward for information. Maybe we would have a better chance of finding her." His eyes brightened with the words. "Whispers have already spread about her disappearance, and I want everyone to know whose side I'm on here."

Valxina raised a brow. "What do you mean?"

Zessfar huffed. "I know what they say about me, Kulrani. I won't allow the folks of this land to believe I'm some sort of heartless lord."

"So you are going into the village?" she asked.

Zessfar nodded.

"I did not know Badawi lords left the palace grounds so casually," Valxina said.

"They don't, not usually." The rays of sunlight gleamed over him. He radiated in the soft light. "Would you like to come with me?"

Chapter 18

Wealth was a thing of show.

Or so, that was what Lord Zessfar believed. On their walk back to the palace, he told Valxina of his wishes, of how he preferred to live casually. Valxina chuckled at the word, casual. She did not believe the lord would know casual or true simplicity if it knocked him to his knees. "But when it comes to the people, when it comes to how they see their ruler," he had said to her during their walk, "they must see the show, the act, the theatrical version of their Badawi lord."

There it was again, theater. The lord had hinted at the similarity between a ruler and a man of the theater during their very first meeting. He seemed to feel like he was trapped. Puppet strings propelled him around Court in a way even Valxina could feel empathetic towards. Valxina could not shake the feeling that perhaps there was more to the wealthy of Court. Maybe they, too, had their own buffet of problems. Even so, she would swap lives with them in a heartbeat. To Valxina, power meant protection. And even if puppet strings hovered above her on stage, there was a sense of safety to it all. After all, if the Court was nothing but a theatrical show, and Zessfar was the star. Valxina, at least in her life before her status of keeper, was a concession. She only was meant to be devoured.

Valxina released a deep breath as they approached the archways of the Court. The smell of the pit no longer lingered; rather, it stayed trapped behind, harnessed by the powers of the king's obeah women.

"And what will the audiences of the town say when they see you with a servant girl?"

Zessfar smiled. "Is that what you believe you are?"

She didn't, at least, not entirely. Valxina knew she was no longer the girl who lit fires and disposed of trash. She was no longer the woman who had trained for the ceremony either. While she was no longer a concession, she did not expect others to change the way they perceived her—not the wealthy of the Court. She certainly did not expect the lord to see her as more, no matter how much she tried. No matter how much he seemed to fall into *her plan*.

Valxina lowered her eyes. The plan was going to waste. She could see it already. It wasn't that the lord had not fallen for her, but she found herself unsettled by her own brewing emotions. Could she... be falling for him?

"You are a keeper now, you know?" His words ran through the archways. When he spotted the way she glanced around, the way she seemed to cower from the attention, he laughed. "Let them."

"Let them what?" Valxina whispered.

"Let them talk if they wish. I thought you said you were not afraid of rumors?"

It was like he had read her mind and unlocked her greatest fear in life. She forced a smile, one so shallow it barely reached her eyes. "I am not."

It was true and yet untrue. Valxina did not fear what rumors would do to her. She almost always feared what they would do to others. Although that didn't really matter to her before, when it came to Zessfar now, fear crept through her, tensing her muscles at the thought.

"Good, then," Zessfar replied.

When they reached his rooms, Valxina stopped in the doorway.

"Wait here," he instructed. "I'll have someone come and dress you."

Valxina lifted a brow. "What is wrong with the way I am dressed?" Valxina looked down at her keeper robe.

Lord Zessfar smiled. "Nothing, absolutely nothing." His finger reached for her face and caressed her cheek. "But it's a show, remember? And if you are to be my leading lady, then I suppose we shall both dress for the roles."

He disappeared with the words.

Valxina stood in the empty doorway. The guards did not look at her, standing silent in the space. She bit her lip. Her life had truly changed. Valxina paced around the hall as she waited. She considered sending word back to the tower—surely Mylo would have gone mad at her escape; perhaps he had even gone and told Ky. She wondered whether she should have sent word to Pax. But Zessfar had assured her they would return in time for her to attend her scheduled crypt duty.

"Valxina?" The woman's voice rang through the hallway. The keeper snapped her head forward. It was a sound all too familiar. She had not seen this woman since she had left the candidates' room for the ceremony. She clenched her trembling fists, her nails digging into her skin. Valxina released a deep breath and turned towards the woman. She held her head high and gritted her teeth. As soon as the woman's gray eyes met hers, Valxina forced a sweet smile. "Lady Masha."

The woman's eyes widened. "What are you doing here?"

Valxina chose her next words wisely. "Lord Z—"

Lady Masha waved her hand between them, cutting Valxina short and dismissing her words. "My lord has sent for me to dress—"

Valxina smiled as she stepped forward. "Zessfar has sent for you to dress me, Lady Masha."

She feasted at the sight of the woman's confusion. Masha's head shook in disbelief. "You?" She scoffed, sucking her teeth.

"You will dress me, Lady Masha." Her eyes bore into her.

But the woman stepped back and shook her head again, her dark tresses swaying wildly with the movement. "I will not dress the likes of you."

The woman appeared different. As Valxina studied her now, she could see her clearly, the bits of gray that washed through her hair and the darkened circles that spread beneath her eyes. She had never noticed the way the woman's wrinkles shaped her face in a perpetual frown nor the fragility that stirred beneath her eyes. Perhaps Valxina was only now able to see her, to truly see her.

"In case you have forgotten, Masha, I am now a keeper. I outrank even you." Valxina asserted. The woman's mouth opened at the words—at the familiar use of her name. "What?" Valxina whispered between them. "I think we are more familiar than most people are. Or does your abuse count for nothing?"

Lady Masha's mouth snapped closed. She studied Valxina as if she could see the look of vengeance in the woman's eyes or feel her emboldened spirit. Valxina straightened her back. Zessfar and his words had made her bold.

Masha lowered her head and turned. "Follow me."

Valxina reached behind and gripped her javelin as she followed. *I am safe. I am safe,* she told herself. Lady Masha could not hurt her, not anymore.

✦

Lady Masha brought her to a private bath chamber. Valxina had never seen this place, for she had only spent her life in shared spaces. The concept of having the water of a bath to oneself was a cry of luxury.

"Go on," Lady Masha urged as she motioned towards the water. Valxina could see it was still hot. Steam lifted from its surface, reaching for the skylight above. Valxina shrugged her robe off and reached her fingers for her neck. After she untied the cloth at her head and folded it, she placed it on top of the robe and settled her items down neatly on a stool.

When Lady Masha reached for Valxina's back, Valxina squirmed and turned away, Masha's fingers cold against her skin.

"Let me remove it," Masha said.

Valxina shook her head. "No, leave it be."

"It needs to be washed."

Valxina lifted her head and took a deep breath before moving forward to the bath. As she turned, she reached her fingers behind her. "I can remove it myself. Turn around."

When the woman looked at her, brows raised, Valxina repeated herself. Authority seeped into her tone. "Turn around." Her voice bounced around the marble room, almost unrecognizable to Valxina.

Lady Masha rolled her eyes, but she obeyed the keeper's wish. Valxina tore the bandage off with one swift movement, inciting a flash of red before her eyes. She muffled a cuss at the pain.

"You should watch your mouth," Masha muttered as she turned back around. Valxina stepped into the water and lowered herself slowly. "Someone who outranks even me—someone who is to be seen with the Lord—should not cuss."

Valxina chuckled. "I do believe our training is complete." She leaned against the bath. "I think I'll pass on any further lessons or advice. Especially from you." She paused and looked up at the woman. Lady Masha's arms crossed over her chest. "What is it?" Valxina muttered. "*Tell me,* how badly do you wish to lash me right now, Masha? How much do you lust for my cry, my pain?"

Masha tightened her hands into fists, and Valxina studied her for a moment. A sliver of worry ebbed itself within Valxina, but she released the fear. *She cannot hurt me.* After all, Lord Zessfar was expecting her. He had sent Masha to care for her.

Valxina did most of her washing herself. Despite the new luxury, she did not feel comfortable with Masha cleaning her. She did not want to feel the woman's touch on her skin. And she certainly did not want Masha to come close enough to see her, truly see her, and her mark. When she was done, Masha wrapped Valxina in keeper-blue linen. It differed from the fabric she had been given by Keeper Sera. This cloth's embroideries were more delicately woven. Masha fashioned the fabric into a dress that swooped at the neckline. It left little to the imagination and exposed the midriff. But Valxina made sure it covered what counted, the mark on her back.

When she was done, Masha reached for Valxina's hair. She wrapped the bandeau about her head and pinned her waves up. Valxina's tresses seemed to vine themselves against the fabric at her head. Last, Masha pinned Valxina's veil over her face once more.

After she finished, Masha walked the keeper to the stalls. The horses had already been tacked up to the carriage. As she neared, Valxina draped a piece of fabric around an arm. Ahead, Lord Zessfar waited, and when he turned, gold glittered in his hands.

Chapter 19

The disappearance of a woman brought the best and the worst out of people.

While some searched for answers out of care and goodwill, others found pleasure in the details. They wished for the worst, and they hoped for a good story. Eleni had gone missing years ago. Valxina remembered the way her heart dropped at the news. But no one searched for her, no lord rose from his throne or vowed to discover her whereabouts. Months had passed with Valxina in a fog until someone finally told her, until the whispers reached her. Eleni had been sent home. She did not bother to uncover the details, although she ached for a reason, although she craved a goodbye. A proper parting never came. So, Valxina allowed the servant gossip to inform her of the details through sly remarks and occasional midnight chatter. She filtered through them in her head. Some were simply too wild to believe in. But she did not seek the truth out herself. She feared it.

Valxina watched the palm trees rush through the carriage window. A pair of golden earrings, twisted into the form of two eels, dangled to her shoulders. They resembled the ones that lived on the lord's crest, the ones that twisted into the Badawi "B." Spotting them in her reflection, Valxina reached a hand up to touch one, and the gold felt cold against her fingertip. They pulled at her earlobes, stretching them in a way she had never felt before. And while they hurt, she reveled in the pain. Most servants did not have their ears pierced. Why would they be when they could not afford the metals that fit into them?

Valxina sighed. If only Eleni could see her now. It was her idea to pierce their ears together in the first place. The needle and four safety pins had been stolen from the desk of a palace seamstress. They were so giddy with excitement and nerves. "One day," Eleni had told her, her short dark hair framing her face like a real-life portrait or masterpiece. "One day, I'll buy us both earrings. Not the kind our fathers buy our mothers after years of saving. The kind people like us can't even dream of. They'll be gold, maybe even a set with pearls. One day, we'll hold our heads up high and sweep the hair behind our ears, looking just like the ladies and noblewomen of Court. Our heads will hurt from the weight of them. But we'll smile through the pain and bask in it. Until then, we'll wear the safety pins and wait for them."

Valxina released a deep breath. She had removed the pins from her ears years ago, under Masha's direction. They still sat in the box of trinkets in her room, the same container that held the lock of Eleni's hair. She lifted her head at the memory. *We'll smile through the pain and bask in it.* While Eleni was no longer here, while it was not she who gifted her the earrings, Valxina felt the need to keep her word.

Lord Zessfar observed her. "They frame you well."

Valxina lowered her hand. "You noticed my ears have been pierced?"

"Of course. I saw the bare markings and knew I had to acquire a pair for you. It's like they were made for you." He ran an index finger over his lip as he watched her. "You look beautiful."

Valxina smiled. "I knew someone once... It was she who stuck the needle through them. I wore safety pins in my ears for years. She said one day I'd wear earrings so heavy that they'd hurt my head."

Zessfar grinned. "And here you are." He motioned a hand before her. "Your friend must have been an obeah woman herself, one who could see right into your future."

Valxina looked out the window. The sky stretched out before her. "I don't think she held those sorts of powers. But she was... she was magical."

"And so are you."

Valxina looked up at him. He wore a jacket of deep blue, and his family emblem rested on his chest. While the morning breeze had left her reaching for her robe, the day had progressed to unbearable heat. The sun beat down on their carriage. Its golden wheels flashed those who stood by. Children, families with mothers and fathers hoisted their pickneys into the air, crowded onto the streets. They twisted their necks as the carriage passed by, hoping for a glimpse of the lord from the palace.

Valxina turned to him. "Are you not hot?"

Zessfar shrugged. "I'm fine."

"Are you?"

She watched the way he lifted the bottom edge of his jacket. He smiled as he said, "If I am honest, Kulrani, I shall probably perish from heat exhaustion by the day's end."

Valxina shook her head. "Then why all of this?"

"Ah, it's part of the act. You see, the people don't want to see their lord in their clothes. They want a ruler that defies the elements himself." His voice mocked the words.

"Even if you expire for the sake of it?"

"Yes, even if it brings me death."

Valxina did not reply immediately. But that was just it... It was not possible—the lord could not die, not that easily. It would take more for the light in his body to be put out.

"I'm sorry, you know," Zessfar continued. When she looked at him, he reached a hand out and placed it on her thigh, which sent shivers up Valxina's body. "I did not mean for you to leave so abruptly the other night. I just... I know you have vows as a keeper. I felt guilty last night for overstepping those sacraments. I went straight to the ceremonial fountain and prayed after your departure."

Valxina held her breath. She wanted to tell him he could—they were his rules. After all, *those* rules came not from the scriptures but from the Badawi family themselves. But Valxina only nodded. "I understand."

"But would it be the unholiest of actions if I kissed you

once more?" Zessfar asked, his voice soft and smooth.

Valxina smiled at the question. She never expected the lord of Badawi to ask her such a question. She looked up at him and hesitated, biting the edge of her lip.

"No," she replied, speaking not with her head but with her heart. "It wouldn't be the unholiest of actions."

Valxina tried to conceal her pounding heartbeat as Zessfar inched closer. His lips pressed onto hers, and Valxina closed her eyes. She flexed a hand at her side and held her breath. The kiss was slow and as graceful as the man in front of her. She leaned into Zessfar and felt him smile against her lips.

But then a shout snapped her back into the present. The carriage stopped with a halt. Valxina fell over Zessfar inelegantly. Her leg propped into the air, and heat rose to her cheeks. It left the keeper in a disarray on the floor. When she looked up at the lord, he only laughed. He held a hand out to her. Kind—he was so kind. He was nothing like the gossips of Court said.

Valxina took his outstretched hand and looked out the window. She observed the thatched roofs and garden stalls. She reached for the door eagerly, but a guard appeared in her vision. He wore the Badawi seal against his chest. His head had been shaven bald, and tattoos crept up his neck. The Badawi guard swung the door open and offered a hand. Valxina lingered for a moment before taking it and moving out of the carriage. She stepped out of its doorway, elated.

Visits out of the palace were not something servants were accustomed to. And for Valxina, a child of the lotto, there were strict rules against her leaving the grounds. She had not left the archways and opulence of the Court since her arrival as a child. Valxina held her breath as she spotted a fruit stand. Lord Zessfar followed behind her. The air smelled fresh, filled with the scents of mangoes, peppered channa, and other food from the stalls. Valxina's eyes grazed over the sea of berries, blankets of blues and purples. Whispers spread around them as the two walked through the market square.

"Kulrani," said Zessfar.

Valxina froze. She looked over at him, her eyes wide and lips pressed into a smile.

"I know," he said. "Come, let's step in for a drink."

When he motioned to the door of a tavern, she followed.

Zessfar spoke to people for what seemed like hours. He described Keeper Sera to them with great detail and told them of her status, of her place as a keeper of his Spring. He maneuvered through simple people, farmers, blacksmiths, and tradesmen. The sight of it was shocking, but his openness with his people warmed Valxina. The people all eagerly answered Zessfar's questions. They dropped whatever they were doing, whomever they were speaking to, to hear their ruler's words. And through it all, a crowd had edged its way into the small space and the street outside. Valxina watched the way people pressed their noses against the window and smiled at their faces distorted in the glass. Dew from their breath stuck against the glazed panels.

People from all directions handed Zessfar items. Although he never took it himself. He'd thank the person politely, nod his head, and wait for a guard to receive the tankard of ale, the roll of tobacco, or the box of produce. She supposed it was precautionary. After all, he was the lord. He even had a taster for his food back at home. But the action made her wonder, *Was the immortality of The Spring muted to poison?* Zessfar's father had died after his head had been removed from his body. But could the power of The Spring fail in other ways?

When an elderly merchant handed Valxina a scarf from his latest voyage, she smiled. She reached her fingers out and thanked the man for his kindness. Valxina imagined he could have been in his seventies—*eighties, perhaps?* The wrinkles that danced across his skin were a sign of a long life. Her fingers rubbed against the rose-tinted material, which was soft and vibrant. Opening her mouth to speak again to the man, she wondered where he had acquired the item. But the lord's voice boomed over her.

"Are you dense?" Zessfar snapped, his voice nearly unrecognizable. Valxina's eyes darted to him as he spoke. The table of men around him went silent. Her heart sank. If she pulled her javelin out and attempted to cut the air, she was sure it would work. The lord's eyes bored into the merchant's. His gaze flickered between the item in Valxina's hand and the man.

"Do you know who she is?" The man stayed silent. It was proof that he was far from witless. For even Valxina heard the venom in the words and knew one should not reply to such a tone. "She is *my keeper.*" He rolled his eyes. "She is not permitted to wear anything other than keeper blue."

Valxina furrowed her brows. She had not seen this side of him before. When Zessfar's gaze reached Valxina's, she turned to the merchant. She smiled, whispered a hushed, "Apologies," and handed the scarf back to the man. When she turned to the lord, he had returned to his conversation. He continued on as if it had not happened.

Valxina spent the rest of the afternoon staring out the frosted tavern windows. And like a world wonder on display, she watched as the townsfolk took their turns admiring her.

Chapter 20

The sun gleamed on Valxina's exposed skin.

While she had politely turned down any gifts of ale or rum, she had drunk four glasses of water by the time Zessfar was ready to leave. It wasn't wise to indulge in the alcohol, especially when the lord was openly doing so himself. She felt on edge, especially after the incident with the merchant. She did not want to falter, to make any more mistakes in his presence. If she could avoid him using that tone again, her chest would ease. It rose the hairs on her neck.

She sighed as they stepped into the market square. The crowd followed them as they walked.

"I'm sorry," Zessfar muttered. He stood so close his arm brushed against hers. The words surprised her.

Valxina kept her eyes forward. "You have nothing to apologize for, my lord."

She knew he would recognize the formality. While her tone was a pat against his back, a soft caress through his hair, her choice of words was the very opposite. "It was foolish of me to take the gift," she continued. She grounded herself for the last words. "Or shall I say, *dense?*"

Lord Zessfar fidgeted beside her. "*Fuck.* It was stupid, I know. I spoke poorly, I know. I- I just wanted to protect you."

"Protect me from what, exactly? From some pink fabric?"

"From impropriety. I wanted them to know your status, to understand it, to know you are an extension of me. I wanted them to know you were not like them. They cannot just speak to you or approach you as they wish."

Valxina's eyes widened, and she took a step back. She hadn't thought twice about the man's gesture because he was exactly like the townspeople. In fact, with her life as a servant, prior to her ceremony, she was probably even below them.

"People should put thought into their actions and words with you as if they were speaking to me, their lord. And they should know better—you are a woman of The Spring."

They continued strolling. When the lord's dark eyes roamed a stand of bucketed wildflowers, he moved quicker. He reached for a bunch and smiled at the woman. When he turned, the bouquet fresh in his hands, he extended them to her. "Let me make it up to you?"

They smelled fresh and sweet. Most were poppies—a bouquet of rosewood pinks and bright scarlet blooms. Mauve-tinted bellflowers rose above the others as if reaching for the cyan sky.

Valxina crossed her arms and let out a breath. "It'll take more than flowers to make up for that tone. The poor man looked terrified in there. Besides, you haven't even paid for those."

Eyes enlarging, he turned to a guard, who nodded and walked over to the woman at the stand. He handed her some coin. Valxina could tell by the way the woman's hazel eyes widened that the amount had been too much. *He was showing off.* Zessfar turned back to face the keeper with an eager glare.

"As I said, it will take more than some flowers, no matter how beautiful they are, to make up for your tone with that man."

Zessfar nodded. "Ok." He looked away in thought. "We should head back now to the palace. But may I take you somewhere along the way?"

"I'm tired," Valxina answered. "And I must get back by six; you know that. I have crypt duty tonight."

The lord shook his head. "I'll get you back in time, I promise." When her eyes softened, he continued with a grin, "You will love it, I promise."

"Don't go around making promises you cannot keep, my lord," Valxina teased.

✦

Valxina had always loved the water. As a child, she would sneak off to the green pond near the gardens and splash away for relief. She enjoyed the way the world silenced when she was in it, under it, around it. Valxina adored the feeling of droplets on her skin. She treasured the silent moments while she held her breath and swam deep. It was one of the many reasons she had wanted to become a keeper of The Spring. So when the lord's carriage stopped at the crest of a lake, Valxina's breath hitched.

The lake was colossal. The keeper raised her hand above her brows and blocked the reflection of the sun. She roamed the edges and watched the way the ends seemed to blur against the land. Palm trees danced among the surface as if in welcome, as if calling her in.

"I thought you might enjoy a swim?" Zessfar beamed beside her.

"And you know me so well?" She tried to be cheeky, but the words fell short. Her joy was apparent.

The lord smiled. "If you want to leave, we can."

But Valxina shook her head. "Absolutely not." She lifted the hem of her dress.

Valxina allowed the rays of the sun to beat against her. She ran toward the edge and kicked her shoes off in the dirt. Zessfar's mouth dropped at the sight of her reaching for her dress. He turned to his guards and instructed them to stay at the carriage.

But Valxina did not care. She stripped the draped fabric off her body, and when she felt her mark would show, she turned to her side and plunged herself into the coolness. It had been years since she last swam for fun. Her latest experiences with water had been forced in training. She pushed back at the flashes of the ceremony. She tried to shake off the memories of her head underwater, of her stifled breath.

Valxina dunked her head beneath the water. It was cold and fresh, sparkling in the brightest shade of blue she had ever seen. It reminded her of keeper blue—of its hints of emerald. Valxina kicked her feet up and floated before closing her eyes. The water welcomed her in a soft embrace. It whispered words she wished to hear; it reminded her of her journey here. She did not bother to look for Zessfar. But he had taken her here. And while she had been upset as she waited in the tavern, she took a moment to think of it. He had done it without ill intentions. He had spoken of his need, his want, to protect her. And now, he had brought her to the most beautiful place in the world.

She squinted her eyes and looked up from the water. A flock of cranes flew above. She admired the way they glided, unaware of the world beneath them, unaware of the thoughts and worries of man. She watched until they disappeared from her vision. What did it feel like to bear wings, to know no boundaries, to settle wherever one wished?

The lord was perched on the edge of the water. He had removed his boots and rolled the fabric of his trousers up. He braced his hands on his waist and watched her. Zessfar kicked at the shallow water beneath him. A smile was plastered across his face. *He had brought them here for her.*

"Are you not coming in?" Valxina called out.

Zessfar shook his head, his dark hair moving with the motion. "Not today," he answered. "Today, this is just for you."

"So you plan to splash and creep around the entire time?"

Zessfar lifted his head. The golden band on his arm glistened in the sunlight. He was beaming, glowing. She thought back to the portrait that hung in his chambers. It was an image of life and death. But as Valxina watched the man on the shore, she smiled. The only image of him that mattered was this one. She closed her eyes and tried to paint it in her head. She tried to brush invisible strokes to represent his skin—the way the light reflected against his tan flesh. He would remain this way forever. He was forever preserved by the water—time would not change his skin. His hair would not gray through the years. Life would not weather him down. She tried to memorize the lines of his smile and the way his eyes narrowed as he laughed. But she could not do so. It was impossible to savor. It could not be done.

Chapter 21

Valxina returned to the tower with damp hair, and a smile lingering on her face. But

when she stepped into the courtyard, Mylo and Ky blocked her path.

"Thank the gods," Mylo said when he saw her face. A look of relief passed through him as Mylo ran a hand through his golden hair and let out a sigh.

"Where the fuck were you?" Ky's voice echoed through the yard. He studied her appearance and raised his brows at her smile. The commander stalked over to Valxina and placed a hand on her arm. She was still cool from her swim, but his hands were hot to the touch. "Mylo saw you with Lord Zessfar. Where did you go?" The words were rough and erratic.

Valxina raised her brow at his tone.

"I saw you get into his carriage, Keeper Val." Mylo barely looked at her.

Valxina lifted her chin. "I was safe. Mylo may not have

been with me, but there were House guards with us."

The commander scoffed at the words. "Like the House guards who took Sera away? Like the House guards who probably stuck Eno's head in the courtyard?"

Valxina lifted her gaze to Ky. She huffed as she steadied herself. "Keeper Sera is missing. I went into town with the lord to spread the word of her disappearance. Eno had taken her, so Zessfar had his head placed in the courtyard as a gift to us keepers, a reminder that he will cut down anyone who threatens our safety."

The words sounded childish on her tongue, and she knew it. She didn't wait to see Ky's face—she could taste the sweetness of naivety on her lips.

"Are you so blind you cannot see through his flashing grin and polished band?"

Valxina froze at his words, so careless, so rash, said out in the courtyard for all to hear. Her eyes flashed about, seeking any tower guards or keepers who may have overheard. But the courtyard was quiet, free of keepers, and the tower guards present did not dare to lift their gazes.

Valxina narrowed her eyes. She was not blind. She knew what she was doing, or at least, had known and planned for this. Valxina straightened her back. "You are not allowed to do this."

Ky snapped, "You are not Zessfar's wife. You are not the lady of the Badawi House. You have no hold there, and you have no power in that way. Do not tell me what I am and am not to do." The commander leaned closer to her. "It was you who told me to stay away. I am allowed to feel what I feel. I am allowed to do what I want. I am not the boy you met in the ring."

Valxina stepped back. "I know that. I see that."

Ky shook his head. "You have heard the rumors about him, little mouse. I know you have." His voice softened with his last words.

"And you believe rumors now?"

"Usually no, I do not. Especially rumors of women in this Court. But when it comes to men or the whispers that spread about powerful men, people do not say those with ease. Members of Court do not go around sharing baseless gossip about powerful men for fun or out of boredom." Ky closed his eyes. "He is dangerous."

"And how are you so sure of that?"

The commander opened his eyes, lifted a hand, and pointed up to the tower. "This place and your change of clothes do not protect you from the horrors of Court. I know you wish they did. I wish they did too. But your ceremony did not create a new set of rules—no matter how much you believed it would." Ky's eyes hardened, and his fingers tightened into a fist. Valxina held her breath as Ky leaned into her. "Into my quarters."

Valxina rolled her eyes at the soft order. She pushed against him and called out, "I'm going in and changing. I'm on crypt duty tonight."

But the commander reached for her once more. "Listen to me!"

Valxina brushed past him and stormed towards the tower doorway. She could hear his footsteps behind her, heavy and fast. And when her feet lifted into the air against her will, she thrashed against him. Ky slung Valxina across his shoulders, out in the open, no less, for all to see. Heat rose through her body as she screamed. She called for Mylo to help her, but he only frowned at her.

"Let me go, you insufferable bastard!" she yelled as Ky carried her towards his quarters. "What the fuck are you doing with me?"

She yanked at his locks. She knew it hurt when he grumbled, "Fuck" under his breath and tightened his grip around her.

They shuffled into the room with no grace. Ky tossed her into the armchair in the dimly lit room. She sunk into it with a thud. Mylo followed in behind them.

"What is wrong with you?" Valxina screamed. She opened her mouth to accost him more.

But Valxina could sense other people in the room. A blur of shadows stood in the corners as if awaiting a welcome, hungry for an invitation. Valxina's heart raced. What were they planning on doing to her? She looked up at Ky, fear hiding behind her eyes. "Please," she cried. Her voice had turned soft.

Ky only nodded and moved to the side. The others in the room whispered. Their shadows stepped out into the light. One, in particular, jolted into the space between them.

Valxina gasped at their face. They were bloodied and tattered. A look of wild desperation cried from the person's large unnatural eyes.

"W-What?" Valxina looked up at the woman. "Keeper Sera?"

A large cut rested across her right brow. A thick layer of

dirt and mud covered her clothes, and she was not wearing her robe. In fact, she was not wearing keeper blue at all. She wore what looked like... servant's clothes. The woman's chest rose wildly as her eyes hardened on. While someone had attempted to clean out her wounds, crimson stained her skin.

Keeper Pax revealed herself from the shadows next. Her face was red and puffy with tears. A light dusting of dirt marked her skirt and choli. Like a thin layer of powder, the dust marked her skin.

Valxina glanced around the room. Ky propped himself against his desk, his arms crossing his body.

"That's enough pretending," the commander muttered to Valxina. When Valxina looked up at him, she dropped the look of shock on her face. "Unless you are so deep into the falsehood you've fallen for him?"

Valxina held her breath. She looked up at the commander. A soft curse released under her breath, *"Fuck."*

Chapter 22

When Danae moved out of the shadows, Valxina froze. Her eyes drilled into Valxina, causing every muscle of Valxina's body to tense. Valxina could feel the energy waft through the room—so explosive she dared not to speak. She turned to Sera. Dark circles stretched beneath her sunken eyes. The woman looked exhausted.

"What happened?" Valxina whispered as she stood. She flattened her hands over her attire and moved to let the woman sit.

Sera's eyes narrowed. She huffed as she plopped into the armchair and gazed beyond the others. "Zessfar," she spat his name like venom, "and I got into an argument yesterday. After I saw he healed your head but not your mark, I went to speak to him."

Inara moved out of the doorway. She knelt next to the woman and handed her a glass.

"Things got... intense." Sera's eyes looked as if the life had been drawn out of them. Her chest rose and fell so deeply, like she had never had a taste for the air before. "He told me to be careful, to watch my mouth and what I said. He said it wasn't my place to question his decisions." She took a long pause. "I knew things were rocky, I knew he was upset, but I didn't expect Eno to take shit into his own fucking hands."

"What do you mean?" Valxina questioned. "Wait... Did Zessfar lay his hands on you?"

Sera took a deep sip from her glass. "No, not necessarily. The blood Pax saw at dinner on my leg... It was an accident. I allowed my emotions to get the best of me, blinding me from grace. I slipped." She pinched at her nose and rolled her eyes as if embarrassed. "But the reason I was taken... It was Eno. He took me to this... place. It was a detention cell. I had heard whispers of its existence, but I did not think it truly existed."

"Were you alone?" Keeper Pax asked.

Sera shook her head. "There were others. Servants... even noblemen and women."

Whispers broke between them. Danae gritted her teeth at the revelation.

Ky snarled. "And how did you get out?"

Something sinister flicked beneath Sera's eyes. Behind them, the fire cracked, and a breeze traveled down the chimney of the hearth. It danced between their bodies. Sera broke the silence once more, "They underestimate us, you know? They do not think much of us keepers—not as much as they pretend they do. Women, even armed ones, are not something they are trained to fear." Sera scoffed. "The late King Elijah had the first Badawi lord implement an army—a legion of men and women to protect The Spring from all who would use it out of vain and greed. Only months later it was discovered that not one, not two, but many of the men had drunk the waters themselves, bottled it, and even sold it to others. Men—they are the blight of this world. They are the ones who take and steal and destroy. That is why the keepers are all women. The first Badawi lord found that women seemed to understand the waters more, that they held more respect for its powers. That isn't to say that no woman has ever stolen from The Spring, just not in the way men have. Women took for their families—for their husbands and children. That is why we are not permitted to marry, have babes, or to even be touched. It is a fear that men will corrupt us. And yet, after years of diligence, of strength, and of devotion... what do they think of us? *Nothing*. I suppose it's a downfall of us not training with them. I suppose it's because they do not work with us, not in the way the tower guards do. I fought two of them during a change of shift. One of the two felt some sort of pity on me as I told him I needed to relieve myself, and as a keeper, I did not wish to do so in a cell. I suppose the pit was near, as he said he would take me there. The other tried to convince him otherwise. But I believe the one—his name was Rohan—I believe he was a man of the gods. He felt guilty for leaving a keeper, a protector of The Spring to shit herself in the dark."

Keeper Pax winced at the words. But Sera continued, "When we reached the doorway, I fought them. I sprinted out to the jungle behind the palace. I thought about running, but I had to warn you all. So I waited on the outskirts until a produce cart came in. When a delivery from San Divolax passed by, I snuck into the carriage. I smuggled myself through the servants' quarters underground. I stole the clothes from a laundry room, and that's when I bumped into Mylo."

Mylo. The tower guard nodded at his name on her tongue. He had found Keeper Sera in the servant's quarters. He had been chasing after Val when he came across her.

Ky stirred in the corner. "Do you know where the detention center is? Do you know how to find it?"

Sera nodded. "I think I might be able to do so. I can take you there. But with Eno gone, I am not sure who the keys have passed on to."

"We need to get the others out of there," said Ky.

"And how are we supposed to do that?" Keeper Pax questioned. "We can't just walk into the place."

"It was under lock and key," Sera added. "There seemed to be only two copies. One with the guards and one held by Eno."

"We can try to take on the Badawi House guards?" Mylo muttered.

Quiet rage rang with his words. Shadows shifted within his eyes.

Ky lifted a brow. "While I know you would enjoy nothing more than knocking the skulls out of Badawi Guards, that is not wise. They probably have guards even before the door. Sera could only see what they looked like during a shift change. There's no way to know how many men are on duty at any given time. We cannot be certain we can get in."

"And what if we have a key?" It was Danae's voice that rang through the room.

Silence spread.

"What do you mean?" Inara asked.

"You said Eno had a key?" Danae turned to Sera.

"Yes, but it was you who informed me of his death."

Danae smiled a wicked grin. "Yes, but I've seen his body. I have seen where he was dumped—clothing, items, trinkets—and all."

The room shuddered at the thought. Valxina bit the inner skin of her cheek. She wondered, *Did Zessfar have any knowledge of the cell Sera had escaped from? Would he know how to enter the premises... or how to enter the place?* The questions brought heat to her face. She was confused, conflicted—angry, even. Even if he hadn't known, what kind of lord sat blindly to the imprisonment of his Court members? It made little sense.

Chapter 23

Crypt duty could not be missed. If anyone noticed a keeper missing from entering or exiting the caverns, all would know. Keeper Sera was the only person who could dismiss a keeper from her schedule. But with her missing, Keeper Pax held that job.

While some in the group believed their plan would only work if they appeared normal—any glimpse of divergence would raise red flags—they decided otherwise. With Sera hiding out in the commander's quarters, it was imperative that no one knew of their movements. Distraction, that was what they truly needed. The tower guards accompanied their keepers—those who were not believed to be missing—to the building. Danae and Inara left for the changing chambers first. Valxina followed, not far behind.

Sera and Pax had instructed them to make their presence known. They were to cause such a commotion the others could not forget they were on duty. They were to attract so much attention as they entered the crypt that no one would doubt their presence. Valxina knew what would elicit the reaction they hoped for. She nodded silently at the command and waited for the moment. But even so, she feared the words prepared at the tip of her tongue.

Beside her, Danae adjusted the surujin on her belt. She had dressed in a keeper's robe. Inara clipped the high neck of her choli next to her. Valxina reached for the material draped around her. She was still wearing the dress Lady Masha had wrapped on her body. She took a deep breath before she spoke, then straightened her back and turned to the women.

"You won't believe who I saw today," Valxina started, "who wrapped me up in this contraption."

Inara turned to look at her, but Danae kept her head straight. Even now, she insisted on being insufferable.

"Are you going to tell us, or is this the start of a silly guessing game?" Danae replied.

Valxina rolled her eyes. "It was Lady Masha."

Inara's eyes widened and she reached a hand to her chest. Danae turned to Valxina, her teeth bared. "I hope you plunged your javelin into that woman's vile throat."

Valxina shook her head. Grasping the end of the material, she began to unwrap it. "I didn't. I let her dress me instead." Her voice was soft and tinged with regret. She wished she had acted with such vigor, instead taking the moment to lock the woman in a closet or force her into a luggage case. She regretted not baring her teeth and showing the woman more. But she needed Masha to be oblivious. Valxina needed the lord off her scent. And if she had murdered Lady Masha, the woman who had spent years torturing her, well, that would cause many to speak. That would leave Zessfar with many questions. Valxina allowed the material to gather at her waist.

"Is that what you would have done?" she asked Danae. "And why? I'm sure she treated you just fine? You're the daughter of a nobleman, are you not?"

Danae clenched her jaw. "Here we go. I've wondered when we would have this conversation—when the innocent child of the lotto would come swinging."

Valxina cringed at her choice of words.

"Danae," Inara started. But her mouth snapped shut, most likely remembering the task at hand. She took in a large gulp.

Valxina's hands shook. "She locked me in closets and luggage cases. She beat me when I failed tests of the scriptures. Sometimes, when Lady Masha was feeling especially spiteful, she'd bring chains with her." Valxina lifted her arms. "From time to time, she'd clamp them so hard they'd leave me bleeding at the wrists."

Danae's glare lowered. She stilled at the sight of the scars on Valxina's wrists. "And that night of the test... the first test..." Valxina's chest rose and fell like that of a frenzied beast. "She and a collection of noblemen and women took their anger out on me. All of them." Valxina shook her head. "What did they do to *you*, Danae? Did you feast with them in that room? Did you chat about your shared lives?"

Her voice had grown so loud the other keepers in the

chambers whispered behind. She could feel their glare on her—she could sense the tension at her words. These were the aspects of becoming a keeper that the women never spoke of. These were the rituals they refused to remember. These were not conversations to be had.

Danae furrowed her brows. She parted her lips and looked at Valxina with a softened look in her eyes. Valxina grew uneasy.

"She made me kneel on grains of rice," Inara said in a soft voice. "I had to kneel there for hours while I prayed. She said I held no intellect, that I wasn't smart enough to become a keeper, that I had to pray to the gods to not lash me down during the ceremony."

Valxina stilled at the mention of the ceremony. When Valxina and Danae turned to Inara, she reached up to collect her braids. They watched as she pinned them up. Sadness washed over her face. "I was so afraid of the ceremony—I swore I would be dead by the end of the night. I thought I would chicken out and be drowned by the guards. And if I somehow found the strength to not tap out, I truly believed the gods would drown me themselves."

The murmurs around them had grown louder. No one dared to speak of the ceremony once it had finished. It was an event meant to be forgotten, to live quietly in their minds for the rest of eternity—but to never be spoken out loud.

"The ceremony..." Valxina said, her words shaky. She took a deep breath and reached for the last bit of her dress. She undid it, revealing the mark on her back. "It was the ceremony where you two and the others did *this*." Valxina motioned to her back. A chill pushed its way up her spine.

The voices around them were apparent. By now, the attention they had wished to garner had been collected. Every eye turned to the woman who stood bare before them. Valxina held her breath, lifted her chin, and matched the gazes of Danae and Inara.

Inara gasped. She reached for her mouth and furrowed her brows. "I-I am so sorry." Soft sobs crept through her voice.

Valxina could feel the lump rising in her throat. She forced it down. But she could not stop her irrational breaths, nor could she hide the tears that formed in the corners of her eyes. She wanted to conceal herself, to cover her body and pretend it had not happened. But when the group decided they needed to attract the attention of the other keepers on duty, Valxina knew—this would do it. She bit her trembling lip as she looked at the other women.

"I know for a fact that you two did not receive the steel the way I did. I know you did not face the things I did. I know you may have faced a fraction of what I did, but you were not tormented." Valxina held her breath.

Danae reached over to one of Valxina's hooks. She stretched for the robe and grasped it with her fingers. When she removed it, she turned to Valxina. Their eyes locked as she handed Valxina the coverage. It was a side of Danae Valxina had never seen before. Her eyes glossed over, and her brows lowered.

"You are right," she muttered. "We were not marked

the way you were. I am sorry for my part in your pain. But know that Inara had very little to do with it. She did not apply pressure."

Valxina took a step towards the other keeper. "Then why did you do it?" she said through gritted teeth. "Does your prejudice truly run that deep?"

Valxina watched as Danae lifted her face. Ice radiated from her stare. "No, I did it because I had to." *Hesitation.* Danae's nostrils flared. "I did it because Lady Masha told me to do so."

Valxina's heart collapsed. The voices of the room seemed to distance themselves. Sounds echoed within her head.

Danae and Inara steadied her with their hands. "You were wrong about one thing—I, too, was tormented."

Valxina could see the woman was battling emotion as well.

"We don't need to do this anymore," Inara whispered to them. "We did it. We can leave it here."

"No," Danae snapped. "I want her to hear it—I want you to hear it. I want people to know."

To know what?

"Yes?" Valxina murmured.

"You speak of the test—of the first trial of our knowledge and loyalty. My father is a nobleman; you are right. And even he stood present at my trial." Danae sucked her teeth. "He knew this was not a life I truly longed for. Believe it or not, this was not my first choice of paths. I was free once. I knew what it felt like to live, to truly live. I did not want to be locked into a tower, placed into the dark, and forbidden to..." She paused as if to consider her next words carefully. But she continued, "I did not want to be forbidden to fuck. But my father had other plans for me. He told me I was wild. He told me how disappointed he was in me. I was the slut of a daughter he wished he had not had. I was a wild heretic who needed to be tamed. He told me no one, no right man, would wish to have me in the future. I had soiled all hopes of becoming the daughter of his dreams. I know what people think of me. I know I am crude. I know darkness follows me. I know there is emptiness in my eyes. I am aware of this... I put it there." Danae shifted as she spoke. "Lady Masha told me to mark you, Valxina. She told me to mark you with every ounce of evil and darkness within me. She told me it would cleanse me of my sins—she told me it was necessary. And when I did not believe that, she told me she would reveal my secret."

Valxina shuddered, and her eyes narrowed. "What did she have to reveal?"

The room had grown loud from the keepers chattering, repeating the words to one another.

"I am not afraid of the world knowing I enjoy company in my bed, if that is what you are thinking. That was not something I was afraid to parade through the Court." Danae's voice had grown softer.

"Then what?" Inara asked.

The three seemed to forget they were not alone in the room. It did not matter anymore. And while they did not need to continue, while they had accomplished their task, they pressed on. Valxina wrapped her robe tighter around her body, pinned the buttons up, and reached for her javelin. When she turned to Danae, the woman continued.

"At the test, my father had me do something. I didn't see it then, I was too clouded by my emotion, but it was a task so that they would rule me forever. They wanted to hold something over my head. They wanted a reason for me to listen. I think that's the worst part about it... It was just a sequence in their plot."

"*They?*" Valxina muttered.

"My family, the Court, the noblemen and women... and others."

"What did they make you do?" Inara questioned.

Danae clenched her jaw. The words seemed to lodge in her throat. When she opened her mouth, no answer released. She shook her head and tried again. "During the first test ..." She paused, whispering her next words so only the two could hear her, "They—my father... He made me kill someone."

There it was. The last blow.

That was when Keeper Pax stormed in.

Chapter 24

While Keeper Sera was known for her stern looks and sharp tongue, Keeper Pax was not. Pax was her calmer half, her less judgmental and more sympathetic side. Kindness usually radiated from her bright, holy eyes. Her hair, shoulder-length and dark as the night, usually swayed with her movement. The woman practically skipped with her steps. But today, things were different.

When Pax jolted through the room with a ring of authority and rage in her voice, all the keepers froze. Women turned to look at her slowly as if in disbelief. They had never seen her like this. She had never risen her voice to any one of them. And now, as Keeper Pax thundered through the room, her eyes fixed on the three women before her, those in her way parted with wide eyes and a look of terror. They turned quickly and grabbed their weapons before making their way toward the crypt. Pax straightened her back and raised her chin. If this were to work, she would have to deliver a performance, a production so realistic no one would question them.

"You three!" Pax shouted across the room. "What is going on here?"

Valxina and the others played their part. They shared a glance at one another before redirecting their eyes to their feet.

"I heard the commotion from the courtyard!" Pax continued. "Can you believe it?"

No one replied.

"By the time I reached the bottom of the tower, I heard your names. Now, what exactly were you talking about to cause such unrest?"

Danae lifted her gaze to the woman. "The ceremony."

"The tests," Valxina added.

"Lady Masha," Inara said.

Keeper Pax took a step back as if she were not expecting to hear Masha's name on Inara's tongue.

"My quarters," she asserted in a low tone. When she looked back to see the last of the keepers entering the crypt, she repeated herself louder, "My quarters!"

Even if it was just an act, Pax shuddered at her own tone.

✦

Sneaking through the palace archways under the guise of night was one thing, but going to the pit to search for a body was another venture entirely.

Valxina held her breath as she pressed against the stone of the tower. She looked up at the sky. The stars, glaring and mystical, flashed their warnings above. When Valxina turned back, she watched the way Desil's arms seemed to hover around his keeper, Inara. Her strong jawline and deep brown eyes were highlighted by a scarf wrapped over her head. Valxina had once heard that Inara's ancestors worshipped different gods. There was a rumor that while her family practices all the faiths, they still spend a significant amount of time in their ancestor's temple. It wasn't wrong to practice a different faith in Qeshm, but it didn't come without its prejudices. Besides, when it came down to it, they all worshipped and prayed to the same gods. The only difference lay in the names they gave them and how they practiced faith. At least, that was what Valxina believed. But perhaps that was why Inara worried about whether she would be deemed worthy during the ceremony. Did she think her ancestry's faith would hurt her? Did she think the gods that looked over The Spring would punish her? Valxina knew the people Inara was rumored to share the blood of. Women like them worked with her in the kitchen. Some of them wore scarves, beautiful and intricate fabrics that had been passed through generations, around their faces, just as Inara did now. Inara's face lit up with a wild expression. She had the appearance of a young fawn on the run.

Valxina flexed her hand as they awaited the word from Ky. He crept into an opening, a space between the tower and the building adjacent. He wore his uniform, although he had forgone his jacket. Valxina watched the way he nodded at those around him. And when he decided the space was clear, he whistled. It was a sharp, clear sound that sent the group fleeing.

Valxina's feet hurried under her. To her right, Mylo ushered her forward. The seconds stretched and warped. The moments were slivers of frozen time. Their footsteps echoed within their heads—like bolts of thunder from the gods above. Valxina did not breathe. She held everything within her as the group slid through the shadows.

Danae, to the left of Valxina, kissed the marble before her. Valxina could not help but look at the woman. Her revelation in the changing chamber left her in a haze. Valxina studied the way Danae twisted her face and scouted the enclaves. The memory of her removing Eno's head from the stake flashed before her. Had the woman been so removed from death? Had Danae truly seen more of death than they knew? Did death flow through her—had she welcomed it at her fingertips?

Danae's eyes shot from one person to another, to the space ahead, and to the shadows behind. And when she stepped into the moonlight and turned, Valxina could not help but admire her. Her golden hair was collected tightly at her skull. It swung gracefully as she ran. Danae's hair, too, appeared to be a weapon. It was swift and agile. She took a step forward, waiting for Ky's next message with her face elevated. Valxina, on the other hand, continued to watch her. Valxina studied the way the woman's nose turned up slightly. While others seemed to narrow their eyes and brows, awaiting the next sign, Danae raised hers. The breathing of others seemed quick and shallow, but hers was deep and slow. As if in an attempt to take in each bit of air, Danae's chest rose and fell profoundly.

The sound of a door opening brought the gang to a halt. Valxina pressed her hands against the marble wall, and Ky's eyes widened as he looked at them. He put his finger to his lips. As they waited, Valxina's throat bobbed. She stood there watching as he walked into the light. A slight night breeze rustled his hair. The group was startled when he whistled again.

The smell of the pit hit them before they saw it. They had passed through the barrier created by the king's obeah women. The distinctions between the pit and the surrounding places seemed to blur in the darkness. Valxina groped for the bandeau at her head, took it off, and wrapped it around her face as a layer of protection over the translucent veil. While the stench of decay was shielded from her nose and mouth, it wasn't enough. As she twisted, Inara lifted her robe to her face. Even Mylo raised an eyebrow and clenched his jaw in response to the aroma.

But Danae only shifted on her feet and scanned the pit. Her eyes were sharp. Her nose had not crinkled. She was a statue, a steady cut of marble against the current. Valxina's eyes lifted as she witnessed the woman move forward. Had she spent so much time in the shadows, had she distanced herself so much, that she stood blind to the fierce aura of the woman in front of her? Danae lowered herself from the crest and stepped into the shallow imprint.

"Do you remember where you saw it?" Ky asked.

Danae shook her head. "I was standing on the south

end when I saw them dump it." She dusted the dirt off her hands with her robe. "I came here to dump Eno's head myself. But I unexpectedly came across a group of House guards. I hid in the trees when I saw them. And I watched as they dumped a body in here. It was strange. I didn't hear them in the distance. It was like they were muffled, like something separated them from the rest of the grounds."

Valxina shifted. Whatever spell that had been cast by the king's obeah women concealed their sounds.

"And you are sure it was Adviser Eno's?" Mylo questioned.

Danae raised her brow. "Who else would be dumped in here without a head?" The words were devastatingly calm. A coldness crept through Valxina's veins.

When Danae moved forward, the others held their breath. Her boots sank into the mud. Behind, Valxina could hear Inara mutter a prayer before she lowered herself to the crest. She placed her hands on the ground to her side and swung her feet around. Ky and the others followed behind.

Valxina had not seen the pit under moonlight since her time as a kitchen servant. Even on the nights the two would sneak off to the gardens and pond, Ky and Valxina never came this close. She shuddered at the memory of them—and at the times she would spill the contents of her basket and run. Of course, she had been here just hours ago. She had stood at the crest with the lord himself. But under the darkness of night, the pit had transformed.

"Danae?" Valxina said as the group moved through

the pit. Her boots drooped farther into decay, now ankle-deep in rot. Its scent tangoed around the decorative barrier at Valxina's face. Vomit rose from her stomach. She coughed, hoping to push the feeling down.

Danae was deafeningly silent. She took a step forward. She crossed over bones and bodies with haste. The way Danae swung her legs and leaped over bodies lengthened her appearance. In contrast, Valxina felt too close to the ground. As she peered down, she cringed. The maggots danced iridescently under the moonlight.

"Danae, did you see the lord out here earlier?" asked Valxina.

"No, *your lover*, Lord Zessfar, was not among the guards," Danae mocked.

"He's not my lover." She had told them of her closeness with the lord, but that she had only approached him for information. She had told them all in Ky's quarters that she had not truly fallen for the lord. It was all part of their plan. *But was that the truth?*

"Oh please," Danae muttered ahead. "I saw you get into his carriage. I watched him as he gifted you jewels."

Valxina did not know why, but the thought of Danae witnessing her with Zessfar made her cringe. She wished she hadn't.

"It's been one day," Valxina started. "You truly can't believe—"

"I think I may know more about these things than you do. And I know you haven't asked my opinion, but you should know he's not what he seems. He's a man, after all. He's powerful and handsome, and I'm sure you feel right and safe when you are around him. Especially given your past."

Valxina gritted her teeth at the words. Was she that easy to read? Heat rose to her cheeks as she lifted her chin to the air as if searching the sky for a break—a moment of salvation from the dreaded conversation.

"You should be more..." Danae paused. She shifted her head and reached down at a body. She pulled at it, abandoning whatever else she had wished to say. "Fuck," she whispered when she saw the man's head still attached.

"Any luck?" Ky asked the group as he trudged through the mess.

"None here," Inara answered.

"Nor here," Mylo said besides Valxina.

"I've yet to find our headless body," added Valxina.

"Wait, I think..." Danae called out. She looked out ahead. Had she seen it? Had Danae spotted a body fresher than the others with the dressings of a nobleman, not that of a guard? But Danae had stilled, and no words escaped her lips as if she had seen the goddess of death herself, as if one syllable could drag her down to hell. Valxina's eyes widened as she stared ahead of them.

There was motion among the shadows. It stilled them all.

Chapter 25

Valxina knew animals swarmed in the pit to feast.

As a kitchen maid, she would catch glimpses of the animals—of the wild cats, bears, and vultures. She would pray to never come across the vultures who would feed on the decay. After tossing her contents, she would sprint back to the palace. Valxina had considered the danger before lowering herself from the crest. But Valxina never imagined creatures of the *scriptures* to exist out there.

As the pit and its contents had changed, so had the vultures. A different kind of darkness lingered. A growl vibrated through the group so swiftly, so loudly, hands went straight to weapons. It catapulted skin to bitter steel. Valxina drew her javelin while holding her breath. She snatched it from its holder and sank her toes into the mud. The soil formed around her feet.

A grave sound traveled around the group, and each member turned. They stepped slowly back to one another.

Mylo, Desil, Agnar, and Ky stopped ahead of the others to guard the keepers. The women huddled close to one another, so close Valxina could *feel* her fellow keepers breathing. They settled at angles—Inara to her right and Danae to her left. Ahead, Mylo and Ky's swords glinted in the night.

"What the fuck was that?" Mylo muttered. His fingers tightened.

"Animals feast on the rot of the pit," Valxina answered. *It couldn't be anything more than a wild creature in search of its dinner.*

"This is no animal," Ky whispered.

Danae's fingers tightened on her weapon. "That is no creature of this world."

Inara turned to the others. "It's the bodies," she said. "They attract a different kind of vulture... They attract..."

Valxina steadied herself. *Of course, there were vultures far more terrifying than bears or cobos.* "It's the death," she said.

The creature growled again. It sent their heads shifting from one side to the other.

"It's a creature of the scripture," said Inara.

Valxina's eyes scanned the darkness. While it wasn't as dark as the crypt, visibility was limited. Chains echoed beyond.

"What *kind* of creature?" Ky asked.

Shadows rushed around them.

When they stepped out of the darkness, a coldness rushed through Valxina's veins. Inara gasped beside her.

"*Creatures,*" Valxina corrected. More than one played among the shadows.

There were stories of beasts in the scriptures—creatures of the night that revealed themselves only in the most unholy of places. Bright golden eyes glared at them. Fur, thick and pitch black, rose before them. Claws ripped at the ground beneath them. Pointed ears twisted as if listening from behind. Sharpened teeth promised destruction. Blood dripped from their mouths. Scattered breaths huffed into the air at the sight. At the sound of their growls, at the vibration between them, the group stiffened. Like man, the creatures lifted, moving onto their hind legs. Chains with large links swung from their necks.

"Stay behind me," Mylo instructed.

The other tower guards echoed similar sentiments to their keepers. But Valxina shifted her gaze to the commander.

"Kyrad?" said Mylo.

Ky turned to look at the keepers. When his eyes met Valxina's, he only nodded silently. And when he nodded to Mylo beside him, all hell broke loose.

The beasts broke out into feverish barks. They bit at the air and circled the group. They charged, leaping over the bodies of the dead. Their claws ripped into skin beneath them as they advanced.

Quickly, Valxina surveyed their surroundings. Decaying bodies and the skulls of men formed tiny towers of death. In the distance, the lights and comforts of Court twinkled away. The juxtaposition was deafening. She shut her eyes for a moment and recalled her lessons of the gods. There was something they hated the most—something they found most unforgiving.

As if reading Valxina's mind, Inara whispered, "They put them here." The woman's voice was erratic. "The gods..."

Danae replied, "The lord has disrespected them. He's shown disregard for life—he's treated the deceased like scrap. He has treated life—the life gifted from them—like trash. Quite literally."

Valxina said, "And these are a sign?"

"Warnings," Inara replied.

"To the lord?"

But before anyone could answer, the guards' formation shattered.

"Fuck!" Agnar muttered when a beast knocked into him.

Danae grunted as she swung her surujin with haste. She did not wait for instructions before she moved forward. Ahead, Valxina watched as Ky and Mylo battled another beast. Each attempt to strike at the creature before them left them swinging at the air. She opened her mouth to speak to Inara at her side, but the sight of the third beast silenced her.

It appeared graver than the others. Marks slashed across its body—tears across its fur and flesh had been left to fester and turn. It bared its teeth—sharp and bloodstained. A knot formed in Valxina's throat. Desil steadied the arrow strung at his bow. Valxina could not tell if minutes or seconds had gone by; they appeared to watch the man for hours, their eyes glued to the tip of the weapon. As it glided through the air, they followed it, muttering whispers of prayers. They watched as the beast stomped its feet and salivated. And when the creature jumped into the air, catching the arrow like a mere toy, Inara screamed.

Valxina flung her javelin, sweat dripping down her back, and ran toward the creature. Desil grasped for another arrow as she batted at the creature's claws. Across, Inara charged the beast with her curved sword. But the beast only averted. It grunted and shoved itself forward. Valxina's javelin vibrated within her hands. She took a deep breath and studied the creature's eyes. No sign of life stirred within it—only the emptiness of death—the kind that surrounded them, slung across mounds of bodies and mud. When the beast jolted toward Valxina, she increased her pace. She swung the blade and aimed for its chest. Instead of the impact she expected—wished for—a claw sent her spiraling toward the ground, slashing her arm. Bitter blood, bright and warm, splattered into the air. A scream released from Valxina's throat. It raged through the air and cut through the grunts and murmurs of others.

Then a sharp ring emerged with the pain of the wound. Heat raced through Valxina's body. She reached out to grab the torn slivers of her robe and clenched at her exposed skin. Valxina thumped into a pile of decaying bodies, face first. The ringing in her head heightened in response. Behind, she could faintly hear the creature wail. Valxina let out a cry as she attempted to lift herself up, her hands sinking into the decay. The ground was moist and gluey and left her slipping and falling into the trodden mess. Maggots, fat and slimy, crawled up her fingers and across her hands. Valxina's eyes widened, and she squealed as she shook them off and turned on her back.

Feet away, Desil had managed to get an arrow into the third beast. It stuck out of the creature's back like a thorn. She twisted in time to see Ky and Mylo sink their swords into the belly of a fallen creature. When her eyes searched for Danae and Agnar, her breathing quickened. She could not see them. *Fuck.* Her eyes blurred with tears of pain and shock. She bit at her lip and scanned the bodies around her.

"Val!" Ky screamed. "Val!"

But it was another voice that brought Valxina to her feet. "Get the fuck up!" Danae yelled.

Covered in blood, Valxina gritted her teeth and shook her head. All her years of training were for this. She pressed her feet into the ground and lifted herself.

Chapter 26

Horrified, Valxina staggered toward her javelin. It had landed feet away and into a corpse. Valxina steadied herself as she approached. She tried to drown out the noise, but the grunts and cries of the others circled through the air like an unwanted, haunted song. Her fingers wrapped across the center of her weapon as she tugged at it, the movements as wild as the beasts. The fabric around her face had fallen off. Strands of wet hair slicked against her skin. Valxina snatched her weapon out of the body of a fallen guard still in uniform. A hand still clenching at her arm, she ran toward the others. Out of the shadows, Danae jolted toward them. She was drenched, covered in mud and blood.

"Danae?" Inara called out to her, worry echoing through her voice.

But Danae only shook her head.

"Where's Agnar? Have you two taken it down?" the commander bellowed.

Danae had not stopped the shaking of her head. "It's down," she said before adding, "H-He's dead."

Valxina's heart dropped.

"Fuck!" Desil screamed ahead.

There was one beast left.

The ragged creature let out a cry. It stomped its feet against the ground and snapped at them. Valxina and Danae joined the others and surrounded it. Danae swung her surujin, while Mylo and Ky charged.

Valxina took flight beside them.

"Stay back!" Mylo commanded.

But she did not abide.

"Stay back!"

She did not.

The creature shook its head. Its eyes pierced into them. Then, under the glint of the moonlight, Valxina saw the pain in the creature's eyes.

"Wait!"

The command escaped her lips before she could think. Ahead, Ky hesitated at her word—but Mylo continued charging on. There wasn't enough time. They watched as the already released arrow sped through the air. It landed between the eyes of the beast within seconds. And when it dropped to the ground, it released a desperate whimper.

"Wait?" Danae snapped.

Valxina moved toward the creature. It kicked involuntarily. When she assessed it would not live, she knelt beside the beast.

"What is it?" Inara questioned as if she could see the guilt that plagued Valxina. But Valxina could not explain why the word had left her lips. Valxina could not understand her hesitation. She squeezed her eyes shut and took a deep breath.

Ky approached her slowly. "It's dying, Val. We must find Eno's body and get out of here. There could be others."

"No luck," Danae replied. "I-I saw his body out there." She motioned her chin in the direction she had emerged from. "Found the body after... after Agnar was torn to shreds. There was no key." Danae lowered her gaze. "Someone must have taken it." While Danae remained calm, regret seemed to linger in her tone.

Ky took a deep breath. His chest rose and fell with defeat. "We need to get back." His hands gripped Valxina's shoulders.

"Are you ok?" Danae asked, her eyes lingering on the fresh blood.

Valxina nodded.

When she moved aside, Valxina watched as the commander lifted his sword. He struck the beast with one final blow. Valxina lifted a brow at the gesture, but he only shrugged. "Even the unholiest of beasts deserve a clean ending."

✦

Valxina headed straight to Zessfar's quarters. No amount of quarrel or comments could stop her. She had seen creatures of the night—unholy beasts sent from the gods to warn him. She wondered, *Had he been aware of the evils that lurked his palace boundaries? Surely, he was not.* Valxina did not care that she was covered in mud and blood. She was completely oblivious to the few maggots that still clung to her robe, their bodies soft as silk. She strutted through the castle corridors without her head covering or veil, on a mission to tell Zessfar what she had seen— she had to tell him about the darkness that lingered and the tower guard he had lost. Agnar. The rest of the group had carried his body out of the pit. Ky swore he would be burned, not left for the beasts to feed on. Although Danae disagreed—she claimed the act would attract too much attention. As they left, Valxina caught Ky's scan of the others. He shook his head at the bodies that were left in the decay.

"Fitting place for Eno," Danae had muttered in response as she looked over the pit, "but not for the rest of them."

As she dashed under the archways, Valxina clenched her javelin. Approaching the doors of the lord's chambers, she held her head high. His usual guards stood watch.

"Is he in there?"

They shared a glance with one another. Neither answered.

"Is Lord Zessfar in there?" she demanded. This time, her voice rang with more authority.

"I do not believe the lord is expecting company—"

"Fuck you," Valxina bit out. "We aren't doing this again. Is he in there or not?"

But her choice of words stirred the men.

"You are no keeper," one spat.

The other, the one who wore the crest tattooed to his skin, gritted his teeth. "You are just as they say."

Valxina edged them on, "And what is that? What do they say?"

The man eyed her down, studying the mud and blood that stained her skin. His glare burned into her flesh. He stared at her face, at her exposed skin and lips.

"You are a servant," the other muttered. "A servant who does not know of boundaries. You are—"

"You are nothing but a distraction to our lord. You are a disgrace to your title. You are no keeper, nothing more than a common whore," the larger man finished. "Now get along and leave him."

Valxina's eyes widened at the words.

"Get going, *lotto child*."

Blood boiled in Valxina's veins. Her breath hitched.

"You're the one who was caught when you were younger," the man with the tattoo continued. "What? Your poor servant girlfriend left you, and now you think you can have the lord?"

Valxina's heart banged against her chest. "Zessfar!" she roared. She positioned herself between them and squared her shoulders. "Zessfar!"

She looked at the two men and sized them down. "I have information for the lord. Now tell me, Is he fucking in there or not? Or would you two rather stand there and tell me how much of a whor—"

The doors opened immediately.

And there he was.

Zessfar's eyes widened at the sight of Valxina. He looked over at the guards and waved them away. "Why did you not let her in?" he shouted. When he studied the distress plastered across Valxina's face and the blood on her arm, he stepped forward, ignoring the men completely.

"What is wrong?" Zessfar questioned. "What has happened?"

Valxina lifted her chin once more. She moved past the guards and into Zessfar's doorway. He held a hand out for her and raised a brow.

Yes, she had been a child of the lotto. Yes, she had been a servant of the palace. Yes, he had been left behind by someone she had once loved. But no, the other insults the guards had flung at her were wrong. She did not *think* she had Lord Zessfar. By the way his face dropped at the sight of her, by the walls that came crashing down in her presence, by his lifted hand and the worry in his deep dark eyes, Valxina knew they were wrong. She did not *think* she had the lord. *She knew she had him.*

Chapter 27

Zessfar cringed at the sight of Valxina's muddied attire, her blood-stained skin, and the wretched smell of decay. His brows furrowed as he looked at her, lifting the back of his hand to his nostrils. "Who did this to you?" His voice was calm but demanding as he clenched a fist at his side.

"The pit." Her voice quivered. While he kept his distance, Valxina moved forward. "I went to the pit tonight."

"You *what*? Why?" He scanned her eyes for more. Fear trembled in his words. It billowed between them.

Valxina halted. His face appeared baffled but responsive. Could she tell him the truth? Valxina's lips parted as she prepared her next words, but Zessfar cut her short.

"Kulrani," he said, his eyes still wide at her appearance. He signaled toward a doorway, one farther into his chambers. "I can't speak to you like this."

"Like how?" She narrowed her eyes, agitated by his interruption. Did he not want to hear about the happenings of his own Court grounds?

"It isn't that I do not wish to know what has happened to you; I do. But you are hurt, you're bleeding, and you're covered in..." Zessfar stopped as if incapable of speaking.

Valxina lowered her gaze. But she could feel Zessfar's eyes that remained fixed on her.

"Through those doors," he said with the tilt of his head. "We need to get you washed up. I promise to listen to all you have to say. In fact, I am eager to learn more about what has occurred. But you can tell me while you are washing... while you bathe."

He was calmer than she expected. Valxina's heart sank at the prospect of wiping the mud, death, and rot off her. She took a breath of death into her lungs before answering, causing her to twitch in revulsion.

"Thank you," she replied with a relieved sigh.

✦

Valxina had never made it farther than the lord's study and waiting room. A wide desk sat near the window, in addition to the couches and chairs that ornamented it. The room's focal point was a bar cart. The blaze of the fireplace illuminated the books and paintings, giving life to the leather and oil.

Valxina could not help but scoff as she walked through the doors into the bathroom. There was a huge vanity in the room, and the already drawn bath glowed with candlelight.

"Were you about to bathe for the night?" Valxina questioned. "I'm sorry to have interrupted."

Zessfar shook his head. He crossed his arms and leaned against the doorway.

"There's no need for you to apologize." He motioned to a stall in the room's corner. "If you'd like to rinse off before bathing, you are welcome to do so. I'll sit here and wait for you to tell me what happened. Take your time."

Valxina approached the stall. The space was separated from the tub room by a wall. She spotted a marble bench, towels, sponges, and a large basin of water when she glanced through the doorframe.

"Go ahead," said Zessfar. He pulled a stool out for himself and perched against the wall of the stall. She waited for him to face the bath before stepping into the small room.

"So?" Zessfar's voice echoed through the room.

Valxina looked up as she reached for the buttons of her robe. The walls of the stall stopped only inches above her head. She hesitated, wondering if she should truly trust him with the information about Sera's reemergence. But Zessfar had helped; he had gone into town asking for her. He had punished Eno for his actions against the santu woman. Her robe dropped to the ground. She reached for a sponge and dipped it into the basin. "Keeper Sera," Valxina whispered. "We found her."

Zessfar was silent on the other end of the wall. Had he heard her? Valxina considered ducking her head out, but she stilled herself.

"Seraphine?" He said her name like a song—like a

melancholy melody. "You found Seraphine?"

The sponge made her fresh cut sting and caused Valxina to flinch. She hesitated, releasing a deep breath before saying, "She came to us."

Zessfar asked, "So she is ok?"

"She's..." *Was Sera ok?*

"She's fine." Valxina ran the sponge across her skin and up her legs. Excess water, stained dark with dirt and blood, trickled down to the drain on the floor. "She's fine," Valxina repeated, unsure whether she was referring to Seraphine or herself. While the water was warm, Valxina wished it was steaming. She wanted to boil the feeling off her. She never wanted to smell that stench again. But no amount of scrubbing could get the pit off her, not truly—it was with her forever.

When Valxina was done, she wrapped herself in a fresh towel. It had been sitting on the stool, waiting for her. Zessfar stood as she stepped out.

"Where is she now?"

"Sera's safe," Valxina answered, her voice hushed. While she said the words, the question remained with her. *Was Keeper Sera truly safe?* With what she had seen in the darkness of the pit, were any of them safe? And with Eno gone, was the threat of being arrested under Badawi House guards actually gone? "Keeper Sera has escaped a detention cell. It seems Eno has been detaining those who speak ill against you. I am assuming you knew nothing of this? Just as you did not know of his arrest of her?" She studied his tightened fingers and worked her way up to his frown. His forehead wrinkled with displeasure and shock.

Zessfar shook his head. It was a slow and guarded movement. "A detainment cell? Kulrani, I had no idea..."

"I know you had him executed for his actions, but did he say anything before he died? Was there anything Eno said that indicated where the detention cells may be hidden? Sera claims other individuals are still being imprisoned there. She even said there were noblemen and women being kept captive." She hurriedly added the final bit. It shouldn't have mattered whether the center was stocked with servants, maids, or noblewomen—but she knew how this Court worked.

Zessfar dropped to the bathroom stool and pressed his forehead against his palms. It was a shield, a movement of protection. But no barriers could protect him from the truth—from the actions of the Court that had taken place right under his nose.

"How could I have been this stupid?" His voice sounded anything but royal. "How could I have been so blind?"

A stone fell into the pit of Valxina's stomach. His tone sent a shiver down her body. The quiet words echoed between them. Valxina rested a hand on Zessfar's shoulder. When he looked up at her, his eyes wide like pools of honey, her fingers glided across his shirt. "You didn't know. You *don't* know."

"And why were you at the pit?" Zessfar asked. "What happened to you?" His gaze lingered on the gash across her arm.

Valxina released a stifled breath. "Zessfar, I went with some others to see if Eno's body held a key."

"A key to the cells?"

"We couldn't find anything. But we were met with something else... Zessfar, the gods are unhappy with your use of the pit. It's like the scriptures said... It seems they have unleashed unholy beasts. They are feasting on your people's bodies—they are eating away at their flesh. We were attacked by three of them."

Zessfar looked up at her. His eyes glossed over. "You think there are unholy beasts in the pit sent from the gods? But those... those are just stories."

Valxina shook her head. "I do not think, I know. *I saw them.* They attacked me—they attacked us."

"Who else was with you?"

"Danae, Inara, Desil, Agnar, Mylo, and Ky."

Lord Zessfar rose a brow. "Ky?"

"Commander Kyrad," Valxina corrected. "And Zessfar, it's... about Agnar." She lifted her gaze. "One of the tower guards."

Zessfar blinked slowly, with a look of astonishment across his eyes.

"One of the creatures killed him."

"These beasts took down a tower guard? So it is true? Everything you are saying?" Zessfar stood.

Valxina bit at her lip. "I'm sorry."

"You're sorry?" Zessfar asked. "I-I've fucked up to the point of vengeful gods, and you are... you are sorry?" While the words were drenched in sadness, Valxina noted the tinge of tempered laughter.

Valxina reached back for his hand. So much pain radiated from the man before her. "I am sorry this is happening to you. I am sorry to tell you this news. But you must know."

Zessfar shook his head. He reached his free hand to Valxina's cheek. "You fought them?" He motioned to the wound on her arm.

Valxina nodded. "We did."

"I'll have to thank you all for what you did. And I think it's only right to include you all in the conversations about what is to come—how we should address these matters."

Valxina tilted her chin. She had not expected this. "You... You would do that?"

"Of course, Kulrani. I must keep you and the others close. You all seem to know more about the happenings of my Court than I do."

The edges of her lips curled upward. "Well, I do not believe that is true."

"Believe what you wish," Lord Zessfar replied. "But I must start with making this up to you."

"And how do you plan to do that?" Valxina replied.

Zessfar nodded to the drawn bath behind them.

"Are you inviting me to bathe in the lord's tub?" she asked, a brow raised. While she had wiped and scrubbed at her skin, she still did not feel clean, not completely.

Zessfar nodded.

"Where is your attendant? If you stuck me with Lady Masha earlier, surely you have a man of your own? Oh, please do not call for her."

Zessfar tilted his head. "I'm not a fan of attendants. I prefer to do those things on my own."

"Me too," Valxina replied. "You know, for future reference."

"Future reference? Do you plan on accompanying me

often in the future?" Zessfar grinned, flashing a set of teeth so perfect they could not be real.

Valxina dipped a hand into the tub. The water was still warm. "I guess that depends on if you want me around."

The lord took a step toward her. "I want you around."

She held her breath. "They'll continue to call me names," Valxina said. She didn't want to care. She did not want to say the words.

"Call you what? Who?" Zessfar rested a hand on her arm. His fingers lingered on her exposed skin.

Valxina shook her head. "I-It doesn't matter."

Zessfar smiled at her. "I know you said no attendants, Kulrani. But would you... would you allow me?"

Chapter 28

Valxina remained silent as Zessfar reached for her towel, still wrapped around her torso. She took a deep breath and held it. The pause felt like an eternity. A gentle caress stroked across a small bloodstain on her neck, and she clenched her eyes at the touch, at his tenderness. In his wake, gooseflesh arose. The blood within Valxina's veins roared. She nodded, sending his fingers straight for the towel. The action was lightning fast.

"It's the least I could do," Zessfar said, "for a keeper who stands before me, stained with blood and mud, a woman dirtied while protecting my Court, my people—*me*."

Was this his way of thanking her?

As Zessfar's fingers glided across the towel, just a touch away from her skin, Valxina held her breath. His brown eyes had darkened. When he got closer, her breathing became labored. His gaze swept over her body, focusing on the covered peaks of her breasts. They had risen, hard against the fabric. It was *he*. The lord of Badawi was undressing her. It was *his* soft and tender fingers on her. His gaze lingered on her as if he were tracing her lips, sketching them in his mind to cherish forever. Valxina hesitated for a moment. *Was Danae right? Were the guards that stood before his door right? No.* She forced the thoughts out of her head. Their presence was not welcomed here. And she certainly did not want to think about Danae at this moment. This wasn't a part of the plan, *no*—but this was real on his end. And for her... this was something she wanted. It was real for her too. The night had left Valxina so full of death and decay, and she wished for nothing more than to clean her body and be reminded of life. So when Zessfar hooked his fingers into the folding of her towel and allowed it to drop, she leaned in.

The Court fell into silence. The sounds of the beasts in the pit blew away with the breeze of the open window. Valxina leaned in closer, her eyelashes fluttering at the movement. As Zessfar's fingertips stretched for her exposed skin, she suppressed a small quiver. She pressed her lips against his. He was cold. So very cold. And when Valxina dipped her head, breaking the connection between them, she pressed her lips together and bit at her skin. He must have had the wine again tonight. He tasted of palm trees, sunshine, and peaches. It was sweet. She reached for him, for the white shirt he wore, and his body inches away. When she searched for the edge of it, she saw the glimmer of a smirk from the corner of her eye. There was that Badawi arrogance—even present now, as they undressed.

Zessfar reached his hands for his shirt. Silently, he

removed it above his head. He did so with grace. His eyes never averted from her—from the way her brown skin shimmered in the light. When he glided a hand across her chin, her eyes widened silently and held yearning.

"Are you sure you want to do this, Kulrani?" Her name had never sounded so powerful. Her name had never sounded so rich or affluent. But here, with him in possession of her name, it was different.

Valxina nodded as she reached for him. She brushed a hand through his soft dark curls and pulled him in closer.

"Are you sure you want to do this, *Zessfar*?"

His name—so clear, so informal, so open, was all it took. Zessfar cupped her face in his hands—soft like satin. He drew her close. Their bodies pressed against one another. Heat—sweltering summer heat—tangoed around them. Zessfar's hands roamed across Valxina. He pushed her back, maneuvering toward the tub.

"Let's get you cleaned up," Zessfar muttered as he motioned behind her.

Valxina had never felt so lavish. She swallowed the knot in her throat and moved toward the tub. She maintained her position, taking sideways steps to the porcelain in the center of the room. This was not the time for him to see her scar; this was not the time for anyone to lay eyes on the mark that still branded her skin like an ugly memory, a reminder of her past more gruesome than it ever should have been. She lifted a naked leg into the water. While steam no longer rose from its surface, it was still warm enough to soothe her. He withered at the noise she made as she slipped in.

"Will you be joining me, my lord?" she asked as she dipped in. She knew the formality would annoy him.

Zessfar shook his head. "What did we say about calling me so?" He stalked over to her. She studied his fingers, the way they reached for his belt at his waist.

Valxina dipped her head under the water as the lord removed the last of his clothing. When she emerged and broke the surface, once again like a darkened nymph, Zessfar stood at the edge. Valxina's hair slicked behind her. Streams of water ran down her face. A series of blinks followed her emergence. The room had gone blurry.

"You are a creature of magic," he muttered gently. "You are absolutely bewitching."

That word. Valxina smiled. "You think me a witch, don't you?" A lord with a witch—an obeah woman—what will they say? But the words were not of worry; unlike in the past, she cared not what Court members would say. Because in this moment, she wanted this. She wanted him. She wanted a moment to give in to her desire and to put herself, not the thoughts or reputations of others, first.

Zessfar grinned as he lifted himself into the tub. He was a tall man, or at least he seemed so to Valxina. His body was not toned or bulked like that of a warrior—but she appreciated that. It was a sign of his life, of his position. And from his chiseled outline, she could tell, he did spend time maintaining his ability in the sparing ring.

It was not a tub like the shared ones of the tower or servants' quarters. This was not made for hordes of folks. At his entrance, water spilled off the edges of the rim. Swooshes of water fell against the tiles crested in Badawi blue. Valxina watched the way the water stirred about.

When he settled, facing her, Zessfar reached a hand out. He brushed a finger across Valxina's cheek and tucked a loose strand of hair behind her ear. "I have a riddle for you."

"Is this really the moment for riddles, my lord?"

Zessfar smirked. "Will you oblige me?"

Valxina hesitated. She fought the knot in her throat and replied, "Always."

Zessfar lifted a brow. "Always?"

Rumors and whispers had been wrong, so wrong. The man before her was kind. He was tender. He welcomed her with open arms. He held her close despite her past. He could have anyone here, but he chose *her*.

"I swear, Kulrani, you are everything I have ever longed for. How could I have lived with you right here... right under my nose, without knowing?" Zessfar said as he pulled her to his side. "Come here," he whispered, his tone so soft and fragile she swore it could break. "Come here."

"And what of the riddle?"

"Fuck the riddle," he said. "Come here."

She abided, and the water stilled. Candle flames heightened. The heat rose. Valxina held her breath as the lord pressed his body against her. A quiet moan escaped her lips. At the sound, Zessfar's kissing erupted into disorderly attempts to devour her. And while her younger self—the last drop of who she had been before the ceremony—reminded her to stay safe, to say vigilant, she did not. For in the moment, she felt awakened, like she was no longer a woman of her background. She didn't need to protect him. She could be herself—the new version of herself who walked with her head high, javelin strapped to her back, and with the lord, the Badawi lord, at her side. Valxina wished she could savor it, she wished she could grasp a vial and bottle the feeling forever. Her heart quickened at the thought. For she knew it couldn't last forever. No, the truth lingered in the shadows—and one day, Zessfar would learn she had planned this. Only, she hadn't accounted for herself. She had not prepared for how she would feel now, with the golden specs of his eyes watching her, or the feel of his fingers caressing her skin. Valxina swallowed at the thought. She moved toward him and lifted her knees, welcoming the lord between her.

Chapter 29

The sound of crashing dishes awakened Valxina from her slumber. She shook her head, trying to erase the cacophony from her mind. As she lifted the pillow over her head, she let out a muffled moan. The magnificent space was bathed in sunlight. She tightened the covers around her. They were soft, like cool, unadulterated clouds. As she shuffled around, they caressed her skin.

"Kulrani?" The voice was faint.

"Mmm?" Valxina muttered.

A soft chuckle spread through the room. "You've slept through both breakfast and lunch," said Zessfar.

Valxina's eyes shot open. A part of her had believed it a dream. Another part of her swore she must have died in the pit and last night was nothing but a slice of nirvana. Her arm seemed to remind her of the nightmare of the pit, pulsing under the weight of her. She tossed the pillow off her and perked up. Still clenching the sheets at her chest, she looked over to the lord. Last night, he had *thanked* her for hours, putting only her needs first. And after they had chatted and shared their favorite riddles and teasers, she had fallen asleep in his bed, tightly tucked under his shoulder.

In daylight, the room appeared different. The four posts of the bed seemed to tower above her. A large jaguar skin rug lay at the foot. And when she saw the sparkle of the lord's golden armband resting so casually at the table, she held her breath.

"I've prepared for a celebration tonight," Zessfar said from the other side of the room.

They weren't alone. While the lord stood in front of an armoire, dressing for the day, a servant collected dishes that had been left about the room. Plates of half-eaten fruit and sticky glasses of wine were scattered about the space.

"A celebration?"

"For you."

The keeper froze at the words. When she looked at the woman across the room, even she seemed to have stilled.

Zessfar continued, "For you and the others—to thank you for what you have uncovered. I would like to celebrate your good work and your dedication. Plus, I'd like to see Seraphine, to make sure she is ok after everything..." He moved toward his armband and outlined its edges with a thumb. And when his eyes averted to the woman in the corner, she followed his glare. "Leave Keeper Valxina some bread and cheese." She did not reply. Her soft nod was answer enough.

When the woman exited the room, Valxina stood from the bed.

"Where are you off to, my enchantress?"

Valxina smiled at the name. "Really leaning into this whole witch thing, aren't you? I should get back to the tower."

"No need," said Zessfar. "I've already sent word to the tower. Commander Kyrad, your tower guard, and your fellow keepers already know you have spent the night here with me."

Valxina's eyes widened. Heat rose to her cheeks. "They know... they *all* know I am here?" Her chest ached.

Zessfar watched the way the woman's eyes lowered. He moved toward her, his features twisted with worry. "Are you ashamed?" His brows pinched together. "Do you regret what we had? Do you wish for it to end?" He stilled. "Just say the word."

Valxina shook her head. "Am *I* ashamed?" She wasn't ashamed, but the words of Lady Masha seemed to echo within her head. Her oath, her vow of celibacy had been broken. She wondered what it meant for her position—her role. Valxina looked up at the lord. "Is it not *you* who should feel such a thing?" She shifted on the bed and propped herself on her knees. "Shame?"

Zessfar rose a brow. "Last night," he began, "was the greatest night of my sorry existence, of all my time as the Badawi lord. If I ran away with you and lived the life of a peasant, I would die a happy, fulfilled man."

Valxina steadied herself. His words were naïve. They were the feverish ramblings of a man who did not know true life in poverty. But still, he had said them. "Stay here, relax. I have some business to attend to. Read a book." He pointed to the shelves on the wall. "Or take another bath if you wish. Perhaps think of me while you do so?" he added with a devilish grin.

Valxina's chest tightened. "And what of my crypt duty tonight?"

"Already taken care of it."

"I am a keeper, Zessfar. It is my duty—"

The lord lifted a hand into the air. He shook his head and looked at her with widened eyes, willing her to stop.

She had worked so hard to become a keeper—to protect The Spring. She did not wish to slack on her duties. But surely, if the lord himself insisted it was safe to take the day off...

"Please," Zessfar added.

It was the need in his voice, the soft demand for her to take the day to rest, that led her to agree. She believed her life would change when she became a keeper. She hoped it would secure her safety—but this, this was a shift on cosmic levels.

"Ok," she finally replied. When his face lit up, she smiled. "Perhaps I'll read—and I will take another bath."

Zessfar walked over to her. He leaned in and pressed his lips against hers. "And will you think of me?"

Valxina shook her head. "You are unholy."

Zessfar pressed into her and placed a kiss against her neck. "You have no idea." He chuckled, his breath warm against her skin.

Chapter 30

No amount of rest would be enough for the night in store for Valxina.

Valxina scanned the dining room, which had been decorated with Badawi flags and keeper blue. At her side, Lord Zessfar grinned.

"Do you like it?" he asked, his voice loud enough for the others to hear.

Valxina checked the eyes of the others. They hovered around the table, their gazes shifting between them. Keepers Sera and Pax were the only two in their robes. Danae had draped herself in a dress so stunning and delicate even Valxina's eyes had gone wide at the sight. Her hair had been knotted into a tight pony at the crest of her head. The golden locks fell softly but stayed put as if instructed not to move. Even the woman's own hair seemed afraid of Danae. Mylo stood, eyes still and hands behind his back. When he looked at Valxina, he hardened his expression. Valxina sighed. She wondered if he was still angry at her for leaving, for visiting the lord's quarters without him. Beside him, Desil rested a hand on Inara's back. She wore her skirt and choli. The fabric complemented her complexion as if designed for her. Her braids cascaded over her shoulders like woven threads. Desil and Inara looked perfect together—too calm and too familiar. Perhaps the night out in the pit had done that to them. Valxina expected to see another tower guard beside Danae. Surely, she would have been reassigned one. She turned to the other figure in the room. He seemed to tower across from the keepers. Valxina lifted the edge of her mouth when she saw the commander. The sight of him in his formal uniform reminded her of the night of his oath. Only two years had passed—but he looked entirely different now.

Lord Zessfar had gifted Valxina a new gown. And like the décor, it held intricate weavings of their two colors—of the lord's House blue and the keepers' shade that shimmered with hints of emerald.

"Do you like it?" Lord Zessfar asked again as they approached the others.

Valxina released a deep breath. "It's *different*."

"Different, in a good way?"

Different used to mean something else entirely to her. Different was a sliver of uncertainty, a chance of being seen too much. Valxina had grown up afraid of being different. The thought of changes used to frighten her. But as she watched the ways the colors intertwined around her, Valxina nodded. It was a good kind of different.

The room was warm. And when she approached the others, she could not fan the stifling heat away. The others conveyed soliloquies within their gazes—paragraphs of emotions and words she could not decipher. She expected it. She was gliding into the room on the Badawi lord's arm after spending the night with him. He had even excused her from crypt duty, no matter how much she protested.

Once seated, Danae was the first to open her mouth. "It is so very kind of you to invite us to dine with you, my lord." Valxina had never heard the woman speak so politely.

Keeper Sera sneered. Valxina watched the way her eyes focused on the lord. But she did not say a word. She knew there would be tension in their reunion—but the act of it, of witnessing it, made her uneasy.

Danae continued, "We were growing worried about our sister when she did not return to the tower last night."

Silence rippled through the table. Fists tightened. Throats bobbed.

The choice of words caused Valxina to tilt her head in thought. *Sister.* "Nothing to worry about," Valxina replied. "I've been fine."

"More than fine, it seems," Danae said, her eyes grazing over Valxina's body.

The lord chuckled. "Keeper Valxina has had me occupied." The word was slow, *occupied*. She watched as he savored it on his tongue, drawing it out as if he did not want it to end. "She has told me of Eno's actions," he added, turning to Keeper Sera. "She has told me what was done to you, Keeper Seraphine." Seraphine rolled her eyes as she reached for the goblet before her. Bruises still painted their way across her face. Freshly forming scars marked her flesh. "Know that I knew nothing of it, please." As if his heart were wounded, he pressed a hand to his chest.

Valxina pressed her goblet of wine to her lips. Again, it was *his*—the bottle he kept in his chambers. She glanced around the table once more. The looks of the others felt distant and unsettling.

She had not realized Zessfar was at her ear until he muttered, "You seemed to enjoy it so much I decided to share it... with your friends."

Her friends.

"Has Val told you about the missing key?" Ky's voice vibrated through the air.

The lord lifted his head slowly, tilting it as if in thought. "*Val*," he murmured under his breath. "Strange to hear your name, so plain, so familiar, on another man's lips."

Valxina stilled. She watched as he clenched his hand beneath the table. He released it, tensing it once more before reaching over. Valxina had not expected the touch. Her eyes widened slightly as Zessfar traced an idle finger across her skin. Zessfar pawed at her thigh, exposed by the high slit of her dress. Her heart quickened as she parted her lips and turned to him.

"She has," Zessfar said, his voice direct. "But I am afraid I have no knowledge of this place or the whereabouts of this so-called detention cell."

Valxina stirred. Her eyes narrowed. *So-called?* He seemed to believe her last night.

Ky grinned as he nodded. He took hold of the meat knife in front of him. The commander radiated irritation as he pressed the tip against the wooden table. He moved the item in a circle, tracing outlines onto the wood. "Do you have knowledge of anything?" Ky sneered. "What kind of lord spends his time seducing keepers instead of ensuring the safety of his people?"

Fuck. Valxina winced. She grimaced not just at the words, but at the lord's fingers on her thigh. He tightened his grip and gritted his teeth as if claiming his possession.

"It would do you good to remember your place, Commander."

"Ah, yes," Ky said. "Even here as we break bread, there are formalities. Even as people are kept captive and tortured, even now..."

Valxina could barely hear Ky's words. She withered under the lord's grip.

"*Zessfar,*" she whispered. He held on too tight.

But he did not release her. Could no one see her in distress? Heat rose from her body.

But Mylo had never removed his eyes from his keeper. "Val?" he said. His tone was hushed. She could barely hear him from the other side of the room.

Zessfar rolled his eyes. "*Val,*" he said again. "Keeper Valxina," the lord corrected with a look of warning.

"*Zessfar,*" Valxina repeated. But he did not release her. His fingers tightened. She held her breath as his nails dug in deeper. The air thickened. The room appeared to shrink. Valxina could hear her heart thumping against her chest.

"I think this has all been a misunderstanding," Valxina croaked.

Danae replied, "No misunderstanding here. The message

was loud and clear when Badawi guards arrived to collect us."

"House guards?" Valxina said. *So this wasn't a celebration. They had not been invited but demanded instead.*

Valxina wasn't sure who stood from their seat first—whether it was Mylo or Ky. And when she looked at them, up from her seat, as if pinned in place, her eyes begged.

"Stand up," the commander said to her. It was a test.

But when she placed her hands against the table, her head went light. The room went blurry. Her heart sank as she tried to focus, as the lord's hands held her in place. Valxina shook her head. She could not.

"Get up," Ky commanded. But then Ky reached a hand to his head, clenching at his forehead as if in pain.

Valxina swallowed the knot in her throat. "I can't." And while his hands grasped at her, it was not only his force that tacked her to her seat. Valxina's heart raced quicker than her mind. She had trusted him. She had believed he was not like the rumors said.

Ky called out to her once again, "For fuck's sake, Val. It's over—release yourself from this foolish masquerade."

From the corner of her eyes, Valxina could see Zessfar sharply turn to face her. Slowly, she scanned the room. Desil had moved to his feet. Keeper Sera watched with bated breath. The woman's hands were pressed against the table as if to steady herself.

"Oh, fuck," Danae muttered as she placed her goblet down. "I was right, wasn't I?"

Zessfar furrowed his brows. "What are they talking about?"

Valxina's heart raced. She lowered her glance, moving her vision to her lap. His fingers, cold and tight, moved upward. It left broken skin in his wake. The metallic scent of blood wafted through the air. His nails, like sharpened blades, dug higher.

"*Please,* my lord," she whispered. "Please let me stand."

Ky moved toward them. "You don't know... Of course you don't know..."

Zessfar didn't release his grip or glare.

Ky continued, "This was all a part of a plan. You can decorate her and this room as much as you wish. You can try to keep her from the rest of us, sure—but she planned this. You were only a tool, a person she needed to get close to in order to—"

Valxina flashed a warning to Ky.

Danae finally stood. Her lips pressed together in a poignant frown. She shook her head as she moved forward a step. "I am sorry," she muttered to Valxina. "I see now what has happened here." But the woman's voice was shaky as if overcome, as if battling a deep slumber.

If last night was a dream, a glimpse of nirvana—tonight was nothing short of a hellish nightmare.

Chapter
31

Fear bellowed through the room.

House guards stormed inside, circling them like cobos in the sky. Their eyes radiated pure hunger.

"Let her go," Keeper Sera demanded as she stood.

"House guards?" Mylo shouted as he unsheathed his sword.

"So this is it," Sera continued, her voice too calm and grave. "Is this who you truly are?"

Valxina squinted—candlelight appeared to blur across the space. She shook her head. "Zessfar," she said, "what have you done?"

When the lord looked down at her, he only nodded to her drink. The wine. He had laced it.

Tears formed, further clouding her vision. She had let her guard down. She had allowed herself to believe the lord had goodness in him. He had told her about himself, he had shared bits of his life—the kind one does not part with easily. She bit at her lip as the others bore their weapons.

Only Inara stared at them with confusion. "We cannot pull our weapons on the lord?" she shouted with confusion, steadying herself with the back of her chair. "This is madness." Desil moved in front of her. He positioned himself like a personal shield. "What would the gods have to say?"

"This *is* madness," Zessfar answered. His voice sent a shiver down Valxina's spine. He seemed too calm. The lord turned to Valxina. "Is this true? Have you snuck yourself into my bed and opened your legs with intentions of"—he gritted his teeth—"what exactly? Perhaps you truly are the whore my guards spoke of."

Valxina shook her head feverishly. The lord released his grip and stood. A deep breath escaped from Valxina as she pushed her chair aside. And when he took a step back, she ran.

"I have been nothing but kind to you, Kulrani. And here I am learning that you only wanted to use me?" Zessfar shook his head. "I thought you were different. I thought we could be something."

Valxina's body crashed into Mylo and Ky, which felt like colliding with a wall. She grabbed at them and placed herself between their bodies. They were bricks she wished to surround and bury herself with. A trickle of blood ran down her left thigh. Zessfar had convinced her to leave her javelin in his quarters for dinner. *"No need to ruin your beauty with the crassness of a weapon, not when we are only dining with your friends."* She had never felt so foolish, so disappointed. She had told herself she could do this, that she could get close to the lord and learn more about the arrest of Sera, about the missing members of Court. It had started with Sera, sure. But when she heard there were others, she couldn't help but wonder, Was it her responsibility to look into it? What would Eleni have done? Years of cowardice had led her to sitting in the shadows, but the status of keeper had filled her with false senses of safety, of power. But she had been wrong. She had failed. She had allowed herself to be blinded. She was sightless when it came to his true nature.

"It's true!" she cried. "But what I felt for you was real, Zessfar. I wanted to know about Sera's arrest. I only wanted you to help me. I didn't think—"

"You *didn't* think," Zessfar shot back. "I find it hard to believe that a woman as smart as you left any detail to chance."

Valxina gripped Ky tighter.

"I expected to at least get to dessert before I placed you all in the cells," Zessfar announced. "You really think I would have allowed you all to walk the halls of my Court? After all that talk last night of me vexing the gods? You should have known, Kulrani, that sort of talk is beyond treasonous. And I surely do not need you lot poking about my Court, asking questions, and raising suspicion." Zessfar snarled. "But suit yourself. I suppose you hadn't even realized this was your last supper."

His words were so cold, so tinged with sarcasm that Valxina froze at the sound. The rumors were true. The whispers were correct. She had been wrong.

"So it was you?" Sera screamed. "You did order my arrest after I questioned you for not healing her mark!"

Pandemonium broke through the room. House guards swarmed the group with the speed of the wildest of cats. Valxina closed her eyes. She recognized the voice that commanded Mylo forward. She did not budge when broad arms wrapped around her like steel.

"I'm sorry!" she cried. She did not know whom her words were directed towards. They spilled out of her. "I'm sorry!" Her voice merged with the sounds of distress around her.

Where the heavy arms could not cover her, delicate hands embraced her. "It's ok," a soft voice said. "You have no one to apologize to."

Valxina shook her head. And when their bodies hit the ground, she cried the words out once more. "I'm sorry!"

The hands around her were torn away. A ringing erupted in her head. Valxina blinked wide, her eyes in terror, but the room was completely dark. She grabbed for her face with her fingers, but they stiffened. They had concealed her face with a sack knotted around her neck.

"Val!" a voice cried out. She could not decipher the owner of the desperate voice.

Valxina squirmed against the tiled ground. She flexed her hands and gritted her teeth. She roared as she attempted to break free. Violent hands grabbed her. Brute force lifted her only to toss her against the ground once more. She cried, but the keeper's bellow was lost in the wails of the others.

The darkness was indescribable. It was unlike the kind she had faced before. She could not pound her fist against its wall, she could not count down the hours until a door would open or light would rise from the cracks. There was no timer to this darkness. A knot formed at the bottom of Valxina's throat. It traveled up as her breathing quickened. Her heart raced, and her blood ran cold. It brought her back to the first time Masha had locked her in the chest. Valxina had believed she had moved past the feeling of overwhelming fear she had once felt in the darkness, but here, this was different. She flexed her hands and screamed out as she reached for her face. She crawled, her exposed leg dragging against the bitter marble ground. But just as she thought she could reach the sack across her face, she was pulled away.

A cold hand reached hungrily at her leg. It pushed the fabric of her dress aside and held her roughly. Struggling to breathe, she could smell the fabric of the sack as it scraped against her face. She kicked her feet out under her. Blindly, she tossed her body aside to free herself of the cold grasp. But the grip tightened again. Its owner dragged her against the floor.

"Let me go!" she screamed. And when a steel-toed blow hit her in her abdomen, the room went silent. She knew who it was—who was touching and hurting her. She recognized his touch. And while last night it was a soft caress, tonight he stung like the kiss of a bitter blade.

Stronger arms flung the keeper back to her feet. Two House guards held her hands back and steadied her. Valxina struggled to stand, and her eyelids fought to keep open. Her head hung from her shoulders.

"Don't worry," the lord muttered into her ear. His voice was entirely different. Valxina's chest rose and fell wildly.

Perhaps it was different—now that she could not see his face. Without his dashing grin and the glint of his eyes, she could see him—truly see him.

Valxina thought back to their conversation when she had woken this morning. She thought back to the way she stood, wrapped in his silken sheets with nothing but the rays of sun on her. She thought back to the words he had used when he pressed his lips against her skin in parting. His embrace had felt so welcomed. Just hours ago, she had enjoyed his touch so much she had wished for more. She thought of him as she bathed. Now, Valxina shook her head at the thought. She had slipped her fingers down her core and rubbed herself with thoughts of him. She had kneaded at her own breasts and straddled her fingers, panting at the thought. Valxina felt sick. She had wanted more. How could she have wanted more of this man just hours ago?

"You are unholy!" Valxina screamed out to him.

Zessfar chuckled, grabbed her by the sack, and pulled her close. Zessfar rubbed a finger over the cloth that concealed her features. He could not see the way her eyes were painted with fear and rage. Valxina could feel him lean in closer. His scent—the smell of the wine on his breath—stirred her stomach.

"I am unholy? You have no idea."

The world went dark.

Chapter 32

Valxina woke on a muddied dirt floor.

She groaned. It was a sound drenched in ache. Her core throbbed in agony. She shifted her head in the mud and curled her knees up. In the fetal position, she tried to steady her breath. Her eyes struggled to adjust as they opened, but a shadowy film tinted her view. It was like peering through a tunnel. Valxina rasped. A croak traveled up her throat as she coughed—uncontrollable, burning coughs that tasted of metal and smelled of rust. Blood splattered into the air, like the rain of scriptures, a mark of the end of days.

Valxina couldn't make sense of the few items she could see. She shivered in a cold sweat as she forced her eyes to focus, grimacing as the vomit traveled up her throat. She tried to hold it back—to will it down and prevent its escape—but she could not swallow. She twisted onto her knees and heaved onto the ground, but her hands refused to follow. Chains shook as she moved. Strands of loose black hair got caught in her sick. She coughed as she felt another wave form in the pit of her stomach. She pressed her head against the cold floor, just inches away from the puddle of vomit, and squeezed her eyes shut. While it was blazing hot and her lips desired water, her body shook. She whimpered, losing her last drip of energy. As she slid into the puddle of her own sick, she gave in; she could not fight it off.

It was hours later when Valxina came to again. Muddled voices spoke in her sleep. They whispered her name and groaned out his—*Zessfar*. At the sound of the lord's name, Valxina shot up. The sudden movement brought a shock of pain to her. But she gritted her teeth and snapped her eyes open, searching. She thrust her hands forward, but they stopped short. Coldness bit at her wrists; she had been chained to a wall. And when she saw the bars of a cell, Valxina let out a confused gasp. She kicked her legs out and pressed her back against the wall. Her breathing hitched. She was not alone. Still shadows lingered in the corners.

"Who is it?" she demanded, her voice cracking. "Leave me alone!"

A figure shifted as Valxina squinted. "Is that you, little mouse?"

Tears rolled down her cheeks. She tried to hold herself back, but they came flooding like the gates of her heart had been blown wide. She sobbed his name out, "Ky!"

"Fuck." Another voice groaned into the darkness.

Valxina never thought she would be grateful for that voice. She recognized that one too—although she had never heard it sound so exhausted, so defeated. "He's locked us away, the bloody bastard, hasn't he?"

It was Danae.

Valxina hung her head and sniffed.

"Mylo?" Ky called out.

But there was no answer.

"Mylo!" he repeated.

A shaky groan replied. Valxina bit her cheek at the response. If that was Mylo, he did not sound well.

Sera's voice emerged from afar. "Pax? Are you ok?"

"I'm ok," Pax answered erratically. She gargled her words as if responding mid-vomit.

"Fuck," Danae hissed. "I'll have to vomit, too, if you all keep to it."

"Val, are you ok?" Mylo said with a grunt.

Words could not form on her lips. Valxina released a weak breath and replied, "Mhmmm."

"Where are we?" Pax asked.

Keeper Sera responded, "I guess he knew about it all along. We're in the detention cell. We're under the Court."

"Is this where you were held before?" Ky coughed.

Sera released a deep breath. "Not this room. There are a series of tunnels and cells. I was held in another. It was smaller."

"Is Inara in here?" Danae's voice echoed through the space. "Inara!"

Silence.

"Desil?" Ky called out.

But there was no answer. The two had not made it to the cell. They were not among them.

"Shit," Danae said softly.

Stillness traveled through the room. Valxina shuddered at the unanswered call. She held her breath and clenched her hands. When she looked down, she frowned. The slit of her dress revealed the blood stains down her leg, which was muddied and smeared. Valxina pressed her lips into a thin line. She lowered her brows and shut her eyes.

"Is everyone ok?" Ky said.

"They threw that bag over my head before I knew it was coming," Keeper Sera answered. "I didn't have time to put up a fight. It was that wine," she added, applying a hand to her head. "He drugged it."

"I froze," Pax said. "I saw them reach for Sera, and I froze." Her voice was tinged with disappointment.

"Bastards got us pretty bad," Danae added. "I saw when they struck Mylo." Her nostrils flared. "Are you bleeding? Is it bad?"

Mylo grunted in response.

"And you, Val?" Ky asked.

She did not know how to answer the question. Her heart ached at the news of Mylo's injury—and of Inara's absence. What had happened to the woman with the sweet smile and soft words?

"Will he be all right?" she asked.

"Who, *Mylo?*" Ky answered. And while he chuckled, Valxina could hear the worry in his tone. "We'll fix him up, make sure he's ok. Mylo will be fine, I promise. But you?"

"Let her be," Danae cut in. "She's talking, isn't she?"

The words were harsh, but Valxina wished for nothing

more in the moment. She signed and whispered a "thanks" when Ky quieted.

"It smells like shit in here. Who keeps puking?" Danae commented.

"Can't help it," Pax cried.

Beyond, a sound stilled them. Mumbled curses released under their breath as a door slammed shut in the distance. Valxina pressed her back against the wall once more. She brought her knees up, and her eyes widened. Her heart raced. She swallowed the bile that traveled up her throat.

A torch appeared in the doorway. The light revealed the battered, muddied group before her. Her lips parted at the sight of them. Pax and Sera sat shackled near the farthest wall in the corner of the room. While Sera seemed fairly unharmed, Pax looked disheveled, her hands clamped at her head with blood running down her face. Her robe was stained with vomit. Clumps still sat at the edges of her mouth and on her chin. Mylo lay on the ground. A chained hand clutched at his abdomen. Dark blood seeped through his uniform. His pale face looked grey. Across, Danae sat with her back pressed against the cell rails. Her chains rooted her near the door. Wild strands of hair framed her face. Trickles of bloodstains covered her torn dress. And to Valxina's right, against the wall, was Ky, with a gash across his arm. His shirt was tattered and clung to his body from sweat.

They all shared slow and exhausted glances across the space, silent assessments of their health. But Valxina did not like the way they looked at her. Even Mylo, with blood pooling beside his body, watched her with heavy eyes.

The gate in the doorway shifted. And so did the group's stares.

Chapter 33

The cell door swung open. Valxina held her breath as a man, much too delicately dressed for his surroundings, stepped inside. His short golden hair glistened under the light of the torch he held. The blues of his eyes washed around wildly as his face crinkled at the sight and his nose twisted at the stench. But he held his chin high as if walking into a throne room, not a cell.

When he turned, his words were sharp and clear. "Do you wish to do nothing but tarnish our name and discredit all we have worked for?" His face was tense as he moved. "If only you had died in your mother's womb." He cast the light across Danae's face, showcasing her battered skin and stern glare.

Danae lifted her chin. "Hello, *Father*. How nice it is to see you too."

Valxina's eyes widened. *Her father.*

"You've scared your mother half to death. Know that I would not be here if it weren't for her. She tried to come here herself when word of your disobedience reached us." Her father narrowed his eyes. "But this is no place for a woman like your mother. This is no place for a noblewoman. You, perhaps. Yes..." He glanced around at the cell. In the distance, vermin scurried about. "Yes, perhaps this is exactly the place for you."

Even Valxina, perched against the wall in the dark corner, gritted her teeth. She tightened her fingers into fists at the man's words.

Bitter ice radiated from Danae as she glared. "What do you want?"

"I want nothing." He dropped a canteen of water to the ground and a roll of bandages. The metal echoed through the room. "From your mother."

Valxina did not remember her parents very much. The day the guards came to collect her from their home was the very last time she saw them. And with all the years that passed, she could barely remember the way they looked or sounded. And while her memory of them was faint, she knew, even now, they were warmer and more loving than this man had ever been to his daughter.

Danae did not say thank you. She held her breath as her father moved toward the gate. "Wait," she muttered as he stepped toward the threshold. Hesitation twirled behind her eyes. Her father paused. He did not turn to look at her but looked forward, out of the cell. "Do you have a key?" She shook at her chains.

Her father laughed. It was deep and haunting. He mocked, "Do you think I would let you out of here? Even if

I could without the lord cutting my head off my shoulders, why would I do so?"

Danae shook her head. "Not for me, not to free me." Her eyes connected with Mylo. "Can you undo my shackles so that I can at least tend to his wounds?" Her face softened, looking over to Ky's gash. "All of theirs."

The request surprised Valxina.

But Danae's father snickered as he turned. He looked at them with pure hatred. Valxina bit the inside of her cheek as she lifted her chin. His gaze met hers.

"What did you all do to end up like this?" When no one answered, he raised a brow. "I have sacrificed so much to earn the lord's trust—to know of his secrets." He examined Danae with a soft shake of his head. "And so have you, Daughter."

"Do lords need much reason to toss their people into cells?" Ky answered. "You've visited your treacherous daughter, so what stops Lord Zessfar from tossing you below the Court as well?"

The man nodded at the words. "The commander of his tower guards? Keepers? Did you, too, learn the truth?"

Keeper Sera spoke up, "That Zessfar is exactly as the rumors say? That he is a snake wrapped in silk—a vulture with a golden armband?"

Danae's father laughed. "You don't know the half of it, do you? To think I lost my daughter, my only true and good daughter, to keep myself out of here." The words were venom and directed to his shackled child in the cell.

Danae tensed.

"Please," Valxina whispered as he turned and reached

for the door. "Please, unshackle just one of us, so we can tend to the others?"

The man rolled his eyes at her. "And who are *you* to ask such a thing from me?"

Valxina lowered her eyes. "I am no one." She thought back to what Danae had shared about her father. "But if we are to die, wouldn't it be grander at the hands of the lord or with the audience of the Court—rather than silently in the dark? It seems like a waste of a lesson."

Danae's father grunted as if considering her words. And just as Valxina wished, the man could not turn down the opportunity to make a show out of disappointment. He held greed for teachings and lessons.

After reaching down, he pulled at his daughter's wrists with force, and Danae's shackles snapped open at the turn of the key. She closed her eyes at the sound as if in silent prayer.

"Tend to the others. Perhaps the gods will forgive you for all you have done. But washing the wounds of these traitors will never wash the blood off your hands." He shoved her to the ground.

Valxina watched with bated breath as Danae's father walked out of the cell. The keys to their shackles shook at his waist. And as the gates slammed, she could feel the questions lingering in the room.

With the torch still fixed on the cell wall, Danae scrambled to Mylo's side. She opened the canteen of water wildly and reached down for his face. With beads of sweat rolling down his features, Mylo gritted his teeth. "I'm fine," he said as she pushed the water toward his mouth.

Her fingers, covered in dirt and dried blood, clenched the canteen with desperation.

Danae shook her head. "Drink the fucking water. Drink some first, and I will share it with the others."

He abided. Mylo gasped as he pulled back from the canteen.

When Ky caught Valxina's worried gaze, he said, "He'll be ok."

But how could he know such a thing?

Danae stood. She reached for the bandages that her father had tossed to the ground and turned to Mylo once more. As she crouched at his side, she tossed the canteen over. The keeper sent the item hurling into the air. And even with the shackles at his wrists, Ky caught it. Valxina studied the way he frowned and shook it.

"I can go last," he said as he turned to Valxina. "You next."

Valxina did not have time to protest. The canteen had already rolled to her feet before she could say a word. When she looked up at Ky, he only smiled. It was forced. She could tell by the way the grin stopped, never reaching his eyes.

"Drink up," Ky instructed.

Valxina could feel the shame rising through her. It was her fault they were locked in here. Her breathing quickened as she shook her head. "No."

Ky only blinked in response.

"I'll go last," she asserted. "I'm the least wounded." She knew it was a lie.

Ky stirred. "Do you think you do not deserve water?"

His brows raised. "Val, please—we all saw what happened to you. Drink it."

Valxina shook her head once more. What *had* happened to her? Zessfar had sunken his nails into her skin; he had clawed at her like a possession. He had instructed his guards to arrest her. And when she was defenseless, when she could not see, he had dragged her across the ground and kicked her at her core. Even now, at the thought of it, her stomach waned in pain.

"Drink it," Ky commanded.

Danae looked up from the ground. Her hands were dripping in Mylo's blood as she wrapped the wound in his abdomen. She stared at Valxina with the most treacherous of oceans behind her eyes. "If I got pulled off you and beaten just for you to die of dehydration," she spat, "I swear to the gods I will find a way to resurrect you so that I may kill you again."

Valxina stilled at the words. Danae was pulled off her? Was it Danae's steady hands that had wrapped around her where Ky's couldn't cover? Her gaze flickered to Ky. He nodded at her lifted brow as if reading the question that stirred within her mind. His eyes moved between the two of them in acknowledgment.

"It was you?" Valxina asked in confusion.

"Doesn't matter," Danae replied. "Drink the water."

"Drink and pass, Val," Ky added with a nod toward Sera and Pax, who sat with her head tucked between her knees.

Valxina reached for the metal container. She untwisted the lid slowly and with caution. She could tell why Ky had frowned. There was so little left. Valxina held her breath as she brought the canteen, which was stained with blood and mud, to her lips. Upon contact, it tasted like bitter, cold metal. As she tilted it farther, Valxina released a deep breath. She moaned and gasped at the taste of the water. It was fresh and crisp. She shut her eyes as she gulped. Her hands shook as she attempted to stop. Tears rolled down her battered face.

"Ok," a soft voice spoke. "That's enough, little mouse."

She cried as she parted with the taste. The remaining water tested her with a calling *plop*.

"You did well."

And while every ounce of her body screamed for more, Valxina rolled the canteen away.

Chapter 34

"Are you hurt?" Danae said as she lowered her body next to Valxina. She rolled her eyes at herself and her choice of words. "Of course you are hurt," she corrected when she turned to the other keeper.

But Valxina only shrugged. She draped her hands over her knees and held them close to her chest.

When Danae noticed the heap of vomit beside her, she motioned toward it with her chin. "From the blow to your stomach or your own guilt?"

Valxina's breath quickened.

"I saw what he did to you. It's embarrassing the bastard could only do so with two House guards holding you down, a sack over your head, and tainted wine coursing through your body."

Valxina swallowed a lump in her throat.

"I tried... I'm sorry," Danae said.

"I-It was you?" Valxina muttered. "Your hands wrapped around me?"

Danae stirred. "Yeah—I thought the commander could use some help. All those muscles and strength, but you still looked so"—she lowered her glare—"vulnerable."

"And why would you help me? You—of all people? Have you not forgotten—what your own hands did to me?"

Danae clenched her fingers at her side and pressed her lips together. "Fucking hell. Of course I haven't forgotten what I did to you. Do you think me a monster? Do you think I enjoyed what I did? I told you... I was instructed to mark you so. And I allowed my own fear, and those bastards, to drive me to it. I know telling you of my regret will not remove the pain or the memories." Danae's voice shook. "I'm sorry for my manner towards you... for my choice of words in the past. But words hold no weight between us. Perhaps guilt made me feel like protecting you out there. Or maybe it was his words, his actions—so possessive and vile. I know what it is like to believe you know someone, to believe you may even love someone... to trust someone... only for them to turn around and hurt and manipulate you. I know the way your heart sinks at the names they call you, as if spreading your legs is reason enough, as if it justifies the pain they inflict on you."

Valxina lifted her chin. "Your father?"

Danae nodded. "He's right. It pains me to say it, but he's right when he says no amount of good will wash the blood off my stained hands. It won't bring Ines back."

"Ines?"

Danae raised her gaze to the ceiling. She blinked before answering, "The person they made me kill—Ines was my sister."

Valxina turned, tightening her stomach and gritting her teeth. "They made you kill your own sister?"

Danae held her gaze. "It was part of the first trial—it was she they made me kill. They said she was going to die anyway. They said if I didn't do it, the House guards would." She rubbed her fingers across her forehead. "She was their favorite. My father treasured her. He called her his prized child... his *darling girl*."

"Then why?"

Danae bit at her lip. "I was told if I ever said anything, they would kill not just me but my mother and father. And while I couldn't give a shit about him, I cannot have my mother's blood on my hands." Danae chuckled. "I don't know why I bother. She isn't blameless."

"If you ever told what?"

"Ines had to die. She had to go, as she knew something she was not supposed to. It was a whisper, a secret clouded in gossip. She didn't even believe it. She didn't think it was true, yet hearing it was enough to rationalize her death to them."

"And what was the gossip?"

"The late Lord Orin could not die because he drank from The Spring. But even immortal lords cannot live without their heads."

Valxina held her breath.

"The men that attacked that night—Chantara's men..." Danae lowered her voice. Tears streamed down her face; she had held this secret for so long. She had lost her sister for it. She had lost herself for it. "Those were not Chantara's men. They were a hired militia."

The others sat silently, listening to Danae's words.

"Danae." Ky's voice was filled with stilled rage. "If those were not Chantara's men, who hired that militia?"

"Do not despise me for not sharing this sooner. Although I would if I were you."

"I-It's ok," Valxina muttered.

"They were hired by Zessfar. They were a distraction, an easy target to blame. And the rumors about Lord Zessfar losing his mind at his father's death? Perhaps there's some truth to it. As Ines had heard, it was he who cut his father's head clean off his neck."

The cell erupted. The room shrank. The words echoed within Valxina's head. Her eyes widened as she turned to Danae. Then she looked ahead at Mylo. He lay still on the ground. The tower guard had almost died protecting Ky in an attack... planned by the lord? They had believed they were protecting The Spring that night. Valxina's heart crashed into her chest. Images of the little boy—the firekeep covered in blood—flashed before her. She shook her head. It was all so senseless. *How could a ruler be so senseless? And how could she have been blind to it?*

"And you?" Valxina said to Danae. "When your father said your family had to make sacrifices, your sister's death kept you all alive and out of the cells?"

Danae nodded. "I... I didn't do it to keep us out of *here*. I didn't even know this place existed. I'll never forget the sound of the dagger hitting the marble ground. It echoed as if shouting to me—as if screaming at me for my sins. How could I have left her to the Badawi House guards? Who knows what more those filthy men would have done to her? Sometimes, death is the release; sometimes, death is not the worst part. So, when she looked at me and smiled the faintest of grins, I knew what she wanted. She wanted me to do it. My fucking sister wanted me to take her life. And I did." Danae lowered her gaze. "My mother does not know, but my family, the rest of us, were allowed to live because of it. She thinks Ines disappeared, like the others of Court. But I knew the truth. Killing Ines saved my life—our lives. The move signaled loyalty to the lord and his adviser. After all, why would we ever share the truth? It would mean owning up to our own sins... my sins... my blood-stained hands."

Shivers moved through Valxina's body. She fought the round of nausea that built up inside her.

"You knew Zessfar was a monster, and you let Valxina walk into his rooms and his bed?" Ky shouted.

Danae's face hardened. "We all knew Zessfar was a monster, so don't tell me you hadn't heard any rumors of him too. Besides, I didn't realize just how serious it had become."

Ky lowered his glare. Valxina reached a chained arm out and rested her hand on Danae's lap. Her thumb traced idle circles against the fabric of Danae's dress. "That was an impossible situation you were placed in. Children should never fear for safety in the presence of their parents. Children should never feel that responsibility. And this... this is so twisted that I just may have to understand why you did what you did to me, to keep you all out of this place."

Danae shook her head as she turned to Valxina. "How

can you speak of forgiveness? When I have marked you for life?"

Valxina looked at her with bright eyes. "Promise me one thing."

"Yes?"

"When we get out of here, you personally will carve out my mark. Be it by flame or by knife. I want his crest off my body. I want no reminder but those in my head of his power. Will you do that?"

Danae's brows lifted. "Fuck," she muttered. "Is that what you truly want?"

Valxina nodded. None of them were safe here. Not even the ones she thought were all along. And when they got out, because she knew they would, she'd make sure he knew how it felt to be afraid.

Danae turned to her. "Our minds can even deceive us. Sometimes we see versions of people, glimpses of others that do not exist. Maybe you saw the good in him—maybe you wished not to see the truth in the rumors and gossip because you thought... Well, just because the rumors about the lord were true, does not mean there is truth to the gossip that surrounds you."

Valxina stirred. She looked over to Keeper Sera across from her. "He told me you two were meant to wed."

Sera's eyes widened, and her brows lowered. "What? Me?"

Valxina nodded.

"He used to call on me," Sera said. "He tried to get my attention, but it never worked." When she noticed the look on Valxina's face, she continued, "Perhaps it would have, but it couldn't with me. I've never had a liking for men."

Even the story he had webbed about caring for the missing Keeper Seraphine, even the words he used to illustrate himself as the castaway lover of a woman who scolded him, was not true.

Valxina could feel the heat rise within her. Vexation swirled around her like a swarm of jack spanias. She bit at her lip and lifted her hands before her. The shackles taunted her at every move.

Chapter 35

Hours later, Valxina thought back to a trick she had learned under Lady Masha's care. She shifted her weight under her and lifted from her sorrowful hunch. Like a new babe, her body cried at the movement, and she whimpered, her legs trembling beneath her. But upon her movement, Danae reached out. Her fingers grasped at Valxina's bent elbows and guided her upward. Valxina hesitated at the initial touch. She wasn't afraid of Danae—her hesitation arose from another fear entirely. Her flinch left softened pale fingers hovering over her. But when she shifted once more and looked at the woman before her, Danae took hold of her again. Her fingers were warm to the touch, just as Ky's hands had been. They were slender but strong. She never expected to find protection in Danae. But the woman surprised her in the darkest of moments.

"Sometimes, when Lady Masha was feeling especially spiteful, she would bring chains with her," Valxina said.

The words were motivation for herself.

The others watched as she bent her knees slightly. Valxina shut her eyes and took a deep breath. She lowered her shackled arms so that they hovered over her legs and stopped when they shook between her knees and her ankles. Valxina motioned her arms through the air in practice. She stopped short right above her legs.

"Val?" Ky said with hesitation.

"I need to get out of these."

He nodded.

Valxina lifted her hands forward and held a breath as she swung. The metal chains hit her legs with alarm. She released a stifled sob, her skin roaring at the impact. But it had not worked. Valxina lifted her arms again and swung downwards. The metal howled against her body and vibrated through the room. Her hands had not been freed. Heat rose from her. Valxina gulped as she lifted her hands again and again. Calls of affliction and suffering echoed through the cell. She shook her head as she lifted her gaze in defeat. Her body, her skin, and her bones—it wouldn't do. These chains were thicker than the ones Masha had used. Valxina was no match for the metal of the shackles.

Valxina looked around the room. Wildness plastered across her face. When she noticed a metal rod, a holder sculpted for a torch against the wall, her breathing quickened. She directed Danae to it and stood trembling as she waited. Danae lifted the item out of its holder and brought it to her fellow keeper.

"Hold it," Valxina instructed. "Grasp it and do not let it go—as if letting the item slip out of your fingers would bring nothing but despair into your life."

Danae lifted her brows. "A bit too late for that, is it not?"

"Just do it."

"Of course," Danae replied with a faint grin.

Valxina placed her hands on either end of the item. She gritted her teeth as she lifted them. When she sent the chains colliding with the iron, the shackles snapped free, unable to withstand the force. She fell to the ground with the momentum. Bits of metal scattered across the floor.

"Well, fuck!" Danae shouted in disbelief.

Valxina lifted herself to her knees. She pressed herself into the ground and held a hand against the wall as she stood. When she did, she looked over at Ky on the ground. The widest of smiles spread across his face, and he shook his head as she rose.

"Unbelievable," he said. His eyes glinted in the torchlight.

"Truly *un-fucking-believable*," Danae said.

"Take the iron to the rest of them," said Valxina as she walked over to the doorway.

Danae moved toward the shackled keepers first.

"Wait," Ky objected as Valxina moved past him.

She froze at his voice. When she looked over to him, he lifted his chin. "Come here, sly little fox."

Valxina lifted a brow. "What happened to *little mouse?*" she mocked.

Ky rested his wrists against his knee and shook his head. "You were never a mouse, Val."

"So why did you call me so?"

Ky grinned. He motioned for her to come closer. Valxina rolled her eyes and lowered herself in front of him.

"I'm not in the mood for games right now, Ky."

"Ask me again."

Valxina huffed.

"Ask me again," he repeated.

"Ok, ok," she whined. "If you never thought me a little mouse, why did you call me so?" Her voice was mocking and uninterested.

"Because all I've ever wanted was to hear you squeal."

Valxina shot up. She gulped down at the knot in her throat and flexed her fingers. Lifting a brow, she said, "Really? Is this truly the place and time for this?" She could feel her skin grow red.

In the distance, Danae taunted, "Mice squeak. Pigs squeal, you idiot."

Valxina pressed her lips together, holding back her own laughter.

Ky looked up at Danae and laughed. "Stop eavesdropping."

"Not eavesdropping if we're all stuck in the same cell."

When Ky faced Valxina once more, he continued, "Well, it also stuck because of how timid and shy you appeared when you first began your training."

Valxina shifted. She had always loved this about Ky—his ability to shift from making her laugh to conversing seriously. She wanted to hate him for turning her cheeks red, for seeking a rise from her, for lightening the mood in a place where jokes should not have been spoken. But she couldn't. She admired him even when he annoyed her the most.

Ky grasped her hand. "I thought I was losing you. I

tried to hold on. Every fiber in my body tried to wrap around you and protect you from his filthy fucking hands. I thought it would be enough. I thought *I* would be enough of a barrier between you two. I saw the way he..."

So, this was what he wanted to talk about. Valxina's smile vanished.

"The way he dragged me across the floor? The way he kicked me while I was down?" She swatted away from his grasp. "*You* weren't enough." She looked over to Danae across the room. She did not intend for the words to sound so rough. Although she wouldn't apologize for it—not now, not with the aching pain pulsing from her abdomen or the sharp sting of regret racing through her head. "But if you two weren't there, who knows what more he would have done." She didn't mean for the words to hurt him—she wasn't sure anyone would be enough to stop Zessfar from his rage.

Ky lowered his face. "There has never been a better time. Will you stop pretending now?"

"Pretending?"

"That you can protect us all. That any of us are safe. That gossip is the greatest threat of this Court."

"Gossip *is* the greatest threat of this Court," Valxina replied.

"And why is that?"

"It's what has kept me away from love and safety."

"And will you continue to allow it?"

Valxina rolled her eyes. "We are in a cell, Ky."

Ky furrowed his brows and scanned the room. "Really? Oh my gods, when did this happen?" He pressed his palms against the ground and flashed a forced grin. "I hadn't realized." He sighed when he spotted the frustrated smile that lifted Valxina's cheeks.

"If not now, when?" he asked in a more serious tone. "I'm not waiting around for someone else to swoop in."

Valxina lowered her gaze. "No one else is swooping in."

Ky's hand moved toward her chin, placing his thumb beneath hers. He lifted Valxina's face. "Are you so sure about that?" he asked, looking not at her but at a figure beyond. "With you, there will always be others. And that's ok."

When she flinched at the movement, he sucked a breath in. "I'll kill him," Ky muttered. "I'll dismember him limb from limb."

Valxina shook her head. "You won't." He was too rash.

"And why not?"

"Because I want to be the one that does so," she replied. "I want to cut his head clean off his neck."

"You're murderous," Ky whispered.

Valxina rolled her eyes as she stood. "Yeah, well, you like it."

Chapter 36

It wasn't long before exhaustion rippled through the cell. Sleep besieged the group of prisoners like a familiar friend. A hollow night's breeze danced through the halls and rose the hairs on their necks. The flames of their torch softened. It hung on to its end the way a child gripped at their mother.

While the others welcomed the rest, Valxina clenched the bars of their cell and waited. She did not know what or who exactly she expected. Although a part of her wished Zessfar would visit, that he would feel a need to speak to her and face her directly. Valxina shook her head. *He wouldn't.* He was too much of a coward. He was too soft. He was too royal. Her fingers gripped at the rails, and her mind battled with her body, her eyelids longing to close.

Footsteps approached. Not from beyond the cell but from behind her. They were slow and steady. Valxina parted her lips to speak, but warm hands surprised her. She flinched and turned to face him, sending an elbow to his gut.

"Did you just... elbow me?" Ky said, clenching his abdomen.

Valxina's eyes widened. "I-I thought..."

"It's ok, really. I get it. I shouldn't be sneaking up on you after everything that has happened today." He placed a steady hand on her shoulder.

Valxina held her breath as he rubbed her tense muscles. "You should get some rest."

Valxina shook her head. "No rest for the wicked."

He placed his left hand on her other shoulder, and with both palms, he pressed against her.

A soft sound released from Valxina, and her friend grinned at the response. "Only, you are not wicked. At least not in the ways that would lead to damnation."

She shifted on her feet. His fingers pressed in harder, bringing relief to her pain.

"Dismiss sleep as it knocks on your door, fine," Ky continued. "But at least rest your legs and your mind. Let me work on wherever ails you."

Valxina huffed. "Even you cannot rub away the pains that haunt me." Visions of Zessfar's hands on her flashed through Valxina's mind. She cringed at the memory of his lips pressed against her skin, of his mouth, his tongue between her thighs. She remembered the way he smelled, the way his scent of summer wine lingered and intertwined between them. The smell had intoxicated her. His soft fingers seemed to trail over her breasts, like a phantom still with her. She pressed a hand against her forehead and shook. "I want to get him out of here. I just want to be rid of him."

Ky released his grip. His hands, broad and worn, hovered above Valxina. He twitched at her words. "You really did fall for him. And he took advantage of your trust..."

"And I took advantage of his," Valxina replied. "Or have you forgotten it was all a part of my plan? I thought I could successfully seduce the lord and uncover what he knew."

"Val..." Ky gripped her once more and turned her body to face him.

He towered over her. Bloodstains still brushed against his dark brown skin. His hands planted her on the ground with ease.

Valxina cringed as she thought of Zessfar's hands on her—the way he had reached for her and pulled her to him. She shook her head at the memory.

"Hey," Ky whispered. His voice broke her thoughts. "Tell me what you want."

Valxina looked up, her eyes wide. She wanted to get Zessfar out of her head. She wanted to wash his hands off her. She wanted to smash her own head against the wall until she could no longer feel him, remember him, taste him. Valxina's breathing quickened. She looked up at Ky and the way his lips parted. He was good. He had always been good. Even the whispers and gossip that bared his name were drenched in compliments and kindness. Valxina clenched her jaw. Her chest rose and fell with vigor.

"Val..." Ky muttered.

Valxina broke their glance. She looked around the room and noted how the others slept silently.

"Whatever you want, little fox."

Valxina returned her gaze to his eyes. Her own darkened at the thought. She bit at her lip and scrunched her brows. "I... I just want him out of my mind." Her voice was a silent cry. "I want to stop thinking about his cold hands on my skin."

Ky nodded. He lowered his hands from her shoulders and moved them down her arms. Every inch of his movement warmed her. He was familiar. *He felt safe.*

"That night in the garden," Ky started as he moved his hands across her arms. "You said I crossed a line when I told you how I felt." He paused, tracing his hands up her shoulders and to her neck. "I was a fool to let you talk me out of it. I was a stupid fucking fool to stay away from you."

Valxina lowered her face. "I did not think you would actually do it."

"I know. I know. I should have checked in on you. I should have been there when you needed me."

Valxina shook her head. "No. You listened to me. I told you to stay away. But that's not what I want, Ky. That's not what I need right now. Shit, it wasn't even what I wanted, truly wanted, then."

Ky stilled. She watched as something flicked beneath his eyes. "Of course," he muttered. "Of course that isn't what you need right now."

His hands fell off her body. It left Valxina cold. "You want to wash the bitterness off of you."

Valxina nodded.

When Ky took her by the hand and moved toward the wall, she followed. The room seemed to dim. Her heart groaned. She hesitated, stopping mid-stride across the room.

Ky did not say a word as he pulled her in. He wrapped his arms around her and lifted her to his chest.

"I..." Valxina began. She had meant what she said about the want, the need, to erase Zessfar from her body. *But not like this.* The moment of reflection plastered across her face. She searched for the words as she wrapped her tired arms across her friend's shoulders.

"Oh, don't worry," Ky whispered. "I'll do nothing more than hold you tight while you rest. I'll keep you warm. I'll keep you safe." He grinned. "If anything—when something—when it does happen, it won't be like this."

A sleepy voice traveled through the room. "Thank the gods." It belonged to Danae. "For a moment I thought you two would actually fuck in here... in a cage surrounded by the rest of us. Fucking animals."

Ky's laughter vibrated through his chest. He looked down at Valxina with a raised brow. "Why, Danae? Is that some secret fantasy of yours? Would you be interested in watching or participating?" He flashed a wicked grin, his eyes never adverting from Valxina's face. "Perhaps some other time we could revisit that."

Valxina elbowed him once more. "Shut up," she muttered as she lay down against the muddied ground. Ky placed an arm beneath her head as a pillow. He leaned in—so close she could feel his breath against her ear. "I have a feeling that would interest you," he added. Although she rolled her eyes, the words sent a bolt of heat down Valxina's spine.

Chapter 37

Valxina barely slept a wink before unwelcome visitors crashed into their cell. A team of Badawi House guards swung the gates of the cell open and swarmed the group. Valxina shuffled off the ground. Danae jumped to her feet. Even Mylo, still clutching his wound, pushed back in protest. Without their weapons, food, and water, they were weak, no match for Lord Zessfar's men.

"Where are you taking us?" Valxina demanded as they grabbed her. She bucked her shoulders at their grasp. Beside her, Mylo and Ky attempted to fight off the House guards that narrowed in on them.

"Just you," one man replied. "Unless..." Valxina raised her eyes to him. It was Lord Zessfar's guard, the man with the tattooed House crest who normally stationed himself outside Zessfar's chambers. At the sight of him, and the feel of his fingers clenching her arms, Valxina screamed. She kicked and shouted.

"Shut up, you foolish whore, or I take her too," said the

guard, his glare pointed to Danae. "I've heard things about you as well," he added with a grin that dripped with horror.

Danae froze. She lifted her chin.

"Fine. I'll go. Take only me." Valxina's voice quivered. "Where are you taking me?"

The guard grinned. "To the lord."

"If you take her, you must take me." Ky's voice boomed through the cell. "I will not breathe the air of this cell if she is not in it."

Valxina shot him a warning glare.

"Don't forget me," Mylo added, almost playfully. He looked surprisingly well compared to the night prior.

"They stay," Valxina ordered. She narrowed her eyes at them.

"Absolutely fucking not," Danae screamed as she struggled with a House guard. "You aren't leaving me in here."

Valxina smirked. "What is it? Afraid you'll piss yourself in here and it is not dark enough to hide?"

Danae pursed her lips. "I'll have you know, if you are to die, I would like to witness the blood run out of you."

Valxina's body jerked. The guards pushed her toward the doorway.

"I'd like to see the blood run out of the lot of you," muttered a guard who had not yet spoken. "It seems they all want to die."

Ky rose a brow at the voice. Valxina studied the look in his eyes, like Ky had recognized something in the guard's tone, muffled behind his helmet. Did he sound familiar?

The tattooed guard was the last thing Valxina saw before they placed the bag over her head.

Indoors. Outdoors. Indoors. Outdoors. Valxina could tell the shift in environment by the breeze. She gasped wildly, hoping to devour every breath of fresh air she could. But the sack, one that resembled the kind used for rice and wheat, stifled her. Valxina's feet scuffled beneath her as the guards edged her on. She could hear the muffled vibrations of the others around her.

Why had the guards brought them all? Valxina wondered as they pressed on. Surely, they would not have cared for their wishes. She did not expect them to abide by Ky's wish or Danae's demand to tag along.

Valxina recognized Ky's voice nearby. "Does the king know Lord Zessfar has keepers in his cells?" He grunted as if absorbing a blow to his gut.

"Don't hold your breath," Danae spoke from behind. "Even if the king did know, do you think His Majesty would take the word of us over the lord?" Her last words trailed off as they were pushed through a doorway.

"Stairs!" Keeper Sera called out. But it was too late. A guard shouted. And for a split second, she was released. Valxina rushed to run, but she could not. Pax's scream was the first to bellow through the air.

Valxina's heart lifted at the sensation. For a moment, she felt as if she were floating... until the first impact. Her shoulder slammed into a stair railing, slowing her momentum down the spiraling staircase. She screamed and waved her hands wildly, attempting to grasp anything nearby. Her heart raced, booming over the sounds of the others—their cries, their shouts, their calls of surprise. She twisted as her foot caught over the body of another, clashing and slamming her back against marble steps. A feral cry released from her. She barely recognized her voice. Valxina lifted her hands to her head as another body crashed into her. She covered her face with haste and curled herself. She tried to make herself small. And when her limbs fell tired with a thump against another, she did not wait. She was not safe. They were not safe.

Valxina's hands shook as she raised them. Her fingers grasped at the bag over her head. She ran them over the material until she found the string at her neck. After untying it, she rapidly removed the sack from her face. It was dark. But even the darkness could not conceal the sight from Valxina.

Blood covered her body. Valxina groaned, her back aching. Ky already moved to stand, but at the sight of her, he froze.

"Shit," he muttered when he locked eyes with her.

Valxina could feel her body shake. Fear radiated from her. She did not want to look down. *Was it hers? Could she be bleeding so?* While she was in pain, she knew this blood did not belong to her. She shifted to her knees and propped herself against the ground. Behind her, something stirred.

Keeper Sera's voice sounded panicked. "Pax?"

Valxina turned. Her collision with the ground had been softened. Her body had not slammed against the ground but against another human. And as she focused her vision on the body that had coincidently saved her, she stifled a horrified gasp.

Keeper Pax lay on the ground, her head and body resting in a puddle of her own blood. Her face was still half-covered with a sack. Valxina crawled over to her, but when she tried to reach for the bag, her hands could not move.

Behind her, Ky held a screaming and distraught Seraphine. Her body shook in shock. The ink within her eyes seemed to darken. "Pax!" she cried, again and again.

Mylo and Danae leaned beside Valxina. Blood trickled from Danae's nose as she crouched. She lifted her fingers and smeared it as she looked at the keeper on the ground.

"Better remove the sack," she muttered.

Mylo, who seemed to have read her mind, reached down. He rested a hand beneath Pax's head and pulled her free.

Her bright santu eyes were wide and still. Her mouth twisted as if she had passed mid-scream. Her short dark hair was slick and wet.

She was kind. She had been kind. Valxina swallowed the ball that rose in her throat and looked back at Sera. "I'm sorry," she whispered, reaching to close the woman's eyes. "I'm so sorry."

Above, the sound of approaching guards increased as if they had broken into a fight amongst themselves.

"We have to go," Mylo said to the others.

Valxina looked at the cavern ahead. "Do you know where we are?"

Every head turned to Sera. "Do you know where we

are?" Ky asked the woman in his arms. He released her, and she ran toward Pax's body lying on the ground.

"I cannot leave her," said Sera. "Go. Go without me. I cannot leave my darling girl like this."

My darling girl. Sera had never appeared so soft.

Danae turned to her. She placed a gentle hand on her cheek. "You loved her," she said, her voice filled with understanding.

Sera nodded.

"You do not need to stay here," Danae responded. "If you stay here, you are on your own."

Keeper Sera nodded. "Then so be it," she replied, her voice haunting. "The caverns run like a maze. Some will lead to The Spring, while others will take you to the edge of the Court walls."

"A maze?" Valxina muttered.

"And how do we know which path to follow?" questioned Mylo.

Sera sighed as she looked down at Pax. She shook her head but did not answer.

"And you are sure? Are you sure you want to stay?" Danae asked. When Sera nodded, she said, "I'll remember what you said to me until the day I die. And while that might be today—I'll remember what you said about us keepers, about the world outside and our need to look after one another, regardless of our past."

Sera pressed her lips together in a frown. "You knew. You knew about Pax and me."

Danae nodded.

"How?"

"It's a gift. I've always been good at recognizing love, real love, between others. And I know that face. The pain you feel—that heat and excruciating sadness is one I once felt too."

"I see it in your face too."

Chapter 38

Valxina had never put much thought into how she would die. But as she ran through the darkness, stale vomit and fresh blood smeared across her, she could not help but wonder, Was this it? Her breathing was erratic, and her lips were so painfully dry. Ky stayed beside her, running with a hand against her back, pushing her forward and farther.

The scrolls of Roseau described death as painless. It was a welcomed relief from the agony of life. Death was certain, it was inevitable. But to the people who lived under the House of Badawi, death had an entirely different meaning. Death was a reminder—a token of the class divide between those permitted to drink from The Spring and those who were not. Keeper Pax had spent her life devoted to The Spring. Like the rest of them, she had said her oath to protect it from the hands of others—those who may use it as a weapon. The scrolls warned against using the magic of The Spring for personal or political gain. Pax had believed the position of keeper was a righteous one, and The Spring was a blessing from the gods. Valxina shuddered at the thought. Now, as she pressed on through the caverns, she could not help but think, *Was there anything holy or righteous about the Badawi House and their immortal Spring?*

She thought back to the beasts of the pit. She had believed their release was a warning by the gods themselves. The memory left her wishing to kick herself. She had believed it a warning, a sign from the gods to the lord himself. But no.

Valxina clenched her jaw as she came to a stop. Two pathways lay ahead.

"Which one?" asked Mylo.

She scanned the two ahead of her. No markers or signs of what appeared ahead. *Did safety lie at the end of either of these?* Valxina bit at her lip as she turned. "I-I don't know."

"We can split," Danae suggested.

Ky growled in response. "There is no fucking way we are splitting up under here."

Mylo added, "Kyrad's right, you're safer if—"

Valxina interjected, "We are no safer with or without you. There is no telling what waits for us at the end of these paths."

"Think about what you are saying, Val," Ky warned.

"I *am* thinking," Valxina answered. "If we all get caught, then death awaits each and every one of us."

"Val—" Mylo replied.

"You heard her," Danae said. "We are splitting."

Ky raised a brow. "And is she the commander now?

Are we taking orders from Valxina?"

Valxina straightened her back. "You are no longer a commander, Ky. Commanders have armies. They have guardsmen and artillery. Look around. It's us. It's only us."

"We're enough to take that bastard down," Mylo replied.

Danae chucked. "Fools. Absolute fools. When will men see how blinded they can be?"

"But what if you *can* collect an army of your own, Ky?" Valxina whispered as she moved toward him.

"What do you mean?"

"Take the tunnel to the left. You and Mylo should go. If you get out of here, go straight to the tower. Collect as many guards as you can. And once you have, come back. Sera mentioned the tunnels lead to The Spring in some way or another. Gather the guards and meet us there. None of us shall be left behind."

Fire burned in Ky's eyes. "And you?"

"Danae and I will take the tunnel to the right. If it leads us out of here, we shall go to the tower. We will do the same as I've suggested you two do—collect as many keepers and their guards who are willing. If we are to find the way out, we will return. We will come find you with an army of our own."

"And *you*?" Ky repeated.

"Find me when you've collected your guards," she whispered.

Ky moved closer. His chest pounded against Valxina. She held her breath as he leaned against her. His dark hair fell, framing their faces as he looked down at her.

✦ 283 ✦

"I will find you with an army," he said as his hands slipped around her waist.

Valxina's breath hitched as he moved two steps closer, pressing her back against the cool of the rocks behind. "And if you don't, I will find *you*," she muttered.

He smiled and glided a hand up her back as another lowered. "Will you stop me?" he said into her ear. "Do rumors and whispers plague you still?"

Valxina scoffed. She lifted a hand to his cheek and wrapped the other around his shoulder. "What do you think?"

"I... I think you know you do not need to protect me anymore."

"And do you feel the same way?"

"I know you do not need protection. I know you can slay monsters and lords alike. But that doesn't mean I won't try. I'll lay my life out—I'd press my skin against my own sword, if it meant you'd be safe forever."

Valxina shook her head. "But you know that is not possible. There is never a guarantee for safety."

"So, you *have* been listening to me, little fox?"

Valxina held her breath as he pressed against her. His lips hovered. She could feel his breath against her skin.

"You shouldn't get used to me listening to you," she murmured.

"I'd never expect it."

"Save it for the reunion," Danae snapped.

Valxina moved to leave, but Ky grabbed at her wrist. He pulled her into him with haste. She held her breath, her eyes widening with surprise. His lips met hers, and she panicked. She reached for his face and held him steady. Before she could realize, his arms wrapped around her. Her heart ached as she tasted him—it was an act of hope. Tight fingers reached behind and grasped at his hair. She, too, needed to part like this.

When the sound of footsteps echoed behind, the two released.

"I'll see you later," Valxina said as she moved away from him.

Danae shot her a glance Valxina could not decipher.

"Get out of here," Danae said as she waved her hands to hurry them away.

When she turned to Valxina, the two took a deep breath. Time seemed to pause as they ventured forward.

Chapter 39

What happens in a person's life to leave them dashing through the darkness with the person once responsible for their pain? What twisted events and spiraling paths leave one glancing over to the person they once thought they understood and knew, not out of wariness—but with fascination? These questions haunted Valxina as she ran through the space with Danae ahead. No response came. The truth eluded her; it rushed away and out of her head.

The woman looked nothing like Valxina had remembered. Her nearly white hair swung wildly behind her. She was muddied and bloody—a far cry from her curated appearance in the years Valxina knew her as a candidate and a Court daughter. Even the energy around her felt different. Valxina knew her as arrogant and often narcissistic—but Danae's words against the men in the cavern had not gone unnoticed. She had supported Valxina. She had listened.

The two ran and ran. And when the footsteps and

echoes of guards behind them dulled, they dashed against the wall to catch their breath. Valxina strained her eyes to survey the way Danae's fingers gripped against the rocks. Even out of breath, slick with sweat, and covered in blood, the woman held her chin high. Danae's face was hardened. Her eyes, as blue as the oceans that surrounded the island, flashed wildly. Valxina followed her glance, her mind miles away. She could see the calculated look, the focus and determination spilling out of Danae. Valxina parted her lips. She heaved, catching her own breath.

But there was a sound, a voice that muttered through the tunnel. It turned Valxina hot with rage. When Danae turned to her, the two women nodded. They crept down the tunnel, their hands balled into fists. The voice grew louder.

"They better return with a fucking army," Danae whispered to Valxina at her side. Her breath, so close against Valxina's ears, sent prickles down her neck. When they came to the end, they ducked behind a pile of rubble.

Valxina peeked over the rocks. They had reached the underground lake.

And the voice... *it was Zessfar's.*

Lord Zessfar paced around the pebbled shore of the water. He ran a frantic hand across his head and through his dark hair, catching on the knots. His lips were tight, pressed together with such force Valxina could barely recognize them. "What do you mean, you lost them?" he shouted to a Badawi guard in full armor. He clenched a hand in the air.

Danae slid farther behind the formation. "Fuck," she

uttered. "So we *do* have to rely on those two idiots to convince the other tower guards and get back here with a group of guards and keepers."

Valxina lifted a brow. "What do you have against them? Do you not think they can do it?"

"Do you think he can truly convince tower guards to follow him?" Danae lifted her brows. "And I don't have anything against *them*. Turns out the boy is all right."

Valxina sent an elbow into her. "Don't call him that."

Danae chuckled as she reached a hand to her side. "Did you just... elbow me?"

Valxina gave Danae a look of warning. "And I'll do it again if you don't call him by his name. Mylo is no boy. What do you have against Ky then?"

Danae looked ahead. "I-I think he's foolish, that's all."

"He's actually sort of brilliant, although you should never tell him I have said so."

Danae shook her head. "Maybe when it comes to guards and artillery and such, but I'm not sure his head is on right when it comes to you."

Valxina froze. What did Danae have to say about her and Ky?

Sensing the shift, Danae continued, "He's rash and a bit fantastical."

Valxina snorted. "Ky's always been a dreamer."

"Yeah," Danae said, her voice softened. "If you say so."

Behind them, the voices grew louder.

"What should we do about him?" Danae said, gesturing over the rock.

"What *can* we do? Just the two of us, unarmed?"

But another voice entered the room—one they recognized.

Valxina and Danae peered over the crest of the formation. There, walking over to Lord Zessfar was a woman who wore her keeper-blue skirt and choli. Her braids fell to her waist. And even with her veil cast across her face, the women recognized her. It was Inara.

"Shit," Danae muttered. "What's she doing here?"

Valxina peered over again. She searched for the keeper's guard—but Desil was nowhere to be found. Then she spotted them... their weapons.

Inara clenched her cutlass in her hand, but at her waist she wore a belt. There, fastened to her belt sat Danae's surujin. And when Valxina's eyes raked up the woman, a rush of adrenaline pumped through her veins. Strapped across Inara's back sat a javelin—*her javelin*. It glinted, catching a ray of torchlight as if calling for her, as if sensing her gaze.

"She's here for us," Valxina uttered.

"Zessfar, the fucking idiot. When Inara hesitated at dinner the other night, when she said it was wrong to attack Badawi House guards, he probably assumed she was on his side. The fucker doesn't know she's got this thing with the gods. She just thought he's some sort of divine man selected by them. She was concerned for her relationship with them, the divine beings, not for him." Danae rolled her eyes. "So conceited, so full of themselves. Men can really get themselves killed over their own vanity. He didn't know she'd see through his whole charade."

"*I* didn't know she'd see through it," Valxina admitted.

"Yeah, well, you don't know Inara as well as I do. Just glad to see she isn't dead."

Valxina grinned. "No, it's only me you'd like to see on the ground bleeding."

"Ah, I thought that would get your attention back there. I was hoping it would get you so mad you'd tell the guards to take me in place of you."

"And why would you want that? Why would anyone want that?"

Danae shifted. "I-I thought it would only be fair after the pain I put you through for me to take your place. I wanted to make up for it. If I can prevent more pain from coming your way, I'd do it so quickly you wouldn't have the time to say no." She paused, her blue eyes glistening like water before them.

Valxina shook her head. Danae did not choose to mark her the way she did. She wasn't the only person who held the metal to her skin. Zessfar and House traditions had created the circumstances for the ceremony and all that torment. Their society had pitted them against one another: a woman of noble birth and a servant child. The Court had placed them on opposite sides of the ring. Valxina watched the way guilt painted its way across the woman's beautiful features. It was tragic, really. She had been forced to do what she did to Valxina. Valxina wondered, *If she had a sister, if she had a mother in her life at Court, would she had done the same thing?* There was no way to tell. There was no way she could place her mind in that situation. She shook her head and looked back out.

"You should go," Valxina whispered.

"What? Why would I leave?"

"You should save yourself." Valxina meant every word. No additional lives should be lost in her ploy for revenge. It was best for the others to leave.

"Save myself?" Danae questioned. The woman took a deep breath and steadied herself. She looked at Valxina and shook her head. "Kyrad would lay down his life and press the metal to his own skin if it meant you would be safe. But I... I would not."

Valxina's eyes narrowed at the words. So this was it. *And Danae would continue her criticism of Ky, even now.*

But Danae continued, "I would not leave you to face this world without me. I would not allow myself to become a distant memory faded by years and pain and future hardship. I know the pain and hardships that come with life will not end here. Do you think I would watch idly? Do you think I would allow you to push me away when all you need, all you have ever needed, is a partner? You don't need them. You never have. And I know, I know in this world controlled by men it often feels like you need them to be safe... Like protection is something you can only have if you are a man or with one. But that is not true. I owe you..."

"You owe me nothing."

"But that's just it. Don't you see? I owe you everything. You felt the pain that saved me and my family. It is you who wears the scars of my past fragility, my fear, my cowardice. But no more, I cannot watch you bear the pain and mistakes of others, not mine nor anyone else's."

Valxina's eyes widened.

Danae's voice trembled as she continued, "I would not lay down my life for you, Valxina. I would burn this Court to the ground. I'd watch as the noblemen and women scurried about in flames. My father included. And if that weren't enough, I'd move on to the island. Don't think for a second I wouldn't unleash pure, unadulterated rage onto anyone who dared to lay a finger on you. And if we were alone, stuck below ground in the caverns with Badawi guards at our heels, I would not take that moment to press you against the wall and waste time with silly fantasies. I'd do anything to get you out alive. I wouldn't question your commands in moments of chaos. You can give me any command you wish. There is only one I will not abide by... and that's saving myself."

Valxina's heart dropped. Her mouth went dry. Her breath hitched as she replied, "Why?"

"I cannot be saved if you are in danger. My soul, it will not rest. I owe you." She parted her lips to say more but stopped.

"So what do we do?" Valxina whispered, her voice shaking.

"We do not sit here and wait for your ex-lover to find us, nor do we wait for your new lover to come save us."

Valxina pressed her lips together.

Seriousness washed over Danae's face. "We go out there, get our weapons, and slice the fucker's head clean off."

It was a plan—an opportunity—Valxina could not turn down.

Chapter 40

Valxina had never stood so close to The Spring. She had dreamed about the moment her feet would touch its shores. She had fantasized what The Spring would look like, how the air would smell around it, how the water would feel against her skin. She watched the way it cascaded down from the rocks and into the lake underneath. It was nothing short of holy. Tears pushed themselves to the surface. Her vision blurred.

The sound of falling water filled the room as she stood. It looked refreshing and cool—but something was wrong. No keepers stood watch over the rocks on Spring duty. No armed women guarded the lake. Instead, Lord Zessfar walked over the rocks, his boots stomping over the sacred ground. In the shadows of the cavern stood a collection of Badawi House guards, and alone, without her tower guard, Inara. Valxina froze at the sight. Men were not allowed in here. Badawi guards were not permitted here.

It didn't make sense. Desil had sworn an oath to the

woman. He, like Mylo, seemed to take the responsibilities of tower guard with the utmost importance. But Mylo was not here. He had changed since her first moments with him. He had gone off without Valxina. He had left her behind. But in this case, it was because she had asked. Valxina held her breath as she moved forward. In the corner of her eye, she could see Danae ready to leap. Zessfar's back faced them. Parts of the simple cotton shirt he wore were left untucked at his waist. And for a moment, Valxina felt transported to the time she had last seen him like this. *He was alone. He tasted like sweet wine and smelled of flowers. His hands caressed her. But the entire time, she had not seen him. She had not truly seen him.* Valxina thought back to the portrait that hung in his chambers. Like the brushstrokes, there were two sides to the man—one for the world to see, and the *other*. Darkness loomed under his skin. She thought back to his touch—how cold his hands had felt when he grabbed her under the dinner table. Perhaps drinking from the fountain gave him the immortality the lords dreamed of, but what had it taken away?

And then, at the crunching of the stones beneath their feet, Lord Zessfar turned. His eyes, once a beacon to Valxina, once a signal of hope and safety, no longer looked so. For a moment, she saw them flash. She watched as pure darkness consumed them, spreading to his irises.

Zessfar lifted his hands at his sides, palms up. He grinned, washing away all the boyish beauty she had once seen in him. "There she is," he announced. "I knew it was only a matter of time."

Valxina froze, with Danae standing between her and Inara, feet away.

"My lord," Valxina said through gritted teeth. "Do you plan to kill us all? To kill everyone who knows your secret?" She shared a worried glance between Danae and Inara. Behind, the House guards moved forward.

A look of surprise was plastered across Zessfar's face.

"I know you lied to me. I lied to you too," said Valxina.

"You mean you tried fuck your way to becoming the lady of the Badawi House?" Zessfar snarled.

Valxina shook her head. "No, my lord. Zessfar, I admit I came to you under the shadow of the night, hoping you would help make sense of Sera's disappearance. I admit, I saw want in your eyes when you watched me, and I planned to use that to my advantage. But..." She held her breath. Valxina lifted her hands and took a step forward. Badawi House guards moved between her and the lord. Even with the guards between them, Valxina kept her eyes on him. "Even with those plans, you charmed me. But you lied to me. You told me you knew nothing of Sera's disappearance. You said you knew nothing about the detention center. You painted yourself as a lost, concerned lord."

Zessfar shouted back at her, "I told you to be careful, Kulrani. We could have been good together. You could have kept your mouth shut and your ass in my bed. But no!" His body shook. "You had to run about my palace grounds with your friends."

Valxina's heart dropped. Was that all he had planned for her? And her eyes widened at the words. *Friends.* She hadn't realized, in just a few days, she had grown close to the keepers, to Mylo, and of course, to Ky once again. He was right in that sense; Valxina had made friends. When she glanced at Inara to her left, she noticed the woman's hands moving. Her movement was slow, almost undetectable.

Valxina, determined to keep the lord's attention, spoke again, "You can try to turn this around on me, Zessfar. It was wrong of me to enter your chambers with my plan, but I am not the problem here. You, despite your kind words and flattery, tossed me into a cell. You have inflicted pain on me, in more than one way. You are the epitome of what it means to belong to the wealth of this empire." She looked at the Badawi House guards that surrounded them. "Do they know? Zessfar, do they know you murdered your own father to take his place in this Court?"

Lord Zessfar pinched the bridge of his nose. "So, *you* know." He released a sound of relief. "I told you I never thought I would ascend to the lordship. I told you what they thought of me, what my father believed, what even the nobles whispered about me."

Valxina shook her head. The hair that framed her face moved with her. "That is not a reason to murder your father. That is not reason enough to cut his head clean off." She watched as Zessfar stuck a hand in his pocket.

"I wanted to prove them wrong."

He fumbled about it until he grasped an object. She watched, eyes like blades, when he removed something small. He held it in the palm of his hand. And when Zessfar tossed it, the item fell to Valxina's feet with a soft thud.

When she looked down, the sight of it was enough to make her uneasy. It was long. Where it had once resembled the color of a light rose, it was rotten, in shades of purple like eminence and plum.

"For you," Zessfar said with a shrug. "I cut off the serpent's tongue so all would hush, so questions and whispers would die out, all so you could feel safe and come into my arms."

Valxina shuddered. "You were never concerned about my safety. You only wanted me to fall into the illusion, to let my guard down, to believe this place could be something it is not. Even in your wildest of dreams, my lord, I would have feared harm. Especially with you, a man who kills his own father and carries around the tongue of his dead adviser."

Zessfar raised his brows. "Is this the portrait you wish to paint of me?" When Valxina's face hardened, he continued, "What can I say, Kulrani—I am a sentimental man. I enjoy my mementos."

Valxina gulped down the knot at her throat. "Are the rumors true about you keeping your father's heart? After his"—she shifted on her feet—"death?"

Zessfar nodded slowly.

"And do you plan on keeping a memento of me?" she asked, half-afraid of his answer.

Zessfar moved forward. But before he could answer, chaos erupted.

Chapter 41

Inara called out her name. Danae sprang into the air and grabbed her surujin. She whipped it above her head, and it cracked like a flash of lightning in the air. The House guards drew their weapons from their holsters and pushed ahead to safeguard their lord. Valxina took a step back. Just feet behind her, her javelin landed upright on the ground.

Valxina ran. Behind, the growing sound of footsteps echoed. She reached for her javelin and pulled it out of the ground. Valxina twisted and kicked a guard who reached for her with eager hands. Her breathing quickened. The fool had not even pulled his weapon. She whipped hers around and pressed it into the exposed sliver of the man's neck. Valxina did not hesitate as she slipped the blade over the man's skin. Blood splattered, projecting patterns across her face. As she looked down at him, her hands shook. The first man she had ever killed. And he wasn't a soldier from Chantara's army—he was a guard, a House guard. Her chest rose and fell wildly. This was never how she expected her first kill to pan out.

Inara swung her cutlass through the air ahead of her. She slashed through men like grass blades. Valxina dashed toward them, both hands clutching the javelin's center. She swung wildly, striking a Badawi's blade. The guard pushed back, clenching his teeth as he pressed into her, harder. Valxina released. She dodged and lowered herself to the ground, avoiding the lash. Commander Hu referred to her as a fox. She couldn't overpower them with force, but she could creep up on them and wear them down. Valxina trailed the man at every step. He rotated to capture her as he flashed fevered, enraged eyes. But Valxina yanked his feet from beneath him. She slung her javelin and slammed the metal against his skin. She twisted it before removing it.

Footsteps in the distance had grown louder. Valxina did not need to turn to know who was there. Inara stood surrounded by guards. She planted her feet on the ground and screamed as she lunged at a man ahead of her. Valxina had not seen the man behind her, a guard with his sword drawn. She froze. But a single arrow zipped through the air. It traveled through the man's head. He dropped almost instantly. Again and again, the arrows fell from the sky. They hit every target—Badawi guards. Blood splattered across Valxina's skin as she sliced the back of a man before her and he fell to his knees. Before she could finish him, an arrow did. She took a moment to look up at the formation as she wiped her face with the back of her hand. Desil stood where she had sheltered with Danae only minutes before. When she saw him, her eyes narrowed. He wasn't dressed in his customary tower guard garb. The man, instead, was dressed as a Badawi House guard. For a brief period, she stilled, recalling the happenings on the stairwell.

Desil had worn the Badawi guard uniform and had been among the others who removed them from their cell. It was Desil who had pushed them. *Was it an attempt to save them time? Had Inara known? Is that why she arrived at the lake armed to the teeth? Had the two been planning on rescuing them all along?*

Ahead, Danae wrapped her surujin around the neck of a House guard. With all her weight, she pulled at it, bringing the man to the ground. She reached down, grabbed his sword that had fallen at his side, and ended him. Before the man took his last breath, she had already sent her weapon spiraling into the air for another.

Valxina's heart raced. She searched through the violence for the one life, the only life she wished to take. She snarled when she saw him. Zessfar had been moved to the far end of the shore. Nearly twenty Badawi House guards surrounded him. He wouldn't get his hands dirty.

"What is it?" Valxina screamed over to him. "Surely you aren't afraid of some women?" She paused, remembering his words to his chamber guards. "Even if we are armed." Valxina studied the way he stepped back. "Do you fear death?"

Valxina pressed on, but she faltered at the sound of a woman's exasperated groan. It was Inara's. Valxina locked eyes with Danae, who swept the feet of a guard and dragged him to the ground. Valxina ran beside her, slicing the man with her javelin without a word. The two searched again for Inara. She had been knocked to the ground, and her cutlass had dropped from her hands. A Badawi guard advanced on her. Valxina glanced behind. Desil had run out of arrows. Valxina watched his hands reach for more, but his sack was empty. He gave off a harrowed expression. So he grabbed his sword from his belt and charged them.

Meanwhile, Inara had snatched a rock from the ground. She threw it at the guard a few feet away, but he dodged it. She crawled near her cutlass, turning to her stomach. The man drew his sword and raised it. The beautiful lake's blue reflected in the metal. Danae lifted her hand and swung her surujin into the air. Valxina gripped the javelin with both hands. They were close, *so close*. Chains wrapped around the man's hand as he swung. But it wasn't enough. He had too much momentum; Danae would be unable to stop him. He roared as he charged toward Inara.

Ahead, another guard stepped between Valxina and the man. She jumped, tossing her weight onto Danae. She hoped their weight would be enough, that it would take the man down by his hands. Danae shouted as they tumbled into the ground, Valxina colliding head-on with Danae. Her face was caked with dirt, Valxina coughed as she struggled to stand up. Danae's eyes widened beneath her. An arrow sailed through the air once more. Inara hoisted herself up with her cutlass in her hand, but the man was already dead.

Desil had run out of arrows, *hadn't he?* Desil collided

with Inara as they turned. With ease, he struck and sliced men down. Inara's eyes widened at the sight. But what about the arrow? Valxina shifted her gaze to the granite formation. Keeper Sera stood there, her eyes as blue as the lake. She was soaked in blood and tears. She had arrived. Sera gave a nod to the two women on the ground.

"Maybe not the time or place?" Danae said from under Valxina in a smoky tone. Heat rose to Valxina's cheeks. She scrambled, rolled off, and stood. Danae grasped her extended hand.

"So she made it, after all," Danae said as she looked behind at Sera.

"She has plenty of reasons to fight," Valxina replied.

"We all have our motivations. And she didn't come alone."

While a flood of Badawi guards emerged from behind Lord Zessfar, others revealed themselves behind Sera. Only those were not House guards; they were from the tower.

"Sorry to have doubted them," Danae confessed. "Maybe your man isn't so bad, after all."

Valxina laughed as Danae reached out. Her warm fingers wiped at the blood on Valxina's face. Valxina stilled at the touch and asked, "Are you saying you like him now?"

Danae twisted her surujin in the air and knocked down an incoming guard. Valxina swung her javelin into him. More blood to spurt onto their skin. Behind, Ky's face tensed at the scene. He roared in command to his guards.

"I'll give him one thing," said Danae as she turned to

watch Ky and Mylo emerge from the tunnels. "He definitely isn't bad to look at."

Valxina's heart swelled with jealousy. But she couldn't decipher it: Was she protective over Ky or *envious* of Danae's compliment? She shook the feeling off and charged back into the fight.

Chapter 42

No amount of training could have prepared Valxina for the emotions of battle—real battle. And while Commander Hu had trained her well, Valxina had never felt her blood pump as wildly as it did now.

Even though the three had never trained together before, Danae, Inara, and Valxina kept an eye on each other. Desil stayed close to Inara, working side by side with her as if they were meant to be together. Ky and Mylo didn't take long to join them at their sides. They cut their way to the others as if slicing down sugarcane, not men. Valxina had seen Ky in training before, but the sight of his strained face, the energy in his strides, it was all new to her. Valxina moved, working in tandem with Danae. Like a fisherman, Danae swung her surujin into the air, ready for the catch. She'd aim for their necks and pull back at them with all her weight. Some died instantly when their heads snapped from their necks. Valxina swung at the others, aiming for their necks. It was practice. After all, there was only one known way to kill the man Valxina truly wished to lay dead. Zessfar. *How many heads would she remove until she reached his?*

The air felt heavy and dark. Valxina never imagined this would be how she would meet the lake and The Spring. She had pictured tears of joy, not the kind that trickles down your face as you collide with your fate. Valxina had once imagined a feast. She had once dreamed about the water against her skin. Now, the waters turned dark with bloodshed. And then she realized... their solution was there. They battled Badawi guards with fear in their hearts, but what if there was no need for fear? If she could get to Zessfar, if she could reach him, could she face him on an even playing field? Sera had warned too much water could lead to death. She shuddered at the thought. The Spring had been gifted to the Badawi family by the gods. *At least, that was what they were taught.* Valxina slammed her javelin into a House guard, letting Ky finish him behind. When she moved toward the edge of the lake, a voice called out for her.

"Valxina!" Inara said, her voice vibrating with terror.

Valxina took another step forward. She stood so close to the edge the slightest of ripples would bring water to her feet. She hovered in indecisiveness.

"Val," Inara warned, "don't."

Valxina turned to those around her. "Get me to him! If you help me get to him, I can do this. I know I can. But we need to be equals. He is immortal."

Behind, Danae turned to her. Her eyes widened, and her heart dropped. Shock rippled through her face. "Don't be stupid!" she called out.

"I didn't know *you* were one to believe in the superstition," Valxina shot back.

Danae huffed. "I'm not, but I know whatever is in there is not worth it. Ingesting too much is deadly. *You* know that too!"

"What do you mean?" Ky asked, his voice and sword cutting through men.

"It's sacred," Inara replied. "We are meant to protect it but not to take from it."

"But protect it from *whom?*" Valxina asked. While she understood the need to protect the waters from the hands of enemies like Chantara, she wondered, *Were they meant to protect it from the lord himself?*

Silence rippled between them. Understanding bellowed through the air.

Danae narrowed her eyes. "You aren't going in there." She stormed over to Valxina and cocked her head. Heat emitted from her body. "The Spring isn't here for us to protect. The Badawi House is nothing but a greedy family who believes this is their possession." She waved her hands into the air. "But it never was theirs. And The Spring never needed our protection. Not truly."

"And why wouldn't it?" Ky questioned.

It was Keeper Sera's voice that boomed in response. "Because The Spring can protect itself."

Valxina lifted a brow as the woman continued. Tower guards created a formation around them.

"It takes from its hosts, from those who drink from it. It feeds off their life while simultaneously allowing them to live longer. But an immortal life from The Spring is no life to live. It drowns out your humanity, slowly but surely. It's the gods' decision who shall be able to withstand the effects of the waters. It's rumored that generations of ingestion have tainted the Badawi family line. It's rumored that it's led to madness. If Valxina drinks it... well, too much could kill her!"

Ky balled his fingers into a fist. "What do you mean?" he screamed, anger piercing through him.

Why would this news anger Ky?

Sera shook her head. "I did not know. I only learned the truth after."

Valxina narrowed her brows. *After what?* Her eyes darted between the two while Sera continued.

"Otherwise I would have done anything to keep Pax alive. There would have been no thought to it." Sera reached inside her robe and dropped a vial to the floor. It was filled with water from The Spring. "I would have used this on her so quickly."

"Why are you so upset?" Mylo asked Ky in a soft and concerning voice.

Sera looked at him with a heavy sadness. She pressed her lips together and sighed.

"I am so sorry," she said. "I'll leave you to it." Then she rejoined the battle.

"What?" Mylo asked Ky again.

Ky furrowed his eyebrows. He shook his head in disbelief as his eyes filled with tears. "No," he mumbled as he looked at the man who had once saved him. "But you seem fine."

Mylo's eyes widened. He took a step forward. "What did you do?" he asked, not with anger but with the softness of fear.

Ky did not answer.

"Kyrad, what did you do?" Danae echoed as she took a step toward Mylo.

"I gave you the water," Ky whispered to Mylo. "Your head was nearly severed. I had Sera and Pax stitch you up. You didn't look like you would make it. But I had to do something. You had saved me. You were too young to go like that..."

"You gave him water?" said Valxina. She needed to hear the words leave his lips.

Ky lifted a fist to his lips and muttered a curse under his breath. "I just wanted you to live."

Even Danae listened in silence, no witty remark positioned at the tip of her tongue. She stood quiet, her back toward them, fighting off the occasional House guard who broke through the tower guards who surrounded them.

Mylo took one step forward, then another. His face was like marble, emotionless.

Valxina held her breath as he reached out. He placed a heavy hand onto Ky's shoulders. He squeezed at him before resting the next on his other shoulder. "Are you telling me... that I am immortal?"

Ky nodded. "I am sorry. I am so sorry, Brother."

Mylo shook his head. "No. You have no reason to be sorry. You saw a path to save me, and you took it. I did the same for you. It's what left me nearly decapitated in the first place. And whatever darkness lingers in me because of this sacrifice, well, I am happy to face it, with you at my side."

Ky lifted his face. "You are not upset?"

"Are you fucking kidding me? You have made me immortal!" He shook Ky's body in a playful motion. "Is that why my wounds had healed so much by the morning? Why I did not die from the loss of so much blood?"

Ky nodded.

Before anyone could say another word, Mylo turned toward the bloodshed and ran right into it.

Chapter 43

Death awaited in the corners.

Behind the brute force of Mylo and Ky, Valxina pressed on. Sweat danced along her skin and raced down her back. She swiped, jabbed, and pressed the metal of her javelin as she continued on. And then, there was a moment.

Mylo jumped forward like a man possessed by madness. While he was never a man with much fear, it was clear now that nothing was holding him back. Valxina had never felt so secure, with the vision of Ky's broad shoulders, of his tense muscles, and his almost godlike maneuvering of the sea of weapons, and with Danae to her side. Even to her right, Valxina could see the flash of Sera's eyes and hear the sound of her grief and pain. The woman sliced through men as if their deaths would return Pax to her side.

And then, in a flash of blues and greens, Valxina saw them. *Keepers.* A swarm of keepers ran through the tunnel, their weapons in tow. They screamed and shouted a sound so wild and unfitting for the women who had been deemed holy and devoted. Valxina knew this would be her moment.

As the keepers ran up from behind, the Badawi guards hesitated. Confusion washed over their faces as they watched the women running toward them. They shared grunts and awkward glances with one another. They looked back at their lord for direction.

And in that moment, Valxina jolted. She pushed her way past Ky's and Mylo's bodies. She zipped between frozen House guards and fallen men. Her heart raced, and her chest pounded, her lips parting as she gasped for air. Zessfar was so close. Standing like statues in the grandest of temples, Zessfar's guards had not budged. They stood, eyes wide and alert. They saw her coming. But they saw someone else. Valxina was not alone. Behind, footsteps crashed against the ground.

Valxina glanced to her right to see Mylo. His golden hair was slick with sweat. His bright eyes had seemed to darken. He looked at her and grinned. He flexed his hand and, in a cocky move, twisted his blade in his hand. It was Mylo who broke the barrier between Valxina and Zessfar.

"Go on!" a voice screamed at her. It was Danae. Her face was tense and wild. She was covered in blood and dirt, and strands of stained hair stuck to her face.

And then another body collided with the wall of guards. *Ky.*

Valxina's eyes widened. They had followed her into the chaos. They had blindly tossed their bodies into the danger. When Ky looked over at her, she saw rage in his eyes.

"Go!" he shouted, moving his glare to Zessfar, who was alone. He was clenching the sword of a Badawi House guard.

Valxina froze.

"Go!" Danae commanded. "You'll be all right."

"Why did you come?" Valxina hollered at them. "Why would you—"

"We had to get you to him," Danae said, rolling her eyes. "Now go cut off his fucking head!"

Ky turned back to her once more. "You are safe." And even with the blood splattered across his body, she had never felt it was more true. "I'll do everything I can to make sure you are safe. No matter where you are—no matter who you are with. As long as I am alive, I will do everything in my power to ensure that you are safe. Perhaps this isn't the greatest place to declare such a thing, surrounded by Badawi guards and a lord who wants us dead. But until I die, even if that may happen today, I will make sure no harm comes your way."

Valxina felt her heart sigh. She tensed, pressing lips together.

"*We*," Danae corrected. "We will ensure your safety. Now go before we are all fucking dead."

Valxina nodded. Her feet took flight before she could give it much thought. Ky cut a man down, paving a clear path to Zessfar. Ahead, the lord had climbed his way into the mouth of another tunnel. He held his sword in hand and glared down at her with arrogance. Valxina pressed on. She pushed herself higher by putting her feet into the crevices of the rocks. Under her weight, dirt and pebbles shifted. She groaned as she ascended, knowing what awaited her at the summit. Valxina raised her hand and leaned over the edge, gritting her teeth in anticipation of the execution.

When she rolled herself to the ledge, she gasped for air. His dark eyes roamed over her. The edge of Zessfar's lips rose into a smirk. Valxina shot him the most daring of scowls. If it was possible to perish from the look in her eyes, the lord would have died on the spot.

"Here we are again," Zessfar said. "You, injured and feeble, looking up at me like that... It's like your ceremony all over again, isn't it?"

Valxina did not reply as she rose to her feet.

"What is it, darling?" Zessfar cooed. "You're right, I much preferred the way you looked up at me that night in my quarters. You know, during our little sleepover..."

Valxina set her jaw. Her nostrils flared. "It won't work."

"What won't work?" he asked calmly.

"Your attempt to instill guilt in me. Your attempt to make me feel small and insignificant. You want me to believe that because I allowed myself to fall for you, that it makes me a bad person."

"And you are not?" Zessfar replied. "Did you not use me as a part of some silly ploy or plot?"

Valxina took a step forward. She released a hollow breath. As she rose a brow, she said, "I did fall for you, Zessfar. I ignored the rumors, the whispers, hell, I even ignored the warnings from the gods themselves."

Zessfar spat, "What warnings of the gods?"

"The beasts of the pit, *Zessfar*," she said in a chilling

voice. "I had believed they were there as a warning for you, but no." Valxina gripped her javelin tighter. "I read into the sign, blinded by my own version of you. Do you remember the scrolls of Roseau? The bit about the gods and beginning of the end?"

Zessfar rolled his eyes. "Of course I know about the scrolls of Roseau and their description of the end of man."

Valxina smiled. "And the gods shall unleash them—beasts as unholy as the men who defy life. Creatures shall roam the land, beings of life and death, of their world and ours. A clever man would see them as a signal, a sign of shifts to come. But a holy man... A holy man would see them as damnation, as punishment." She paused, remembering all those years, all those "lessons" Lady Masha had taught her, which had finally come to some purpose. "You, Lord Zessfar of the Badawi House, are being punished. Those beasts were not a warning *for* you, but a sign of damnation, a warning *against* you. You and your family house have taken life and death into your own hands. And the gods have spoken." She swung her javelin in hand.

Something sparked behind Zessfar's eyes. "I did not choose to be born to the Badawi family."

"And yet you upheld their traditions. You steal children from families. You brainwash folks into believing you—*you*—are chosen by the gods." She scoffed.

"And who are you to talk of the gods as if you know them?"

Valxina laughed. "It's the one thing you told us keepers. We are holy. We are divine. The gods have spoken. And I have listened. Do you remember the night I came to you?

Fresh from the pit, covered in blood and maggots?" Valxina sneered. "Do you remember what you asked? 'Who did this to you?'" Valxina shook her head. "Now I know. It was *you*. You have done this. You are to blame."

Chapter 44

Javelin in hand, Valxina moved toward Zessfar.

But a sound, a scream so loud and wild, filled the caverns like shouts from the gods themselves. She turned to watch below. Valxina's eyes widened, and her lips parted in fear. She watched as a House guard swiped into the air. And when he hit his target, all air seemed to dissipate.

Even immortals cannot live without their heads.

Mylo's head rolled and rolled. It stopped at Danae's feet. And while previous events and conversation had led Valxina to believe the woman cared not for the tower guard, her scream said otherwise. The woman, the one who had removed Eno's head from the stake with ease and spoke of death like a friend, looked shattered. Her fingers clawed at her face, long and distorted. Valxina watched as Ky brought a man to the ground and twisted to see the guard who he called "brother" lying dead. Ky shouted. He'd lost another. Valxina, through the distance and the chaos, could not decipher his words.

Her heart dropped. She cried out at the sight of them, at the image of Mylo's decapitated head against the ground. His soft blonde curls dripped with blood. While static, dead silent static, filled her head, she could *hear* his head roll. It was wrong. It should not have been him. It should have been Zessfar's head rolling on the ground like a child's ball made for play. Tears fell down her cheeks as she gasped for air.

The space frenzied. It was so loud she could barely hear herself think. Valxina watched below as Ky dropped to his knees. He seemed unaware of all around him. Danae stood at his back, protecting him from undetected blows. Danae, the woman who seemed to dislike everyone—including the commander—became his line of defense. The sight had Valxina biting her lips against their quiver.

"Well, well," Zessfar said from behind. His voice rose. "It seems your tower guard is dead, Kulrani. What are you to do?"

Valxina took a deep breath. The back of her free hand swiped at the tears on her cheek, and she whipped around to face Zessfar. She knew what she had to do now. She could not lose the rest of them. And when she heard Inara's scream, she straightened her back and steadied her feet on the ground. She would not look back. Not now. Her heart banged against her chest. She raised her javelin and charged towards the man.

Zessfar. Lord Zessfar. Only days had passed since he had sanctioned the mutilation of her skin. She had disregarded years of gossip and whispers about him. Perhaps she wanted to see good in him where others could not.

While he claimed he had not asked to be born to the Badawi House, Valxina knew he had turned into the very person he had despised. He was not only a Badawi man but also *the* Badawi man. Power had led him to murder his own father. Power had him disregarding basic rites and rituals. He had spat at life itself. Power had him clawing his way into her skin as if she were his possession.

She was too quick for him. She was too stealthy for him. Valxina evaded his first swipe at her and moved to his back. But it wouldn't do. She wished for him to watch as she took his life. And like she did with the men below, she turned with him, waiting for him to grow confused and exhausted. She dodged his strikes and blows with ease. Perhaps more time in the training ring and less gambling away his family's fortune in town would have done the man good.

Valxina swung her javelin against his legs, bringing Lord Zessfar to his knees. And when he looked up, his eyes somewhat lighter with fear and a plea heavy on his gaze, Valxina shook her head. She kicked his weapon away as he muttered, "You will never be safe. You cannot get away with murdering an immortal lord."

"I'll be just fine," she spat through her narrow gaze, "and you are not immortal. Not truly. As even immortal men cannot live without their heads."

But before she could finish the thought, she paused. Could she truly do it?

Zessfar slammed into her body before she could think. Valxina's feet left the ground, and her vision blurred. His hold on her was tight and overbearing. She tried to squirm out of his arms, but she froze. She was falling. They were falling. He had taken her off the cliff.

The world was spinning. For a moment, Valxina watched the ceiling of the caverns, filled with dripping icicles of stalactite, holding her breath. They grew smaller and smaller in her vision. She could feel him against her chest, his body cold and his heart racing. Zessfar's grip loosened as Valxina's body turned toward the ground. Ky and Danae dashed below. Tears streamed down her face as Valxina saw their features. Closer and closer. The ground called to her. It whispered her name like a hungry siren.

Valxina screamed as she fell toward the ground. But the impact cut her call short, stifling her cries of distress. Someone had softened her fall. His scent, so familiar, wrapped around her in an embrace.

"Val?" Ky said from beneath her. He had reached her. He had placed his body between her and the ground. Even with the chaos and turmoil below, he had seen her, had watched her, had run to catch her.

"Mhmmm," Valxina muttered, the impact shaking her. She winced. She couldn't get to her feet fast enough.

Lord Zessfar groveled. He staggered, barely lifting himself with the sword in hand. The guards, both tower and House, seemed frozen by the sight. They watched the man shake with each step he took.

"I told you to be careful," he warned, his voice hard.

Ky's grip on Valxina tightened.

When Valxina turned, she saw Danae. Her weapon had been stripped from her grasp, and she shifted on her feet. Guards moved to surround her. Danae's eyes widened, her breathing wild and erratic. And then she turned to them.

Valxina released a bated breath as Danae collided with them. She draped her body over Valxina. Like a mother to a child, a goddess to her creation, one lover to another, she laid her hands over them and crouched against the ground.

"Danae," Valxina said.

The woman looked down at them. She locked eyes with Ky, and her eyes seemed to soften. When she looked at Valxina, she whispered, "I suppose I can see why he would lay his life down." When Danae turned to Ky, she asked, "What would you do if you were to live without her?"

Ky blinked. "There would be no life without her." He turned to Valxina. "There would be no life without you. I have waited too long to tell you. I have been an absolute fool, Val. I love you."

The words sent lightning down her spine. He loved her.

Danae nodded. "I'm sorry. I misjudged you." She turned to Valxina and placed a soft hand on her cheek. "I am so sorry." Tears streamed down her face. "For all the pain I have caused you."

"Danae—"

"No, let me finish—"

"I forgive you. I understand. I forgive you. You don't need to—"

Danae hushed her. Across the way, Zessfar moved closer to them.

"I owe you this," Danae said before springing to her feet. Danae charged towards the lord, no weapon in hand, and he grinned at her. A scream escaped Valxina's lips at the sight. She reached her hands out, hoping to grab the woman, to pull her back, to keep her within their grasp. But it was too late.

Valxina braced herself for impact. Her vision went blurry with tears. But an arrow cut through the air. It brought the lord to his knees. Behind them, Keeper Sera watched with a bow in her hand. She had shot the lord right through his head. He stumbled to the ground, but he was not dead. It would take more than that to kill him.

Danae knocked the man to the ground. She kicked the sword out of his hand and took it in her grasp. When she looked back, her eyes wild and her face full of rage, Valxina saw her. Truly saw her. She was asking for permission. Valxina nodded. And another head thumped to the ground. Another immortal head. Lord Zessfar of the Badawi House was dead.

Even the unholiest of creatures deserve a clean ending.

Chapter 45

The fighting ended almost immediately. But Valxina and Ky did not move. She watched from Ky's tight hold as Danae removed and piked the lord's head, securing it to the ground. Then, still covered in blood and her eyes blurred with tears, Danae approached Mylo's body—her feet practically dragging behind. Valxina and Ky watched as Danae ripped at her clothing, creating a wrap for the fallen tower guard. She wrapped Mylo's face, still twisted with pain. She held his face close to her, so tight against her chest that Mylo would have been able to hear the fierce beating of her heart as she neared the others.

Danae lowered herself against Valxina and Ky, perched against a pile of rubble. Valxina offered her a hand as she lowered herself to the ground.

"What you did was stupid," said Danae.

Ky nodded.

"But it was brave," Danae added.

"Mylo," Valxina muttered.

Ky tightened his arms around her, bringing her in close and tight. He smelt as rich as the jungle.

Danae settled in next to them. When she felt Ky shake, she whispered, "I've got you." She buried herself against them and laid a hand on Ky's shoulder.

Valxina looked over to Inara. She hovered over an injured man. *Desil.* The cry that had vibrated through the caverns had been for Desil.

"We need to get out of here," Danae said. She rested a tender hand on Valxina's, which still lay against Ky's chest. The three of them exchanged a quiet glance.

Ky only looked at them both. He moved closer to Valxina and let his lips hover before hers. "I do not know what I would have done if something happened to you."

Valxina shook her head. "I was safe." *She was safe.*

Danae moved to stand, but Valxina reached out. She grasped the woman's hand and guided her back down.

When Ky kissed her, Valxina cradled his face. Still shaken from her fall, she stabilized herself with his body. Her chest pressed against him as their lips met one another. Valxina closed her eyes, attempting to memorize the moment for eternity.

When they parted, she looked over at Danae. "We need to leave," she said. Danae nodded, her eyes focused on their hands, their fingers still interwoven. Valxina hadn't let go even as she kissed Ky before her. Even Ky had not seemed bothered by her presence. He watched her with welcoming eyes—as if knowing the thoughts that ran through her head. Danae tightened her grip. "But first, we should set up a pyre. We should give those who have died a proper send-off. Including Pax and Mylo."

"And the men in the pit?" Ky replied.

"We should release them too, don't you think?"

"Yes," Danae answered, "we should."

We. The sound was kindling to fire.

✦

They had hours to themselves under the flames of the pyre. They needed the time to make it right, to give them a proper goodbye. Danae reached for Valxina. Her eyes studied her with awe and longing. When she offered her hand, a shoulder to balance herself on, Valxina took it.

"I told you," Danae said as they watched from the distance.

"What is that?" asked Valxina.

"That I would burn the entire Court to the ground. And here we are, watching it all blaze."

Valxina looked at the woman once more. This time, Danae smiled.

"Fuck," Valxina muttered.

"What?"

"You're smiling."

Danae rolled her eyes. "As if you have never seen me smile."

Valxina shook her head. "I can say with absolute certainty that I have never seen you smile."

"Well, you have never paid me much attention."

"As if you paid me any."

"That's not true," Danae said, her brows furrowed. "I have always paid attention to you. Even when you thought I didn't."

Valxina hesitated before replying, "I-I have to apologize to you."

"For?" Danae turned to face her.

"You were right. It was me—I did creep around in the shadows. I did keep my distance from you and the others. I-I was afraid of friendships. I loved someone once and lost her. With my background and my class, I thought I would taint anyone who crossed paths with me."

"And now?"

Valxina's expression intensified. She held her breath as a gust of blazing air washed over her. "Now, I know my background has never been something to cower from. My ancestors built the tunnels. I became the first servant child to rise to the status of keeper. And now... I am blessed by the gods." She removed a vial from her pocket.

Danae lifted a brow. "You kept it? The vial from the lake?"

Valxina nodded. "I-I drank from it. Before climbing the cliff to Zessfar. Although Ky softened my fall, I think this is the reason I did not need to be scraped off the ground. I am blessed."

Danae reached out for a wild strand of Valxina's hair. She tucked it behind the woman's ear. "You have always been a woman blessed by the gods." Her eyes deepened. "How can anyone look at you and not smile?"

Valxina narrowed her eyes as Danae moved closer.

Valxina's heart quickened. She held her breath. "And what are you doing now?"

Danae grinned. "I'm trying to kiss you. May I?"

Valxina bit at her lip as she leaned in. Danae rested a hand across Valxina's cheek, her thumb tracing idle circles over her skin. When their lips met, the world silenced. Valxina lifted to her toes and wrapped her arms around Danae. And Danae kissed her back, so fiercely Val stumbled. Danae wrapped her arms around her torso and lifted her, just slightly.

Night crept through the Court halls and gardens. Whispers and gossip spread themselves wide across the House of Badawi.

Valxina Kulrani, a servant girl, a child of the lotto, had seduced and murdered Lord Zessfar. Whispers said she and her friends stole from The Spring. She radicalized the keepers and tower guards and forced them to destroy the tower and tunnels. She set them aflame. She was wild, she was rash, and she had no care for the life of men.

But who would believe such rumors and whispers? And were they correct?

Valxina stole a glimpse of the chaos as they shuffled into the jungle. Court members hurried about the palace as the fire spread behind the tower.

She held her breath at the sight. Danae had held true to her promise. She had lit the entire Court on fire.

In the distance, Keeper Sera, insistent on staying, on building a new House out of the rubble, freeing the folks left in the cells, and speaking to the king of Zessfar's actions, lifted a hand to her.

Sera did not need to say the words out loud. They seemed to carry themselves in the embers and ashes. Valxina could hear her voice, her message, loud and clear.

Sera had been wrong.

The House of Badawi *was* a place for fire and flames.

And it needed to be burned to the ground.

Valxina turned, hearing the footsteps of another in the distance. Ky emerged into the clearing with the jungle behind. He smiled, nodding at the two women in front of him.

"Come on, Inara and Desil are waiting," he said, his voice calm and his face almost proud as he looked at them. And when Ky lifted a brow, nodding to the unknown behind, they followed.

Note to readers.

I genuinely hope you had as much fun reading this book as I had creating it. If you did (or didn't), I would greatly appreciate a brief review on Goodreads, StoryGraph, Amazon, or your preferred book website. For every author, reviews are vital, and even a few lines or words can make a big difference to us.

Please note, in an effort to keep review spaces safe for readers, I do not monitor or reply to reviews myself. I ask that if you did enjoy my book and find a reviewer with a different opinion, please do not engage with them. Everyone is entitled to share their thoughts on this novel (*unless you have something homophobic, classist, or racist to say... that, will not be tolerated*). I expect responses from all ends of the spectrum. Know that you are safe to leave a review of your honest opinion, without any reaction from me, the author.

Acknowledgements

Thank you, dear readers, for taking a chance on me, Val, and this novel. I picked up the metaphoric pen during the pandemic and did not expect to create an entire world, yet alone share it. Would it be a pandemic related acknowledgement without the mention of #booktok and #bookstagram? It absolutely would not. I am so grateful to the internet strangers that hyped me up and showed interest in this story. I do not think House of Badawi would have made it into your hands without the online community.

A huge shout out and thank you to Katie, Natalie, and Jenny for their honest opinions and suggestions.

And to Kev for supporting and encouraging my wild ideas and dreams.

About the Author

C.J. Khemi is the debut author of House of Badawi. She's Indo-Trinidadian-American, a native New Yorker, and is currently living out her cottage-core dreams in her home outside of NYC. Khemi holds a M.A. in International Affairs and a B.A. in Psychology. She is a content writer by day, covering current affairs and politics in the United States. When C.J. is not working or writing, she is out walking at her local nature preserve, trying to perfect her mom's curry chicken recipe (which she has yet to get *just right*), and binging her latest obsession with her cat, Moon.

You can follow C.J. for more on:
TikTok @cj.khemibooks
Instagram @cj.khemibooks

Check out her website at:
CJKHEMI.COM

CPSIA information can be obtained
at www.ICGtesting.com
Printed in the USA
LVHW090151240922
729141LV00015B/619